PRAISE FOR DAVE WHITE'S f

WHEN ONE

"Dave White has long been regarded in the   the finest
young writers of short fiction
Man Dies, and the results
that is both traditional
much-plowed field with
detective novels will,

—Da

"**A terrific novel**, a uni
procedural with a sto
fatal as your last car wreck. It's a great read."

—James Crumley, Dashiell Hammett Award–winning author of
The Last Good Kiss and The Right Madness

"Derringer Award–winner White's **engrossing, evocative debut novel** will
grab most readers from its opening sentences. . . . Fans of hard-hitting,
uncompromising private investigators will hope that Donne ditches his
college dreams and continues to pound the pavement."
—Publishers Weekly, starred review

"When One Man Dies barrels straight out of the old school and swerves onto the
highway that will take **detective fiction where it's going next.**"

—Sean Doolittle, author of The Cleanup and Rain Dogs

"Every now and then you find a debut novel that carries the clear promise of big
things to come. When One Man Dies is one of those. **Dave White is creating a
winner with Jackson Donne.**"

—Michael Koryta, Edgar-nominated author of A Welcome Grave

"**Jackson Donne takes his place alongside the grim and battered PIs of
yore**—your Archers, your Spades—uncovering painful truths and doling out
what passes in this tarnished world for justice. Bracing stuff."
—Charles Ardai, Edgar Award–winning author
and founder of Hard Case Crime

"**When I read my first Dave White story, I knew that he was going to be
huge someday**—like, Robert Parker huge. When One Man Dies is the first bold
step in fulfilling that promise."

—Duane Swierczynski, author of The Blonde and The Wheelman

NOMINATED FOR THE 2007 STRAND MAGAZINE CRITICS AWARD

ALSO BY
DAVE WHITE

WHEN ONE MAN DIES

THE EVIL THAT MEN DO

a jackson donne novel

DAVE WHITE

THREE RIVERS PRESS
NEW YORK

Copyright © 2008 by Dave White

Published in the United States by Three Rivers Press, an imprint of the Crown
Publishing Group, a division of Random House, Inc., New York.
www.crownpublishing.com

Three Rivers Press and the Tugboat design are registered
trademarks of Random House, Inc.

Library of Congress Cataloging-in-Publication Data
White, Dave, 1979–
The evil that men do: a Jackson Donne novel / Dave White.—1st ed.
1. Private investigators—New Jersey—Fiction.   2. Ex-police officers—
Fiction.   3. Aging parents—Fiction.   4. Brothers and sisters—Fiction.
5. Alzheimer's disease—Fiction.   6. Domestic fiction.   I. Title.
PS3623.H5727E95 2008
813'.6—dc22   2007050921

ISBN 978-0-307-38279-5

Printed in the United States of America

Design by Maria Elias

10 9 8 7 6 5 4 3 2 1

First Edition

To my grandparents,
Mimi, Martin, Harriet, and Paul

acknowledgments

I would like to thank:

My editor, Julian Pavia, and my agent, Allan Guthrie. Both took the drafts of this book and helped shape it into something much better than it originally was.

My parents, Carol and Martin, and my brother, Tom, for their love and support.

My friends who lent their names for the book, and my friends who didn't. I owe drinks all around.

The faculty, staff, and administration of Christopher Columbus Middle School for their continuing support.

The people who picked up *When One Man Dies*. I hope you came back to check this one out as well.

And all the writers out there who've been there for me. You know who you are and you know you're completely awesome.

Thanks, everybody.

The evil that men do lives after them;
The good is oft interred with their bones.

—William Shakespeare, *Julius Caesar*

THE EVIL THAT MEN DO

part one

JOE TENANT

1938

Joe Tenant tied the barge to the dock. The water licked its sides, and the boat swayed back and forth. The chill of the morning air made him shiver, and he wished for the sun to rise a little faster. He pulled the knot tight, made sure it was secure, and stepped onto the wooden planks.

A few men sorted through their lunch boxes, looking for a quick breakfast before starting the day shift. Tenant always thought that odd, because, as long as he'd worked the night shift, the morning had always signaled dinner to him. Working nights was difficult, adjusting to the schedule, keeping a wife happy, but Tenant enjoyed the silence.

"Hey, Tugboat, how's the water today?" one of the daymen asked. "They're transferring me to nights next week, so I want to enjoy it while I can."

Tenant smiled at his nickname. He hadn't liked it at first, thought the men were mocking him, but he'd soon learned that everybody had a nickname on the water.

"How are you, Sops? Water's kind of rocky, might be a storm later in the day."

"Fantastic," Sops said.

Tenant wished them a good day and headed toward the parking lot. The warehouses that surrounded the lot expelled smoke and steam, doing their best to spur the economy. The air smelled like fish and soot, and Tenant would be happy just to get home.

He reached his car and was reminded how lucky he was. In these days, it was good fate to have a car when hardly anyone did. Meanwhile those guys down in Clifton were trying to build that dog park, and doing whatever the hell else FDR wanted them to do. And all that shit out in Europe, he was living a blessed life.

He unlocked the door and got in. And as he sat down, he realized he'd left his lunch box on the barge. He sighed, got out of the car, and started the trek back to the boat. The water slapped against the dock, and it wobbled a bit. He knelt down and reached for his lunch box.

"We warned you."

The voice was loud, rising over the water. Tenant looked to his left toward the source of the sound. About thirty feet away, two men slouched along the shore, staring downward. A thin stream of light reflecting off the river illuminated them. The light came from a docking boat farther down the river.

Tenant could tell the men were out of view to anyone in the parking lot. He'd gone down to the shoreline to fish out his shoe when a coworker played a joke on him. He knew you could be seen only from the dock he stood on.

"No, please." Another voice. "It was only business."

Between the two men, a hand rose out of the water, as if the person needed help standing. One of the men slapped the hand away.

"Don't worry, Maxwell. This is only business too."

The second man raised his arm over his head. In the light Tenant saw a thick shape, probably a blackjack. The man swung it downward, and it landed with a sickening thump. Water splashed around his arm. The man repeated the move three more times.

Tenant should have just turned and run away, but his muscles wouldn't move. His eyes wouldn't look away.

The other man kicked at the body in the water until the current took it. He turned his head to watch it float away, and his pale face faced Tenant, his features caught momentarily in the thin light off the river. Joe Tenant tried to memorize them. The reddish hair, freckles, the crooked smile.

If the man saw Tenant, he didn't react. He just turned back toward land and walked off.

Tenant peered over the edge of the dock. Dark waves ebbed and flowed, and the water was deep enough here that he couldn't see the bottom. The dock rocked again, hard enough that Tenant had to brace himself. He crossed to the other edge and peered over.

At first he didn't notice it, he looked too far left. But once the dock rocked one more time, he looked to the right. Bile rose in his throat.

Facedown in the water, the body of a man in a pin-striped suit bobbed in the current, sleeve caught against the pier.

Tenant closed his eyes and swore.

Maybe he wasn't as lucky as he thought.

CHAPTER 1

JACKSON DONNE HADN'T TALKED TO HIS SISTER IN years. So when Susan buzzed his apartment, he wasn't really expecting it.

"You closed your office," she said as she entered.

"Court ordered."

She didn't respond, save for brushing a strand of her short auburn hair over her ear. Susan had cut her hair since the last time he'd seen her and it was boyish in style, though thick and brushed back. It didn't fit her.

"How are you, Jackson?" she asked.

"Why are you here?"

She stalked past Donne and sat on the couch. Dropping her purse on his coffee table, she said, "No small talk?"

He didn't respond.

"It's Mom," Susan continued. "She's sick, real sick. She doesn't have much time left."

He couldn't help asking, "What's wrong?"

"Alzheimer's, dementia. We put her in a nursing home last year, now she's in a hospice."

"Why didn't you call me?"

"Would you have come help?"

It was a good point. He had separated himself from his family, just as his father had. Unlike his father, however, Donne had good reasons. At least he thought so.

"There's a reason I'm coming to see you now. Mom, she's been talking about stuff I never knew about. I'm not sure if it's rambling truths or she's making things up, but I need your help. You're a detective."

"Not anymore," he said.

"Whatever," she said. "I want your help."

"To do what? You want me to sit by her, read her stories, talk to her?" He shook his head. "I'm busy, Susan. Not going to do it."

"Come on, Jackson. You know how much we mean to her. She had us so late in her life. Please, she should have been in menopause and she was having kids. We should both be there for her."

Donne shook his head.

"Damn it, Jackson. It's time to grow up. Be a son. Be a brother. What else are you doing with your life?"

"I'm starting school at Rutgers in the fall. I'm working."

"I want you to find out about Mom's dad. She's been talking about him."

"What does it matter?"

She grabbed her purse and moved toward the door. Finally.

"Peace of mind," she said as she turned the knob. "Doesn't that matter?"

"What kind of purse is that?" he asked. "Coach, one of those expensive kinds?"

She looked at the purse, then at Donne, confused.

"Franklin buy that for you? Drop a couple hundred on you to keep you happy?"

Her face turned red, and she took a deep breath before speaking. "Think about it, Jackson. You need to see her again before she dies. Peace of mind. I don't think you've ever had it. Not with Jeanne, not with me, not with Mom. Hell, not even with Dad, and you were, what, eight when he left? Maybe you could use a little closure. Help us out."

"No."

"Please, Jackson. She said that our grandfather murdered someone. It's all she's been talking about. I need to know if it's true."

She pulled the door open and stepped into the hallway.

He never should have allowed her up.

Donne worked nighttime security at a storage facility in Piscataway. It was a great job. He got in about eleven and off at seven. No one bothered him, and he could come in a little buzzed after a few drinks at the Olde Towne Tavern. He could even catch a little West Coast baseball on satellite radio or take a nap.

Which was what he was doing when Franklin Carter approached him.

"Wake up, asshole," he said, banging a fist on the desk.

Jackson sat forward, his eyes shot open, and he stifled a yawn.

Carter looked like he'd just come from work, dressed in a pinstriped suit, pale blue shirt, and striped tie. Even his loafers were polished. His dark hair was combed back, his mustache neatly trimmed.

"What do you want, Franklin?" Donne asked. His tongue tasted like leather.

"Your sister came to you for help and you turned her down."

"Yes, I did."

"Why?"

"You know why."

The silence hung in the room. Behind Carter, through the swinging glass door, headlights passed. It had to be earlier than Donne thought for there to be that much traffic.

"I want you to help her," Carter said. "She came home the other day in tears. She had just been with your mother, watching her fade away. She said she went to see you and you two argued. You're hurting her. I won't have that."

Donne shrugged. "It's not my problem."

Franklin Carter slammed his fists on the desk again and leaned in so close Donne smelled his breath. "It is your problem! This is about your mother and your sister. Don't you have any sense of family?"

Donne thought about Jeanne. About what he knew about her now.

"No," he said.

Carter stood back up and reached into his jacket pocket and pulled out a pen and checkbook.

"What's it going to take?" he asked.

"I don't do investigative work anymore."

He took a deep breath, then said, "Everyone has a price."

Donne sat back in his chair and closed his eyes. He didn't have any college scholarships coming in. He hadn't been paid a salary in a long while. The storage facility was an hourly wage and it wasn't much more than rent and drinking money.

"You always were a rich prick," Donne said. "Even in high school. I couldn't stand you. I never understood why our parents were friends."

"What's the price?" Carter said, his voice unbearably confident.

Donne gave his brother-in-law a price. Carter scribbled out a check.

✳

When Carter came through the door, his tie was loosened and his hair was out of place. Susan got off the couch and wrapped her arms around him.

"How was work?"

He pressed his hand against the small of her back and pulled her close. Susan smelled the faint remains of his sweet cologne.

Carter didn't answer her question, so she moved her head away from his neck and looked at him.

"Work?" she asked, nudging his shoulder with her chin. "You know, meals, plates, table settings, schmoozing with customers on the Upper East Side? Or at the very least in Montclair? I asked you a question."

Carter leaned in and kissed her.

"Jackson's going to help."

"You're kidding. He told me he didn't want to see Mom. He seemed pretty adamant."

Carter shrugged. "He's going to help."

"Thank you."

He smiled and kissed her again. "Anything for you, babe."

CHAPTER

BUSINESS at the OLDe towne tavern had been booming in the last few months. Donne didn't know what it was. Even with school out, people would pack the place on weekend nights to the point where you couldn't sit at the bar and couldn't move your elbows when you stood. On weeknights, you had to get there before seven to get a table. Maybe the new chef Artie hired had stopped overcooking the burgers.

Or maybe Artie had finally cleaned the taps.

Either way, Donne made sure he was there at six P.M. on the dot, Molson in front of him, a grilled chicken sandwich on the way. He placed his cell phone on the bar next to his pint glass. It wasn't until Artie approached him that Donne realized he was staring at the phone.

"Waiting for a call?" he asked.

Looking up, Donne said, "No, deciding whether or not to make one."

Artie nodded and waited.

"Bad date?" he asked when Donne didn't elaborate.

"No, my sister."

"You have a sister?"

Donne downed his pint and Artie took it to refill.

"There's a reason you didn't know that."

"And now you have to call her about something?"

"You're quick," Donne said. There was no smile to go along with the comment.

Artie put the pint down so hard he nearly dropped it. He turned on his heel and walked away. Donne picked up his cell phone and dialed.

Susan picked up on the third ring.

"I'll do it," he said without preamble. "I can start tomorrow. Where's Mom staying?"

"Uh," she mumbled. "Grove Estates in Wayne. On Berdan Avenue."

Two women walked into the bar, hair made up like they'd just come from shooting *The Sopranos*. They wore shorts and tank tops and cracked gum.

"I'll be there in the morning."

"Do you want me to be th—"

He snapped the phone shut.

✳

Steve Earle on the CD player. A good way to go, because he did feel all right. Surprisingly so. There weren't any nerves, no sweaty palms, just the job at hand.

The Ryder truck rumbled up Third Avenue, crossing Seventy-sixth. Mike Garibell could see the restaurant up ahead. He was going to need to find parking soon.

Mike Garibell. He smiled at the name.

He was going to have to think of himself that way tonight. That was the name on the fake driver's license. In case he got pulled over.

Hey, Mike, how are you tonight? the bouncer at the bar next door might ask, checking the ID.

I'm fine.

No, don't say anything. Just smile and nod. Act like you belong.

Carter's was on the corner of Seventy-ninth and Third. A banner hung from the canopy advertising "Our 75th Year!" Good a time as any for revenge. The exterior of the restaurant was wood paneled, with glass swing doors that led to a dark hallway. No one was inside. The place had closed down hours earlier.

Mike pulled the truck to a stop on the corner. Put it in park. He figured it would take about two minutes for someone to come out of one of the bars and notice the damn thing and call the cops. Another seven or eight minutes for the cops to get there and check it out. If it hadn't been two in the morning, even less time.

That would give Mike about ten minutes to get some space between him and the truck. Doable. Might even get to suck a pint down before pressing the old button.

They had to learn. Family was the most important thing. Payback started now.

Fuck it, just get the hell out of there. He stepped down from the cab of the truck and crossed the street. He didn't hurry. He walked. He looked like he belonged. Like Mike Garibell was supposed to be there.

He made his way up to Eightieth and turned left. There was an Irish pub on the corner, and he stopped in. The place was nearly empty. Five more minutes and the fuzz would be swarming around the big yellow truck.

When the bartender put a glass full of Smithwick's in front of him, Mike decided it was time. He didn't know how the fucking Arabs did it, sat in the car and pressed the button. Let themselves go with the truck. It didn't make sense.

Even now, a block and a half away, he felt a moment of regret as he reached into his pocket.

Finding the remote, he pressed the button. A moment of hesitation, then an eruption of light and sound rattled the glasses. The bartender swore and hit the ground.

Mike finished the pint in two gulps, dropped a five on the bar, and left.

He was six blocks north when his ears finally stopped ringing.

CHAPTER 3

DONNE'S SISTER CALLED WHEN HE WAS ON VALLEY Road in Wayne, which, he was pretty sure, was the worst place to call anyone with Verizon in New Jersey. The phone buzzed once and then dropped out, sending it right to voice mail. He hoped she thought he was avoiding her.

He made a left onto Berdan and saw Grove Estates just up the street. It looked like a bed-and-breakfast. A house that reached back probably an acre, with a porch at the front door. Its roof pointed toward the sun, and its aluminum siding was pink. It looked comfortable and welcoming, as it was supposed to.

Inside, the reception area looked like the lobby of a hotel. A few senior citizens sat around a fountain, reading or talking with one another. Soft Tony Bennett played over the loudspeakers, and receptionists dressed like nurses smiled at everyone.

He stopped at the welcome desk. A woman with dark hair pulled back in a bun smiled at him.

"Can I help you, sir?"

"Yes," Donne said. "My name's Jackson Donne."

"*You're* Isabelle's son? She talks about you all the time. We were wondering when you were going to come visit."

He felt a wave of guilt and tried to let it pass without showing it to everyone in the room.

"I've been busy," he muttered.

"She's in room three oh eight." The way she spoke, Donne wondered if there was a poster in the break room reminding the employees to answer the phone with a smile.

She pointed to Donne's right. Closed double doors with a combination keypad.

"Through there. Third door on the right. The code is one, five, seven. When you go through, make sure you pull the door closed. There is a pad on the other side for when you leave. Same code."

"Why the security?" he asked.

"We don't want any of the residents in that wing to get out. We have a staff that's outnumbered by residents twenty to one. If the door is left open, one of the residents could wander unsupervised and injure either another resident or themselves."

"Do I have to go in armed?" He smiled.

She didn't. "We change the code every week or so, so be sure to ask. Sometimes the residents find the combination out and sneak through. Have a good day, Mr. Donne."

He pressed the code and opened the door. He stepped into another room, much like the lobby. A large TV played the news—a picture of something that looked like a war zone—and a few people sat on a couch, staring at the screen blankly. A woman in a wheelchair cried. Another in an easy chair seemed comatose. A man screamed that he wanted to see his father. The man had to be nearing eighty.

Four closed doors down a pale, plain hallway, he found room 308. He knocked gently and pushed the door open. A small square room with a twin bed in the middle, his mother lying asleep in it. A dresser with a mirror above it and a small TV across from the bed next to a desk and chair. A long window with drawn curtains let sunlight seep through. He stood in the doorway and watched his mother's chest rise and fall slowly.

Stepping closer, he saw how white her hair had gotten. The last time he'd seen her it had been a light blond, but now it nearly matched the pillowcase. Even as she rested there were wrinkles around her lips, eyes, and nose that hadn't been there before. His mother had had her kids late, but she'd always acted young. Always looked young. Until now. He put his hands in his pockets, closed his eyes, and took a long, slow breath.

Donne's cell phone buzzed and he stepped out of the room. The caller ID informed him it was his sister again. Flicking open the phone, he wasn't even able to say hello before he heard her crying.

"Susan," he said, "are you okay?"

"Jackson, I— Have you seen the news?"

"No. I just got to the nursing home. What's wrong?"

"Franklin . . . the restaurant. I don't know." She couldn't control herself, and the sobs continued, harder now. He was surprised she was able to hold the phone.

"Okay. Calm down. Just tell me what happened. Take a deep breath and go through it from the beginning."

As Donne spoke, he looked up at the TV again. He knew what she was going to say before she said it.

"Franklin's restaurant in New York. Terrorists or something, they don't know. But it's gone. They blew it up."

The war zone on the TV screen wasn't a foreign country. It was New York City.

"Jesus Christ. How many people were hurt?"

"No one is sure what's going on. They haven't found any bodies— Oh God."

"All right. It's okay. Where's Franklin?"

"Trying to get into the city."

"He's not hurt, then?"

"No," she said. "He's all right. There probably wasn't anyone there; it happened in the middle of the night. But just . . ." She trailed off.

"It'll be okay. Could it have been an accident? A gas explosion, something like that?"

"No. They found pieces of a truck."

"Well, keep me posted. I'm going to stay here and wait for Mom to wake up."

Donne went back into the room, pulled out the desk chair next to the bed, and took his mom's hand. For the first time since he'd last seen his mother, he was worried about his family.

✳

The first thing Franklin Carter thought when he got to the site was that he was going to have to have his shoes shined. Here he was dressed to the nines, pin-striped suit, tailored blue shirt, red Armani tie, black shoes, and he was going to get dust all over them. Dust and who knew what else. Blood maybe?

Could someone have been inside?

He doubted it. The restaurant took its last table at ten-thirty and was usually cleared and closed up by one-thirty. The explosion had happened after two in the morning.

But still, blow the place up? That was a tough way to wake up in the morning. Never mind getting to the city when terrorism was suspected. That was a pain in the ass. The FBI had to come get him, in a black car, lights flashing. They tried to look undercover, but they could put on a show when they wanted to.

"Any idea who could have done this?" one of the agents in the front seat had asked.

No, Franklin Carter thought. I *don't have an idea*. I *know*.

But he looked at the agent dead in the eye and said, "No. I don't know anything about this."

CHAPTER

JACKSON DONNE'S MOTHER WOKE UP AN HOUR
later. She didn't jolt awake or sit up, she simply opened her eyes and
let out a deep breath as if she'd been holding it for a while. He
squeezed her hand. She didn't return the squeeze.

"Daddy?" she whispered.

"No, Mom," he said. "It's me, your son. It's Jackson."

"Dad," she said again. "Dad, you can't go there. You'll get hurt."

The words were directed at him. There was fear in her voice, her
hands shook, and she breathed quickly as if she was nervous. Her
dark eyes bored into his, but she didn't see her son, she saw her father. And for some reason, he was in danger.

"Mom," Donne said again. "Your father is dead. He has been for
years."

"Dad, please. Just stay." She whispered the words, but they

contained power. He remembered her ability to do that anytime he came home late. She didn't want to wake up Susan, but she wanted Donne to know she meant business. *You never do what you're told*.

Donne wasn't going anywhere.

She told him or her father—Donne wasn't sure which—to stay one more time, and then her entire body shook and tears ran down her cheeks. He squeezed her hand tighter. He didn't know what she was talking about, but he told her it would be okay.

Eventually her breathing slowed, the crying stopped, and she slipped back to sleep. He let go of her hand and stood up.

It didn't take a doctor to realize she was very ill and there wasn't much time left. His sister had been right to ask him to come here.

He found a box of Kleenex in the desk after he returned to the chair. He took a few tissues and dried the tears off his mother's face.

Donne's throat closed up and he had to leave the room. He stepped out into the hallway and pulled the door of room 308 closed behind him. He dialed his sister.

When she answered, Donne said, "She didn't recognize me."

"What are you talking about?" Susan didn't sound like she was crying anymore, but her voice was thick, as if he'd woken her up from a deep sleep.

"Mom didn't recognize me."

"Jackson, that's just the disease. She doesn't recognize me half the time. Of course, if you'd taken the time to visit earlier, it would be easier for her."

"Fuck you, Susan. She kept calling me 'Dad.'"

"She's been talking about Grandpa Joe a lot lately."

"Did you know him?"

"No. He died before I was born too. Mom always called him Grandpa Joe anyway. Don't you remember?"

To be honest, he didn't. He only remembered his mother crying the day his father walked out on them. It was the dominating memory of his childhood, his mother's sadness. When she was disappointed in him, when she compared him to his father. And now she was comparing him to *her* father.

"Has Mom ever talked about her father being in danger?" he asked.

"What? What are you talking about?"

The old woman in the wheelchair who'd been crying earlier rolled past him and asked him to have a good day.

He told Susan what their mother had said.

"No," Susan said. "She never said anything like that. I told you, she said he killed someone."

"Who would know about Grandpa Joe? Are there any relatives still around I could speak to? Maybe they could tell us what Mom is talking about."

"Aunt Faye is still around. She lives in Rutherford, I think. I'll have to look up her address. Franklin and I send her a Christmas card every year. Hold on. Let me find the address book."

The thought of Susan and her husband actually taking the time to write out Christmas cards was vaguely sickening. She was living a normal life, the kind he never imagined for himself.

Susan came back and gave him the address. Donne memorized it.

For the first time, he noticed the antiseptic smell of the nursing home. It was too clean, like everything had been washed away.

For all the work the staff put into making this a home, it still felt like a hospital, clean, sanitary, and distant.

✳

Mike Garibell burned the fake ID and became Bryan Hackett again.

Standing in the middle of his living room, Hackett smiled as he watched the news. The feds had no idea. They hadn't ruled out terrorism yet. He had plenty of time. And his job wasn't even done yet.

Jill came up behind him, dug her hands into his shoulder muscles, and kneaded. He closed his eyes and rolled his neck.

"It went good," she said. "How long before we get the money?"

"These things take time," he said. "This was only the beginning."

She stopped massaging. Hackett turned to face her.

"You already talked to Carter. He knows you're serious. He

didn't give you the money the first time you asked. Now he damn well better. And fast."

"It's going to take more time. You're right, he knows I'm serious. But knowing him, he's going to try and show me he's serious too. We're going to have to get to the wife."

"You still think you'll need to go through with the whole thing."

Hackett smiled. "I'm *hoping* I need to go through with the whole thing."

"We need the money." Jill crossed her arms and pouted. "Soon."

"I know when the plane leaves. We'll have it by then." Hackett brushed a blond lock of hair behind her ear. "But things might get worse before then. I want you to go to your mother's."

"What? No." She stepped back from him.

"You have to. It's not going to be safe here."

"I want to be a part of this. I want to be there when you get the money."

Hackett nodded. "I'll call you. You'll be in the loop every step of the way. But it's better this way. You won't be hurt."

"This isn't a good idea."

He wrapped her in his arms and held her tight. Jill's hands never touched his back. She kept them at her sides.

"Please," he said. "I love you."

"Only if you promise to call."

"I promise." He felt her finally return the hug. "Now go pack."

Jill broke the embrace and went up the stairs. Watching her go, Hackett thought it almost felt like he hadn't blown up a building only hours before. Just another day of marriage.

But the plan was in motion. One more thing had to be taken care of.

Hackett picked up the phone and dialed Delshawn. When the call was answered, all Hackett said was "Make it happen."

1938

Joe Tenant knew his wife would be worried sick. It wasn't like him to be this late. He didn't go out for a drink after the night shift like the other guys. He went home and walked his daughter to school, kissed his wife, and slept for six or seven hours. It wasn't exciting, but it was his life and that was how he liked it.

After talking to the police, he hoped he could put this behind him and get back to living his life. Three hours had felt like an eternity.

He sat in his car and started it, letting it warm up. The engine rattled and he hoped it wasn't on the verge of breaking down. While he was lucky enough to have a car in these hard times, he wasn't lucky enough to be able to afford fixing it.

"Joe Tenant," a voice behind him said. An Irish brogue, thick and rough.

Before Tenant could turn around, he felt cool metal against his chin. Whoever was behind him was pressing a knife against his skin.

"You saw us, didn't you? That's unfortunate for you."

Tenant had to swallow before he spoke. He felt the saliva curl down his throat and he wondered if it would be the last thing he tasted.

"Who are you?" he asked.

The knife pulled against his skin, and he felt a sharp pain along his jawline.

"Ah, you're not gonna be asking any more questions, okay?"

"Please," Tenant said.

"Now, listen to me, and I won't have to dig this blade any deeper. Do I have your attention?"

"You have my attention," he said.

"Good. Here's what's going to happen. You're going to go home today, back to your wife, and tell her you love her. You're going to sleep and you're going to come back into work tonight. You're going to live your life, do you understand?"

Tenant said yes, though he didn't understand at all.

"What you're not going to do," the Irishman continued, "is go back to the police. You'll know nothing of this day. It didn't happen. The police have the body now and their investigation is under way. You did the right thing. But you're not going to help anymore. You can't help. You didn't see anything else. Understand?"

"Yes."

"We do business a certain way, Mr. Tenant. No one was supposed to find that body. It's unfortunate it surfaced when it did. And that you were there. And it's unfortunate you're going to have a scar from this knife. But let me tell you something: A scar is a small thing compared to what we can do. Have a nice day."

The back door of the car opened and slammed shut. Tenant rubbed his chin, feeling blood on his fingers.

His family was too important. He was going to keep his mouth shut, and they were going to leave him alone.

CHAPTER 5

DONNE CRUISED OVER THE PASSAIC RIVER, ACROSS Route 21, and got off at Park Avenue. Normally, with traffic it was about a twenty-five-minute drive. Today he was going to make it in twenty, and that felt long. He made the requisite turns and found the little Cape Cod home Faye and George lived in.

He wondered if they would remember him. The next thing he wondered was, what did two senior citizens need a black Cadillac Escalade for? The enormous SUV was parked on the curb outside their house. He parked his car across from it and looked at the open front door. This was not a good sign. He immediately reached in the glove compartment for his Glock, then remembered he didn't carry it anymore.

One of the changes Donne was going to have to get used to, no longer being a licensed private investigator.

He crept across the front lawn and pressed himself against the gray siding. The grass needed cutting. Envelopes overflowed in the mailbox next to the front door.

He peeked through the slightly open front door but couldn't see anything except an empty hallway.

The first gunshot sounded like a firecracker. A loud firecracker, but a firecracker nonetheless. Donne hit the dirt because of instinct, but he was immediately on his feet again and moving quickly to the front door. There was no mistaking the second gunshot.

Call the police, he thought. But this was a quiet suburban town. Someone was home and would hear the shots and call the cops. A tall black man dressed in gang colors emerged from the front door as Donne reached for the knob. The man didn't register Donne, and Donne hit him hard, wrapping him up like a linebacker.

"What the fuck?" he said as he hit the ground. "Get off me, nigga." Donne tried to push him hard in the grass by his shoulders, but the guy rolled and hit him in the cheek with something metallic. It was Donne's turn to grunt as he hit the grass.

While Donne was trying to shake off the pain, the guy got into his Escalade. He was down the street before Donne was even able to sit up. A bright blue shirt. What gang was that? When he was a cop, Donne used to know these things, but years away from the force and the shot to the head had slowed him down.

He sat on the grass for a minute, trying to clear his head and let the world come back into focus. As it did, he remembered the two gunshots and pushed himself to his feet.

The inside of the house was quiet, and cleaner than the outside. Everything was neat and dusted. The TV played *The Price Is Right*. He stepped past a brown recliner and through a doorway into the kitchen. The kitchen was not so neat.

Faye and George were strewn across the kitchen tile on their stomachs. Blood stained the tiles, pouring from their heads. They'd both been shot twice in the back of their skulls. Executions. No point trying to resuscitate them. They were undoubtedly dead.

Whatever had happened in here, it was quick, and his aunt and uncle hadn't put up a fight. They probably got to their knees believing that act of submission would save them. They probably believed they would live.

In less than twenty-four hours, two of his relatives were dead and his brother-in-law's restaurant had been blown up. He was going to have to talk to Franklin Carter again.

In the distance he heard police sirens. After a quick sweep of the house, Donne found that nothing seemed to be missing. There was money and jewelry on the dresser in their bedroom. The TV and radio were still there. Even the lockbox in his uncle's office remained intact. He was careful not to touch anything as he stepped out of the room and back onto the front lawn. Standing on the grass, he let it all sink in. The house was so familiar, pictures on the mantel, the piano they'd had for years but he'd never heard played. He remembered having Thanksgiving dinner here when he was ten, two years after his father left.

They sat at the table, Aunt Faye and his mother next to each other across from Susan and him. Uncle George at the head of the table, carving knife in hand, turkey in front of him. It was all smiles that day, the promise of another family holiday ahead of them. The sides had been passed, a full plate of mashed potatoes, carrots, peas, and green beans for everyone. Per tradition, the orange and lime Jell-Os sat untouched. Apparently, his great-grandmother passed the recipe down, but not the original taste. All that was left to pass was the bird. The play-by-play of a football game added an extra rhythm to the meal.

It was a regular Norman Rockwell moment.

Uncle George sank the knife into the turkey. He smiled as he got a whiff of the aroma and said, "Faye, I can tell already you've topped yourself."

Aunt Faye smiled back at him but didn't say anything.

Mom and Susan were engaged in an argument about blue jeans, but there wasn't any anger in the argument. Mom was laughing.

George turned to Donne and asked if he wanted white meat or dark meat.

"Both," Donne said.

"Thattaboy." He laughed. "You know, one day you'll be doing this for your own family. And for us too, I hope."

"You think so?"

"Think? I know it. Look at the way you take care of your mom and sister since your dad— Well, just look. You do a good job of it."

"Thanks, Uncle George."

"Remember that when you get older, okay? Remember moments like these."

"I will," Donne said with a ten-year-old's enthusiasm.

"Family," he said. "It means everything."

Donne nodded. At the time, he believed him.

After dinner, George took him aside. "Remember what I said. Our family has been through a lot, even before you were born. And sometimes you're going to have to fix what the people before you did wrong."

"What do you mean, Uncle George?"

"There's something I'm trying to put right. It might take a few years, but your aunt and I are going to fix it. Maybe I'll even tell you about it one day."

The police sirens grew louder, snapping Donne back to the present. He felt his legs give out. Before today he hadn't seen his mother since he left to spend a year at Villanova. He couldn't remember the last time he'd seen Faye and George. Now his mother was in a bed holding on to life and confusing him with her father. His aunt and uncle were dead, lying motionless on kitchen tiles.

He tried to fight it down, and did, barely. He sat on the grass and waited.

✳

Susan Carter sat on her couch, glued to the TV. She wondered if this was how the families of 9/11 felt during those first few hours watching as their loved ones were trapped inside the two burning buildings. Hoping, praying there was a way out, some way they were still alive.

No, she decided. They felt much worse. Everyone Susan knew was okay, no one was hurt, and no one was killed. It was just her husband's business in ruins. And even then, they still had the restaurant in Montclair. The original Carter's.

The reporter on Channel 4 stood in front of two fire trucks, talking about an "all-too-familiar scene on the Upper East Side." In between the trucks behind the reporter, Susan saw Franklin talking to a man in a suit. Franklin was hunched over and looked exhausted. She wondered what they were talking about. Why would terrorists blow up their restaurant with no one inside? Why hadn't the FBI said anything yet?

The news switched to a traffic report explaining when the bridges and tunnels would open again. All this because of her husband's restaurant. Again, she came back to the question: Why? Things like this didn't happen to her. At least, they didn't before she met Franklin.

The phone rang, startling her. She picked it up. It was Jackson, and she expected an update on Faye and George, to hear what they knew about her grandfather. That wasn't what he told her.

Jackson said that Faye and George were dead.

Shot, he said. Murdered.

She didn't hear the rest, because she dropped the phone. Her entire body tingled and she felt herself racked with sobs so crippling she collapsed on the floor.

CHAPTER

WHEN THE COPS SHOWED UP, THEY WENT THROUGH
the routine of frisking, cuffing, and sitting Donne in the backseat of a
cop car while they checked out his story. Going through it too many
times before, he had hoped this part of his life was over when his private investigator's license was revoked.

Through the back window, Donne watched the first officer on
the scene dry-heave on the front lawn. Probably a rookie, never seen a
murdered body before. In a few moments, two detectives would show
up and do their thing, and a bigger Bergen County city would send a
medical examiner or CSI guys or whatever they were called. Worst-
case scenario, the county would send someone in.

So he waited, watched as two plainclothers he didn't recognize
pulled up in a Chevy. The one in the pin-striped suit talked to the of-

ficer, and the one in a charcoal suit went through the front door while pulling on plastic gloves. Pinstripe followed Charcoal inside.

Donne settled back into the leather seat.

✳

Pinstripe waited twenty minutes before he came out to talk to Donne. If there was a pool, Donne's money would have been on having to wait half an hour. The cop must have had a date.

He opened the back door of the car and crouched in front of Donne.

"I'm Detective Iapicca," he said. He ran a hand through his thick black hair, and with all the oil in it, Donne was surprised the hand came back dry. Then he produced a badge.

"I'm Jackson Donne." He couldn't move his hands. They were cuffed behind him.

Iapicca nodded. "Why don't you tell me what happened?"

Donne told him the entire story. Did not leave a detail out. He had learned the hard way that lying will only get you in more trouble.

When Donne finished, Iapicca said, "You expect me to believe that?"

"Well," Donne said, choosing his words carefully, "it is what happened. And you told me to tell you 'what happened.'"

"Let me ask you something. You know how many times I've interviewed witnesses?"

"No. I've never met you before."

"Lots of times."

"I see."

"And, do you know how many times they've told me a 'black guy' did it?"

"No idea."

"I don't have the exact specifics, but I'd go with ninety percent."

"You don't keep stats?"

"Listen, all I'm saying is your story sounds a bit sketchy. Most of the time someone tells me it's the black guy in gang colors, it turns out they're lying. Gangs are not a problem in Rutherford, New Jersey."

Donne took a deep breath. "This town is right in between Passaic, Paterson, and Newark. Three cities where gangs are extremely prevalent. And you're telling me it's impossible to have a gang member come in and shoot my aunt and uncle."

"I'm saying it's unlikely."

The charcoal-suited cop came out of the front door. He was on a cell phone.

"Then what is likely?" Donne asked.

"You did it."

Donne nodded. Time to shut up.

"But," he continued, "the time for that accusation will come later. Right now there's really no evidence." He flipped a business card on Donne's lap. "The rookie over there is going to uncuff you and you'll be free to go. Call me if you think of anything else."

He winked at Donne.

"Or," Iapicca said, "if you just want to turn yourself in."

<hr />

That was the fucking shit, Carlos thought, walking down the street. Cesar and James were ahead of him, laughing. Cut school and just steal shit. Best day ever. Just fucking around, havin' fun.

"Yo, nigga," James said, "you shoulda D-blocked that sign."

Carlos thought about the neon Budweiser sign. That would look tight in his room, next to the Ludacris poster, but nah, he couldn't carry it. And the police always drove by the bar. Throwing the rocks to break the window was bad enough.

"If five-oh shows up," Cesar said, "just run. We get the hell out. They ain't gonna catch us."

"Nah, yo," Carlos said, looking over his shoulder. "Five-oh come by, walk. They ain't gonna arrest anyone who walkin'. We ain't do nothing wrong then."

Cesar started to laugh, but sure enough, they heard the sirens of a cop car. Carlos didn't even flinch, just kept on walking. Cesar and James, though, they didn't listen.

James took off first, looking like he did when he ran track at school, arms tight to the body, knees up high. Cesar flailed, arms all over the place. You could tell the panic just by the way he ran.

Carlos, though, did not hurry. Nothing bothered him. Especially not the cops.

Cesar and James were a good block and a half ahead when the car blew by Carlos. It screeched to a halt in front of his two friends. Carlos laughed and turned the corner. Walked down the street toward the river. Passaic River smelled like shit, but it was better than walking toward a cop car.

As he reached the bank of the river, he saw a big black Escalade pull off the curb back toward Route 3. Looked just like one of those cars on BET in the videos. He walked toward it, wondering if whoever was inside was somebody famous.

The Escalade was long gone by the time Carlos reached the spot where it had been parked. He looked down at the tracks in the street, like he'd spun the wheels out. He wanted to walk down closer, but man, he just got these Air Forces and he didn't want them to get all muddy.

But something caught his eye reflecting in the light, down by the river. It was sticking out of the mud, stuck there like it had been tossed out the window. And he knew what it was.

He decided it was worth getting his shoes muddy to get a better look.

He reached down and pulled it out of the dirt to look at it.

So much better than a fucking neon beer sign.

Definitely a gun.

CHAPTER

I SHOULD BE WITH MY SISTER.

Sitting in Parkway traffic, Donne pulled out his cell phone and called his job instead. He was supposed to be clocking in in an hour. There was no way he'd get there in time. And deep in his bones, he knew he wouldn't be back there at all.

His boss, Rick Manning, picked up.

"I quit," Donne said.

"What? What are you talking about? You're supposed to be here."

"I quit," Donne said again. He thought about the check from Franklin Carter.

"You can't quit."

"I'm not coming in tonight. I have to take care of things. I won't be in again."

"Why not? What happened?"

Rick's neck muscles were probably taut with anger. Donne didn't hear what he said next. He hung up the phone.

I should be with my sister.

✳

Two hours later, Donne was six beers deep at the Olde Towne Tavern. As Artie filled his pint glass with a seventh Bud, Donne's mind spun through the list of dead that had surrounded his life. Their faces were blurry, as if they were faded into the distance and only the alcohol kept them around. He took the glass from Artie.

Donne didn't want them to leave, either.

Artie watched him take a slug from the pint glass. Before Donne could put the glass to his lips again, Artie said, "All right, what's the problem?"

"I quit my job," Donne said.

Artie nodded.

"My mother has Alzheimer's. She's dying."

He took a sip of beer. Artie said nothing.

"My brother-in-law's restaurant blew up."

Another sip. Still nothing.

"My aunt and uncle were murdered and the cop at the scene thinks I did it."

Artie turned around and started to walk away from him. Donne finished off his beer and said, "Where are you going?"

He stopped at the taps, took two more pint glasses and filled them. Then he found the bottle of Jack and two shot glasses.

"We're both going to have to drink."

He put the glasses down and started pouring the Jack Daniel's. He tried to keep his face straight, but when he made eye contact with Donne, he broke into a huge grin and started laughing.

"Man," Artie said. "When the shit hits the fan for you, it really hits the fan."

After today, his neck tense, the buzz of the alcohol swirling through him, he couldn't help himself. Donne laughed too.

They did a shot, and toasted Donne's aunt and uncle.

"So, what happens tomorrow?" he asked.

"I get back to work."

"Thought you said you quit."

Donne took a deep pull from the pint glass, draining half of it. The beer went down smooth. He was flying high. After the next beer, he wouldn't feel anything until tomorrow morning.

"I have a new job," he said. "I'm going to find out what the hell is going on."

✳

Franklin Carter needed to call his wife. He'd spent all day in the city, and his cell had been ringing nonstop. But he didn't have time now. Special Agent Sam Draxton sat across the table from him. They were in the local Starbucks. Draxton was on his third cup. Carter bit into a black and white cookie.

"So," Draxton said. "You gonna tell me what happened?"

"What do you mean?"

Draxton took a sip of coffee, his eyes never leaving Carter.

"You and I both know this isn't terrorism."

The cookie suddenly tasted stale. He placed it on the napkin. "It isn't?"

"No. Terrorists want casualties. They're not going to blow up a restaurant at three in the morning. So, what's going on here?"

"Why would I know?"

The coffee shop was empty. No one wanted to be in the area. Franklin Carter had never seen the streets this empty. The silence in the neighborhood was eerie.

Draxton's cell phone rang. He answered and quickly said, "Yeah, you can tell 'em. And get the tunnels and bridges open."

He closed the phone and said, "We know things we can't let on. We know this isn't Al Qaeda or any of those organizations. They would have taken credit. So now we have to interview suspects."

"Are you saying I'm a suspect?"

Draxton spread his hands. "I'm saying you probably know something."

"I don't."

Now the agent nodded. "I'm sure you don't. Let me ask you something. Are there people out there who dislike you?"

"I'm sure there are people who aren't happy with me. I'm sure someone didn't like a dish that was served there. Customers are unhappy all the time."

"You know that's not what I mean."

"What would you like me to say? I haven't a clue what's going on. I'm fucking tired and I want to go home to see my wife."

"Have you been in competition with any other restaurants?"

"There's always competition."

"Friendly?"

"Yes. When we opened, the Chicken Roost owners came down to eat at our restaurant. Brought a bottle of wine, spent a fortune, tipped our waitress great. But then they asked us to come eat there. I never went. We've been rivals ever since. But nothing like this would come of it."

Carter shifted in his seat. The damned Starbucks stools were the least comfortable chairs he'd ever sat in. They should have gone for the couches. But Carter was pretty sure Draxton wanted them to sit in these seats for some reason.

"When can I go home?" Carter asked.

"We'll get someone to drive you home now," Draxton said. "Just one more question."

"What's that?"

"Do we have any reason to be worried about your Montclair restaurant?"

Carter shifted again. What should he tell them? There was every reason to be worried about it. But if he said yes, the feds would want to know *why* he was worried. And he couldn't tell them that.

He took a deep breath.

"No," he said. "There is absolutely no reason to be concerned. Now, if you'll excuse me, I have to let my wife know I'll be home soon."

CHAPTER 8

HIS mother was awake when Donne visited her the next morning. She was still lying in the bed, but her eyes were focused as she took him in. Her mouth opened to speak, and he braced himself.

"Jackson?" she said with a hoarse voice.

He reached over to a cup of water and helped her sip some.

"Yeah, Mom. It's me." Today she didn't think he was her father. Progress.

"I want to go home," she said, her voice loosening up a little. Donne wondered when she last spoke. Was it yesterday when he was visiting?

"I know," he said. "Maybe soon."

"Thank you. I miss my house."

She sipped some more water.

Outside the room, Donne could hear a woman screaming. She wanted to go home too. She just announced it more forcefully.

"I miss you too, Jackson," she said.

Donne didn't know how much time he had before his mother's focus faded into oblivion. He wanted her to know what happened. But it could completely mess her up, set her back.

She put her hand in his.

His mother should know. She was still human, she was still alive. She should know about her own brother.

"Mom, I have some bad news."

His mother didn't speak. She blinked.

"Aunt Faye and Uncle George died yesterday. Someone shot them."

Outside the screaming woman stopped. In the hallway, the only sounds were the beeping of medical machines. His mother leaned back in the bed and shut her eyes. Donne wondered if she understood.

"Daddy," she said.

He squeezed her hand, sure he'd lost her focus. The news was too much for her to handle. He had sent her back into the abyss that her life had been swimming in. A small tear trickled from the corner of her left eye. She returned the squeeze.

"This is all your fault, Daddy," she said.

"What?" he asked. "Mom, what did you say?"

Behind him one of the nurses entered. She wore blue coveralls and held a clipboard in her hand. She gave him a brief smile.

"I'm sorry," she said, "it's time for her medication. You'll have to step outside."

"Is the medicine going to put her to sleep?"

The nurse didn't expect such a question and glared at the clipboard, as if consulting her notes.

"She normally sleeps after she takes it, yes."

"You can't give it to her now. I need to talk with her some more."

"Sir, I'm sorry, but this is the scheduled time. We can't mess up the schedule. Now, if you'll excuse me."

She stepped past him and put his mother's hand back on the

bed. "Hi, Isabelle. How are we doing today?" she asked with a saccharine voice.

As he left the room, his mother's words echoed in his head.

This is all your fault, Daddy.

✴

Donne's sister's home was on Upper Mountain Road, a sprawling brick home with a long driveway hidden behind a gate and two large bushes. He parked on the street and walked across the front lawn, hurrying to avoid as much rain as possible.

Susan answered in pajama pants and a Montclair State University T-shirt. Her hair was out of place, there were dark circles under her eyes, and her cheeks were ruddy. He could tell she'd been crying.

"Oh, Jackson," she said, and wrapped him up in her arms. They stood on the porch in the rain, hugging. Donne couldn't remember the last time he had hugged his sister. For a moment, the past melted away and they were just two people in mourning.

When Susan broke the embrace, the dampness of her tears streaked down both their faces.

"Come inside," she said.

Donne followed her into the living room, which had two leather couches, a black leather easy chair, a glass table, wall-to-wall shag carpet, and what had to be a fifty-inch flat-screen TV. The TV was turned to the news.

"The restaurant business has treated you guys well, I see," he said.

"We do okay." Susan didn't make eye contact.

He sat on the couch and ran his hand through his wet hair to push it out of his eyes. Outside, thunder crashed.

"They just said on the news the explosion wasn't terrorism, but it was a bomb," Susan said.

"What did Franklin say?"

"I haven't talked to him. He came home after I fell asleep last night and just kissed me on the cheek. Didn't say anything. He left before I woke up."

"Where was he going?"

"I don't know," Susan said. "Oh my God, Jackson. Between this and Faye and George . . . and Mom. How are we going to deal with this?"

He didn't answer right away. The old grudge still throbbed inside him.

"We?"

"The family. You, me, Franklin? Maybe we should try and get in touch with Faye and George's son."

"Their son? Susan, that was a long time ago. An adoption. You know it didn't work out."

"Still, he should know."

"Do you know what happened to him?"

"No."

"Well, I don't have time now. I'm going to find out what's going on. I need to talk to Franklin. And soon."

"Call him."

"You're going to have to give me his number."

She did. Donne saved it to his contacts list.

"What about the Montclair restaurant?" he asked.

"What do you mean?"

"Are the police concerned about it?"

"I don't know," she said. "Like I said, I haven't gotten the chance to talk to Franklin. All the information I've gotten came from the news reports. And they're all focused on New York. I know they opened the bridges and tunnels late last night. That's it."

She paced the living room with balled fists. It was as if she was attempting to puncture holes in her palms with her nails.

"You have to sit," he said. "Pacing like that isn't going to help. You need to try to go about life, and relax. If you keep worrying, it's just going to make time go slower. And the worry is going to build up until you burst."

"How did you deal with it? When Jeanne died? When you shot that guy in New Brunswick?" she said. "You sank into the bottle, that's how. I'm sorry, Jackson, that's not going to be me."

It was only then he realized how much he wanted a drink. How he would rather be sitting in the Olde Towne Tavern talking to Artie about the Yankees or Mets. Pint glass after pint glass.

"You know it's true," she said.

He stood up.

"I'll call you later," he said. "I have work to do."

As if she regretted her outburst, Susan said, "Be careful."

"I will."

He stepped out into the thunderstorm. It looked like this weather wouldn't ever let up.

※

Franklin Carter took an early break from Carter's on Church Street. The waitresses were setting up for lunch, the finances were in order, and his hostess kept asking annoying questions about the bombing. So, instead of politely not answering her questions, he decided to ignore her totally and go for coffee.

He ordered a coffee and sat facing the street. As far as he could tell, no one from the FBI was staked out near Carter's. He exhaled and took a sip of coffee as the door swung open and a burly man entered.

The man, ruddy faced, with freckles and red hair, sat across from him.

"What the hell are you doing here?" Carter asked.

Hackett laughed. "I have a message for you."

Franklin leaned across the table and his chest tapped his coffee cup. He caught it before it spilled everywhere, but some of the brown liquid splashed onto the tabletop. There went any shot of being intimidating.

"You look nervous, Franklin. Stressed. Is everything okay?"

Carter said nothing.

"Oh, that's right, I've been watching the news. The bombing."

Hackett leaned back. He had a pale smooth face, clean shaven. "That's gotta suck."

"It was you."

"Pay up. I asked you for money months ago. You didn't listen. Next time, the restaurant might not be empty."

Hackett stood up, straightened the collar of his polo shirt, and exited back into the rain. Carter put his head in his hands and tried to breathe deeply.

There was no way he was going to pay.

"They're dead?"

"Yeah."

"Good. Maybe now you should find out what happened to the witness. What did he look like?"

Delshawn described him. Jackson Donne, a bit earlier than expected.

"You want him out of the picture?"

Hackett let the question linger a moment.

"No. It's not time for that yet." Hackett chose his words carefully. "Just slow him down a bit."

"A'ight."

Hackett snapped his cell phone shut.

CHAPTER

DONNE'S NEXT STOP WAS ONLY A MILE AWAY. He took Upper Mountain Road to Bloomfield, where you had to pay a meter. He parked, paid, and walked around the corner.

Along Church and Bloomfield, Montclair was an integration of all three parts of the city's population. It seemed to Donne that the poor made their way south toward the discount shoe stores and fast-food restaurants. The college kids worked their way along the old record shop and toward sushi restaurants. And the wealthy members of the population checked out antique shops and Carter's. Even in the pouring rain.

The town struck him as less segregated than New Brunswick, where the rich hung out in the restaurant and theater districts, the poor stayed north of the theaters, and the students kept mostly on campus. Montclair seemed integrated and more modern. Or maybe he was just cynical about his own city.

He stepped under the purple canopy of Carter's, its name written along the sides in script, and knocked on the glass door. They wouldn't open for lunch for another ten minutes, but he hoped Franklin was there.

Instead, a short blonde who didn't look a day over twenty pushed the door open. She wore a white button-down shirt, black dress pants, and a name tag that read "Kate."

"I'm sorry, sir, we don't open until noon."

Donne checked his watch. "Well, it's almost noon, Kate."

Hearing her name threw her off for a second, but she put on a great condescending smile and said, "Almost isn't noon. I'm sorry, sir."

Kate started to close the door, but he put his hand in and pulled it from her hand. The condescending smile set him off.

"Hey," she said. "You can't do that."

"I'm looking for Franklin Carter. Is he in?"

"No," she said, trying—but failing—to pull the door closed. Donne now had his foot stuck between the door and the jamb. "He won't be in until after noon."

"Well," he said, grabbing the door again. He pulled it wide open. "I guess I'll just have to wait for him."

"You can't—" Kate said as Donne stepped past her into the restaurant. "Who the hell are you?"

"That's not very professional."

He walked toward the hostess table, noticing the dark maroon wallpaper with dark mahogany-trimmed walls. The tables in the middle of the restaurant were wooden as well, all set with paper napkins and silverware.

"I don't care how professional it is. You can't just come barging in here."

Donne took a seat at one of the tables. Not very comfortable. The wooden back of the chair was solid and straight. He couldn't settle into it. They probably wanted the customers uncomfortable so as to move them in and out quickly when the place was busy.

"I'm working for Mr. Carter," Donne said. Then he gave her his best condescending smile. "And I'm his brother-in-law."

He was pretty sure someone put the air-conditioning on at that moment. Kate's stare could have frozen fire.

"Oh," she said. "You."

"Yep, me. Do you think I could get lunch?" He glanced at his watch again. "It is noon now."

Kate's face flushed. "Can I get you something to drink?"

"Beer?"

"We don't have a liquor license. Most of Montclair is bring your own."

"I see. I'll just take an iced tea, then."

"Very well," Kate said. "Your waitress will be right with you."

"You're not my waitress?"

"I'm just the hostess, sir."

"That's a shame."

She disappeared through a curtain into the kitchen. Through the front window he watched the rain splatter and traffic pass. A few people with umbrellas stopped and checked the menu, then moved on.

A tall brunette, dressed the same as Kate but with a name tag that read "Lauren," put a glass of iced tea in front of him and asked if he was ready to order. He told her he'd have a steak sandwich. She gave him a more genuine smile than Kate had and also disappeared into the kitchen.

Framed on the walls were news reviews of Carter's, autographed pictures of a few B-list celebrities who'd frequented the place, and one picture of Franklin Carter standing around a bunch of waitresses posed as if it were a family portrait. He looked happy as hell. Donne had never seen him that way.

"Hey, Lauren," he called.

She poked her head out through the kitchen door.

"Yeah?"

"Has Franklin been in today at all?"

She walked over to his table, leaned over, and spoke in a whisper. "He was here this morning but left to grab some coffee when *somebody* annoyed him." She crooked her head back to the kitchen as she spoke.

He couldn't imagine Kate annoying anyone.

"He'll be back soon, I'm sure," Lauren said. "Your food will be right out."

"Thanks."

She started back toward the kitchen, but he stopped her.

"So," he said. "What's the buzz on what happened in New York?"

"I don't know anything about that."

"Come on," he said. "I'm sure Kate told you that I'm working for Franklin. That I'm kind of a detective. How am I going to figure anything out if I don't ask and you don't tell?"

"Kate said you were working for Franklin's wife. Something about her mother."

Jeez, word got around quick. He wondered what other gossip Franklin had let drop in the past two days.

"Well, you never know what might be related," he said.

"I honestly don't know anything except what's been said on the news."

"Has Franklin been acting strange lately?"

"Nothing more than usual. A few arguments with Kate, but that happens all the time when you have co-owners. There's always restaurant drama. I hate this place."

"Well, listen, if you hear anything, give me a call. I like drama." Donne dropped his old business card on the table. Other than the location of his now-defunct office, the information was up to date.

She picked it up and said, "Let me get your sandwich."

The front door opened and Carter stepped inside. He was soaking wet and looked pale. He made eye contact with Donne. Donne didn't think it was possible, but Carter went even more white.

"Hi, Franklin," Donne said. "I was hoping we could talk."

"More talk is the last thing I need," he said.

✳

Carlos took the gun down to the alleyway across the street from Rutt's. Now that the rain had stopped, he could finally get outside to try the thing. The cars from Route 3 would be loud enough to cover the sounds of the gun, he thought. He wanted to fire it in the alleyway, just to see what it was like. That would be so fucking gansta.

He stood like they did in the movies. The bad guys, not the cops, relaxed with the gun held sideways, and leanin' back like Fat Joe in that video. He pulled the trigger and the thing went off. It sounded like thunder, and his ears were ringing. The recoil from the gun knocked him on his ass. He didn't expect that.

It was fucking cool, though. Too bad school was out.

"What the hell was that?" he heard someone yell.

Shit. Route 3 was nowhere near as loud as he needed it to be.

He shoved the gun into the waistband of his jeans and ran up Delawanna.

CHAPTER **10**

fRANKLIN cARteR RubbeD HIS face IN HIS HANDS.
He sat across from Donne and refused to make eye contact. Droplets
of water soaked into his shirt at the shoulders, and his hair was mat-
ted down from the rain.

He took a deep breath, bit his lip, and said, "I thought you were
dealing with your mother. That's what I'm paying you for."

"I want to know what happened in the city."

"What's there to know? A truck pulled up and blew up. Now
there's nothing. But no one got hurt. That's what happened."

"Who did it?"

He finally met Donne's eyes. But Carter looked at Donne like
Donne was an idiot. "Terrorists? Someone deranged? I don't know."

Lauren came out of the kitchen with the steak sandwich and

placed it, a bottle of ketchup, and a glass of iced tea in front of Donne. He took a sip of the tea.

"The FBI said it's not terrorists. And it seems very interesting that someone 'deranged' picked your restaurant to blow up. At three in the morning. When no one could get hurt."

"Deranged people are called deranged for a reason."

Donne took a bite of the steak sandwich. Better off taking his time and letting Carter sweat. He appeared shaken up and angry. That wasn't like the Carter he knew. Then again, his restaurant had just been bombed. That had to be hard to take.

Donne said, "It just seems like a huge coincidence that your restaurant blows up and two of my relatives are murdered."

"Susan told me they were dead. Nothing else. She was too upset. What happened?"

Donne told him the story, and Carter noticed the bruise on Donne's head from the gun. As Donne finished the story, Carter buried his head in his hands.

"Can you leave, please?" he asked.

"I'd like to finish my sand—"

"Get out!"

Donne put the sandwich down, fixing the silverware into the perfect place setting. He took a twenty out of his wallet and left it on the table. Carter said nothing during the process. Donne stood up and left the restaurant.

Outside the rain had stopped, and he walked to his car slowly. There was no hurry. He wanted to mull over what had just happened.

It could be that Carter was just having a bad day. At the same time, Donne's instinct was telling him otherwise. Carter knew something. He knew why people were dying. And though they hadn't spoken much, Donne remembered that Carter had been the rock for his sister at tough times. When Donne had gone into rehab. When Jeanne died.

Suddenly, it all came flooding back. Right there in the middle of Church Street, Donne almost passed out. He realized he hadn't thought of Jeanne in days.

They'd been separated for a few months, Donne and Jeanne.

Who she slept with in that time was her business. But his old partner? Finding that out only months ago had been like going through her death all over again. The short time they had when they got back together was tainted.

And then she got in the car that night.

What it must have been like, watching the headlights careening across the double yellow line toward her car. The drunk driver who left the scene of the crime never to be heard from again, empty bottles of scotch on the floor of the car the only clue to his state of mind. She died, and he couldn't be there to save her. He'd changed his life for her. And in an instant she was gone.

He got to his car and took a few deep breaths. He needed a drink. Badly.

✳

Delshawn Butler's cell phone rang before he even got out of the park. He looked at the caller ID and picked it up.

"You want the guy you ran into outside the house, you can have him. Beat the shit out of him," Hackett said.

Butler sucked his teeth and gave it some thought. "Yeah, where he at?"

"He's leaving Carter's restaurant." Hackett described the car the guy had been driving. The same one he saw outside of that East Rutherford house.

"How do you know it's him?"

"I just do."

Butler listened, hung up, and went to find his ride. He had some shit to deal with now.

He found the car pulling onto Valley Road just a few minutes later.

1 9 3 8

Joe Tenant opened the door to his kitchen. It was next to the driveway, and his family never used it, but he was too tired to walk back around to the front door like a "civilized man," as his wife would say.

Caroline was scrubbing the dishes in the sink and the kitchen smelled of bacon and maple syrup. She looked up from her work when he closed the door.

"You're late this morning. I had to walk Isabelle to school all by myself."

He started to apologize, to just say something, but the words wouldn't come. The lump in his throat was thick, and for a moment he was happy Isabelle was at school already. He wasn't going to be able to hold back the tears.

He collapsed into Caroline's arms, pulled her close to him, and kissed her neck. He didn't shake when he cried, the tears just rolled down his cheeks and onto the strap of his wife's apron.

"What's the matter?" she asked.

He didn't respond. Instead, he kissed her deeply and she responded, pressing her body against his, letting his tongue explore her mouth. She ran her hands through his hair. He lifted her up and carried her to the bedroom.

*

Before he fell asleep, Joe asked Caroline to wake him when she was going to pick up Isabelle. She did at quarter to three. He dressed and walked with her along Hoover toward the tall brick school. It was one of the best features of their house, being only a block from school. Behind them, he noticed a dark Chevy, its motor idling.

Isabelle was the second to last student out, like she always was. Something about walking in alphabetical order in a line struck Tenant the wrong way. It was like Isabelle was always going to come in last, that the school bred it in her, all because her last name started with T. She was going to have to work just a little bit harder.

When Isabelle saw Tenant, she screamed, "Daddy!" and embraced him. He lifted her off her feet and held her tight. Thankfully, tears did not come. He put her down and the family walked home together.

The Chevy still idled across from their house. Two men sat inside it, making no effort to hide. The one in the passenger seat gave Tenant a little wave while Tenant tried to stare them down.

"Nice kid," the guy in the car said.

"Take her inside," Tenant said to Caroline.

"What are you going to do?" She had seen the car too.

"Just go."

She did as she was told, and Joe went up the driveway and opened the trunk of his car. He took out the crowbar he kept inside. Gripping it in his right hand, he crossed the street. He noticed the Chevy's engine was now shut down.

They didn't know what was going to happen until it was too late. Tenant raised the crowbar over his head and brought it down hard on the windshield. The glass crumpled and shattered against the blow. He raised it again and brought it down upon the hood this time. He heard the engine roar to life.

"Stay the fuck away from my family! I did what you said!" he yelled, bringing the crowbar down twice more.

The car started to roll and pull away from the curb. Tenant stepped out of its path and threw the crowbar at the bumper. It clattered against the ground. The Chevy was gone.

✳

Two hours later, as Tenant dressed for work, he heard the telephone ring. He took it.

"That was a nice stunt today. Did your wife see it?"

He gripped the phone tight. He didn't recognize the voice, but it was definitely Irish.

"We only wanted to make sure you listened to our threat from the morning. You were in no danger at that moment. However, if you go to the police, if you try another stunt like you pulled this afternoon, you and your family's safety will be in danger." The voice trailed off.

Tenant wasn't going to put up with this.

"I told you to stay away from my family," he said. "Or what you saw from me today was just the beginning."

"Then I feel pity for your wife, because she's married to a dead man. I hope you understand."

The line went dead.

chapter **11**

JACKSON DONNE found a DIVE BAR ON vaLLey
Road in Montclair. Getting back to New Brunswick and the Tavern
would have taken too long, so instead he stopped there. The place
was named Tierney's and was incredibly Irish inside, at least by New
Jersey standards. Notre Dame flags, shamrocks, and a "Happy St.
Patrick's Day" sign from the nineties were stapled to the wall. The
wooden walls were old and rotting, and other than the bar and
barstools, there was only a jukebox.

When Donne ordered his beer, the bartender asked him how his
day was going. Donne grunted back a response and hoped it was clear
there wouldn't be any more talking. Just good old-fashioned drinking.

He heard the door to the bar swing open. Whoever came in
must have stood there surveying the bar for a minute, because Donne
didn't hear any footsteps at first. When he did, they were short and

light, as if the feet were barely touching the floor. The guy sat right next to him. Donne didn't even look.

No reason to make eye contact. That might start a conversation.

Half an hour later, Donne was three beers deep and just starting to get a buzz on. The memories of Jeanne were fading. His nerves were calming; one more beer and he'd be comfortable enough to go home.

The guy sitting next to him was only on his first beer.

"Yo, motherfucker, what you say?" He tapped Donne hard on the shoulder.

Donne half-turned toward him and said, "Nothing. I'm just drinking a beer."

"Hey, I said I heard you say something. Now I want to know what it was." He pushed Donne this time.

Donne turned fully toward him and took a look at him. He was thick, muscular, and black. In a bar like this, it would be a lie to say he wasn't noticeable. Especially this early in the afternoon.

"Look, I don't know what you're—" Donne recognized the man from his aunt's home. It was the guy who had pistol-whipped him. "Oh, fuck," he managed before taking a right cross to the head.

He spun off his barstool and onto the ground, just before his beer glass hit the floor. It shattered, sending shards of glass and splashes of beer everywhere. He tried to push himself up, but caught a quick shot to the ribs with the guy's foot.

"Hey," Donne heard someone yell. "Break it up!"

Probably the bartender.

Donne took another shot to the ribs and rolled onto his back. Looking up, he saw the guy lift a barstool over his head. He slammed it down on top of Donne, and Donne was barely able to lift an arm to block it. It shattered, and some of the wood scraped across Donne's face.

When Donne looked at the guy, everything moved in slow motion. He reached into the waistband of his pants, pulled out a large gun, and aimed it at Donne. He began to squeeze the trigger.

Donne braced himself for the inevitable shot, but then heard a large *clack* and everything snapped back into reality.

"I said, break it up." The bartender was aiming a pump-action shotgun at Donne's assailant.

"Yo, man," the asshole said, putting his gun away. "I'm getting the fuck out of here."

"Good idea," the bartender said.

The bastard jogged out the back door. The door slammed shut behind him, and for a moment there was silence. Then three gunshots, quickly followed by the squeal of tires.

Donne pushed himself to his feet and felt the bar sway around him. He would have been better off with the fourth beer.

"You okay?" the bartender asked.

"Yeah," he said.

"What did you say to him?"

"Not a word."

"You assholes can't be doing that sort of thing," he said. "I could lose my liquor license. There are only a few of those in Montclair, and they're expensive as hell."

Donne grunted and walked toward the door. He had to concentrate to walk straight. The pain in his arm and across his face slowed his step. He opened the door slowly, in case the guy was waiting for him, and peeked out. His car had its back windshield shot out, and the back two tires had been blown to shreds.

"Hey," the bartender said. "You're going to have to pay for these damages."

Donne pulled the door open fully and hobbled to his car. He had to rest when he reached it, put his hand on the trunk. His stomach tightened, and he had to fight to keep the beer down.

He didn't hear the bartender open the door.

"The police are on their way," the bartender yelled.

"Good," he said before the world tilted beneath him and black asphalt raced toward his face.

DONNE BLINKED, SPIT, AND COUGHED WATER. HIS body throbbed, and he had two new cuts on his hands from when he fell to the asphalt.

"Wake the fuck up," the bartender said, holding a bucket that dripped a few drops of water. "This is the last thing I need. I can't have you passed out in the parking lot." He looked at the flashing lights parading up the street.

Donne pushed himself into a sitting position. His wet clothes stuck to his skin and to the ground. With the stiffness in his beaten body, pushing himself up felt like it took forever. Two police cruisers pulled into the lot and stopped short in front of him. A major sign he should at least attempt to stand. Donne used his bumper, the shocks sagging under his weight, and got to his feet. Two officers got out of the cars.

"What the hell happened here?" one of them asked.

Donne told him. The bartender was talking to the other cop near the cruiser, his arms waving in the air, looking at him every once in a while. He was much more animated than Donne was.

"We're going to have to impound your car for evidence," the first officer said after Donne was finished. "You might want to get to a hospital."

"I'll be fine."

He didn't seem convinced. "Then are you going to be able to find yourself a ride?"

Donne nodded, thinking about calling Artie but knowing he wouldn't be able to get away from work. He thought about calling Carter or Susan, but decided there was someone else he wanted to talk to. Someone who hadn't believed his story earlier.

✳

Detective Mike Iapicca picked Donne up an hour later. He wasn't happy about it. Donne didn't think the detective thought he'd ever call him, and Iapicca was going to take any opportunity he had to talk to Donne.

"Get the fuck in," he said from his Chevy Impala.

Donne limped around the car and sat in the passenger seat.

"You look like shit," Iapicca said.

"The guy who killed my aunt and uncle yesterday just kicked the shit out of me."

"I see." He took Valley Road away from Montclair. Donne was woozy and wondered if Iapicca would actually take him back to New Brunswick or to East Rutherford. "This black guy dressed in gang colors? He just happens to show up in a bar in Montclair that you're drinking in?"

"Yeah."

"How much did you have to drink?"

"Two beers."

"Everyone says one or two."

"I would have had three, but the punch to the face kept me from finishing it."

Traffic slowed near a shopping area. They got caught at a red light. People sat outside a Starbucks sipping coffee. A few others stared at mannequins in a GAP window. Donne felt the drowsiness in his eyes, and he leaned back in the passenger seat.

"You think I'm going to let you sleep in my car? Jesus, you probably have a concussion and you can't think straight."

Donne couldn't help it. His eyelids drooped and he fell asleep.

✴

Bryan Hackett answered his cell phone. It was Delshawn.

"I beat the shit outta that motherfucker."

"Is he dead?"

"Nah, fuckin' bartender had a shotgun. So I shot the motherfucker's tires and windows out."

"Good. How bad is he hurt?"

"I hit him with a stool. He was bleeding all over the bar. I don't know if he was knocked out or whatnot, but he was hurtin'."

Hackett rubbed his chin. Donne was only momentarily out of the picture, which meant he couldn't slow any of this down. And while Carter might not be willing to pay up, Hackett was pretty sure he could break Carter's wife. Hackett was glad Delshawn had listened and didn't kill Donne. This was turning into a game. And the best games involved challenges. Donne would be a good challenge.

He hung up the phone. This whole business venture might actually be fun.

1 9 3 8

Joe Tenant sat with two police officers. Cigarette smoke layered the air, and the sweet smell made Tenant wish he hadn't quit. But when he'd gotten back in the boxing ring to spar with a friend a few months back, he realized he couldn't breathe as well anymore. This was the first time he'd had a craving since then, even though the thickness of the smoke caused him to wheeze a bit.

"So, since you found the body you've had a knife held to your throat, you've been followed in a car, and been threatened by phone?"

Detective Lacey was heavyset. Too many snacks, too many drinks. Tenant could take him easily, a jab to the gut, right cross to the chin. And the guy's condescending tone was causing Tenant to seriously consider doing just that.

"That's what I said." Tenant balled his fists at his thighs. The detective wouldn't be able to see that under the table.

"And you just decided to contact us now. The last time you saw us, you didn't say anything."

"I was worried before. About my family."

"Why aren't you worried now?"

"He threatened my family anyway. He said he was going to kill me."

Lacey nodded and wrote something on a piece of paper. "Can you describe the man?"

"There were two of them. One I only saw from behind on the docks."

"What did the other one look like? The one in your car?"

Tenant described the pale man he had seen on the docks the other night one more time. Said the one from the backseat had an Irish accent but he didn't see his face. And then he talked about the crowbar incident.

Lacey rubbed his face. Took a deep breath.

"You smashed his car? Why?"

"He threatened my family."

The detective referred to the paper. "I thought he threatened your family by phone."

"Following me in a car while I'm walking my daughter home from school is a threat."

Tenant's nails were digging into his palms. This guy Lacey was the kind of guy who'd get his ass beat if he didn't have a badge. And a gun.

"Did you know the deceased?"

"If I didn't see the guy getting the shit kicked out of him, I would have thought it was just a body floating in the river. They show up from time to time. Sometimes someone decides to commit suicide. I've never been threatened over it before."

"Does the name Maxwell Carter mean anything to you?"

"No. Never heard of it."

Lacey tapped his pen on the table. "That's the man whose body you found the other day. You've never heard the name before."

Tenant spread his hands. He wondered if Lacey could see the nail marks on his palms.

"You don't read the newspapers? Listen to the radio?"

This was infuriating. "What the hell are you getting at?"

"Maxwell Carter is—I should say was—probably the richest businessman in Northern New Jersey."

Tenant smiled. Then he started to laugh.

Lacey waited. Didn't say a word, but Tenant could tell the detective didn't understand.

"Well, then," Tenant said, "I wish I hadn't found him dead. If he was alive, I could have asked him for a loan."

He stood up. The cops weren't going to help. All they were going to do was throw the names of the dead at him.

Like he wanted a hand in any of this.

It was all being forced on him. He just wanted protection for his family.

But what was it his old boxing trainer had told him? The best protection is a good attack?

Yeah. Tenant liked the sound of that.

CHAPTER 13

JACKSON DONNE WOKE UP IN A BED AND IMMEDI-
ately asked where he was.

"You're an asshole. And you're at Mountainside Hospital. You
have a knock on the head, but they want to check you out, make sure it
doesn't get worse. Plus you were drinking, so they want to hydrate you."

The white room came into focus. Donne was in a bed, slightly
inclined. Then he realized he wasn't in a room at all, but instead a
cubicle-like area enclosed in a white curtain. Iapicca was the only one
with him.

An IV tube extended from Donne's left forearm. It pinched his
skin, and pain stabbed up his arm into his shoulder. He didn't want to
move it.

"Gotta be honest," he said. "I'm starting to believe you."

"What are you talking about?"

Donne's head throbbed, and he wanted to go back to sleep.

"I think there really was another guy in there with your aunt and uncle. We found some fingerprints that aren't yours. The lab guys found tire tracks by the curb that aren't matched up with your car."

As if the gods had been watching, a nurse came through the partition in the curtain, holding a clipboard. She smiled at him, then turned to the detective.

"Would you mind excusing us for a moment?"

He grinned back at the nurse, then shot Donne with his thumb and forefinger.

"We'll talk about this later, buddy," he said, and disappeared through the partition.

They wanted to hold Donne overnight, just to keep an eye on him. What choice did he have?

✳

Franklin Carter turned off the lights and locked the door. Being the last to leave the restaurant was a rarity for him, but today he found it to be a refuge. He didn't have to talk to Susan about what had been going on. He didn't have to worry about paying off anyone. The FBI wasn't bothering him. He could just sit and count bills and reflect on how this restaurant was something he'd built, something he created. And it wasn't a pile of rubble in New York City.

After he finished tallying tips, checking time sheets, and calculating expenses, he put all the receipts back in the register, checked all the silverware was put away, and made sure the oven was off. The last thing he needed was a gas explosion here.

Carter noticed the irony of the thought and stepped through the door onto the sidewalk. It was after midnight and the street was nearly empty. A few college kids spilled out of the bar up the street. To his right, on the corner of Church and Bloomfield, a homeless guy eyed him up and started to walk toward him. The last thing Carter wanted to do was hand out money.

So he turned his back to the homeless guy and headed toward

the college kids. He whistled a John Mayer song to himself as he walked, then stopped and cursed the song. It was stuck in his head after Kate made sure she put the CD on the restaurant stereo. On repeat. The worst part was that the speakers were turned so low you didn't even know you were listening to it until three hours later, when all you could think about was how her body was a fucking wonderland.

The waitresses didn't understand music. There were good bands out there, smaller bands that played the same type of music as John without the overdone radio play. Amos Lee, Band of Horses, The Format—Christ, anything but John Mayer.

He turned into the parking garage, thinking that tomorrow he'd bring his iPod. The music would be much more eclectic.

Carter paid the parking fee, a measly two bucks, and started up the stairs to the second floor. He heard footsteps descending above him and thought he'd stay as far to the right as he could when he reached the first landing. The person coming down was definitely moving quickly, maybe one of the college kids late in meeting his boys for shots.

Turning on the landing toward the next flight of stairs, Carter kept his head down and saw only the black boots of the person he was trying to avoid. The feet were coming directly for him, and he looked up much too late.

Pain erupted from the side of his head, and like he was a spectator in his own body, Franklin Carter felt himself slip to his knees. Another shot to the head; the world didn't go completely dark, but Carter was dazed. He wasn't sure what was going on, but he knew he was being dragged along the concrete steps.

He fought to stay conscious and to focus on what was happening, but everything was fuzzy and muddled. He couldn't think clearly. Hearing sliding doors close and feeling rope being tied around his wrists didn't mean much to him. He couldn't put it all together, no matter how he tried to fight through the pain in his head.

The only thing he could think about was John Mayer waiting on the world to change.

God damn John Mayer.

As she typed the code into the lock, Susan Carter decided she was going to have to get used to it. With all the shit that was going on in their lives, there would be nights when Franklin wouldn't come home. And they definitely wouldn't be able to visit her mother together. He was a busy man.

So when he hadn't come home last night, after his late night earlier in the week, she'd just figured this would be par for the course.

That hadn't kept her from almost being sick in the bathroom when she noticed his side of the bed hadn't been disturbed.

She also found it odd that she hadn't heard from Jackson yesterday.

But Susan put it all aside and plastered a smile on her face when she entered her mother's room.

The nurse smiled at Susan and said, "She's awake today. And she seems to be pretty aware."

"Is she getting better?"

The nurse frowned. "No, but it's encouraging that you might be able to talk to her for a while. It can't hurt." She left them alone.

Susan had to fight to keep the smile on her face. The woman in bed wasn't her mother anymore. It was a facsimile. The body was the same, albeit thinner and more pale. But inside it wasn't Isabelle Donne. Even though her mother blinked and smiled when Susan sat, there was a void behind the eyes. There wasn't the same recognition. It wasn't the woman who yelled and grounded her when she took the car without asking. It wasn't the woman who wept in front of her and Jackson when their father ran off one morning.

"Hi, Mom," Susan said.

"Hi." The voice wasn't even the same. There wasn't any strength or conviction behind it.

"Did Jackson come by?"

Her mother nodded. "Jackson looks good."

"When? This morning?"

The question clearly confused her. She squeezed her eyes shut and frowned.

Susan didn't want to push. "I saw him the other day too, Mom. You're right. He does look good."

If you consider the stench of alcohol on him and the lines at his eyes that shouldn't be there good.

The strain on her mom's face disappeared. "I miss him. I miss Daddy."

"Daddy's long gone," Susan said.

"This is his fault. Everything is Dad's fault. I remember. The car outside. The water."

Her mother's voice trembled and the strain reappeared. A tear appeared at the corner of her eye.

Susan kept fighting to keep her composure. Her eyes burned. She put a hand on her mother's arm.

"It's okay, Mom. It's going to be okay."

"Dad should have stayed away. I told him. We told him."

Susan let her own tears flow. Nothing made sense, and it hurt to watch. She wanted so desperately to just be able to have one more normal conversation with her mother. Just some time to say good-bye and have her mother know she was loved.

But that wasn't going to happen. Her mother had disappeared months before.

"Maxwell Carter," her mom said. "Maxwell Carter."

The name sounded so familiar. Was it a relative of Franklin's? Why had she heard it before? "Who are you talking about, Mom?"

But her mother just shook her head slowly and leaned back against the pillow. The grip she'd had on Susan's hand relaxed. There wasn't much more to talk about today.

"I love you, Mom," Susan said, and kissed her gently on the forehead. "Just hang on a little longer. I know Jackson wants to tell you too. You need to hear it. And he needs to say it."

Susan left the room, then reached into her bag. Taking out her cell phone, she checked it to see if Franklin or Jackson had called. She'd had it on silent so she could talk to her mother without interruption;

now she turned the ringer back on. No one had called, but the phone rang almost immediately. It was a number Susan didn't recognize.

She answered anyway.

"Listen to me carefully," a voice said. "I have your husband. He is safe. For now. Instructions will follow. No police."

And like that the line went dead.

part two

SUSAN CARTER

CHAPTER 14

JACKSON WASN'T PICKING UP HIS PHONE. SUSAN
Carter dialed again and got his voice mail again. Where the hell was he?

The parking lot closed in on her, or at least that's how it felt. The cars were too close and she couldn't see her own. She was wandering in circles. Her BMW had to be here somewhere. She had gotten here somehow.

"This is Jackson Donne. I can't get to my phone right now. Please leave a message."

Beep!

"Jackson, this is Susan. Where are you? Call me, please."

Her hands shook hard and she couldn't close her cell phone. It was getting hard to breathe. The corners of her vision started to fade. She called Jackson again.

"This is Jackson Donne. I can't get to my phone right now. Please leave a message."

Beep!

"Please, Jackson. This is an emergency. Call me back."

His cell phone wasn't on. Where was he? She was getting light-headed now. They'd taken her husband.

They? Who was they?

And now Jackson was missing. Had something happened to him too? The sounds of traffic from Berdan Avenue rattled in her ears. Tears flowed from her eyes. She couldn't breathe. It felt like an elephant was standing on her chest.

Beep!

"Jackson! Pick up your goddamned phone!"

She hadn't even realized she'd called again until she heard the beep. Susan didn't know what else to do. Now she felt the asphalt tilt beneath her, and her vision clouded completely. She couldn't fight it anymore. She was going to pass out.

"Oh my God!" someone yelled. "Are you okay?"

But she couldn't answer. Susan couldn't shoulder any more tragedy. She crashed into the asphalt.

❋

Carlos figured he'd try the gun one more time. But there weren't any quiet parks. It was too fucking nice out. Kids were out on the swings. Moms were walking their babies. He even saw one of his asshole teachers out walking his dog. No place to just go and shoot the thing.

And like hell if he was just going to wait for the next rainy day, or fuck that, even wait for nighttime. The gun was fucking boring anyway. None of his friends wanted to come and play around with it. And it's not like he'd ever *really* shoot someone. So he was just going to have to get rid of it.

Maybe dump it back by the river?

Nah, yo, there were always a ton of cops down there. The last thing he needed was to be seen dropping a gun off on a riverbank. They might arrest him and put him in Juvie for that thing yesterday.

Carlos wondered what happened to Cesar and Joseph with the cops. They were probably all locked up. Man, if Cameisha had seen them, she'd laugh her ass off. Running away like that, she wouldn't respect that. No, Carlos had her respect. At least he thought he did, the way she smiled at him and laughed when he made fun of her.

But she always liked it in school when he told on the real punks. Like that time Kurt stole Ms. Caruso's wallet. And Carlos told her what happened. Cameisha said that was good of him. Even kissed him. It wasn't a blow job, but it was something.

Maybe he could get a blow job out of her if he did the right thing. The gun. Maybe if he took the gun to the cops and then told her about it.

He knew snitches got stitches, but yo, this was a shot at a blow job from Cameisha.

There was no question. He would walk down to the police station and turn the gun in. Tell the cops he found that shit and he didn't want any elementary school kids to get hurt playing with it.

A *fuckin' blow job*!

CHAPTER **15**

FRANKLIN CARTER WAS SURE HE WAS TIED TO a wooden chair in a basement. The air was moist, and droplets of water dripped down the concrete walls into puddles. Wooden stairs led to a metal door. The door opened and a figure paused at the top of the stairs, light behind him.

Now the figure was at the bottom of the stairs. Carter could hear feet plop through a puddle as it approached, blanketed in shadow.

"Mr. Carter, you didn't pay like I asked."

"We only talked yesterday."

"We've talked before that! I came to you, nicely! Your family owes mine! You know that."

"What happened is in the past. It's not my fault."

Bryan Hackett undid the belt around his jeans and began to slide it out of the loops. Carter didn't like where this was going.

"Blood runs deep, Franklin. It's as much your fault as anyone's."

"This is stupid, Bryan."

The belt buckle caught him across the face. Carter felt skin tear away from his cheek, felt the sharp sting, and then the drop of blood down his cheek.

"No," Hackett said, his voice even. "This is not stupid. After all that's happened, paying me money means you get off easy."

Carter heard the whiz of the leather and metal through the air, and his head snapped to the side before he realized he'd been hit again. This time from the left. Both of his cheeks were bleeding now, and sweat dripped from his brow, burning into the cuts.

"Well, now you have me, what are you going to do? Kill me?" Carter had to spit the words out.

"Maybe."

Hackett circled Carter's chair. The buckle of the belt scratched the concrete floor slowly as he went.

"Why kill me?" Carter asked. "You kill me, you'll never get your money."

"Oh, I'll get my money." Hackett leaned in toward Carter's ear from behind. His voice was soft. "But I'm going to have some fun first. And if you die? Well, not only will I have to find a different way to get my money, but I'm also going to consider you a pussy. Understand me, boyo? You'll go out a pussy."

The belt buckle caught him in the back of the head this time, right behind the ear. Carter grunted in pain.

"Your wife will pay me. She'll pay to see you alive. And if not, she'll pay to get your body back for the funeral."

"No. Not Susan." Carter squeezed his eyes shut. "Keep her out of this. She has nothing to do with this."

The belt came quick this time. Three shots to the head. Carter tried to roll with the shots, but he couldn't guess the direction they came from. He tried to force the pain out of his head. He thought of music. Guggenheim Grotto. "A Cold Truth."

He sang through clenched teeth. He wouldn't beg. He wouldn't plead. And he most definitely would not be a pussy.

Hackett was in front of him again. Carter, refusing to look in his eyes, could tell from the direction of his voice.

"That's the thing, Franklin," he said. "Susan has *everything* to do with this."

✳

The closest police station in Clifton was in Styretown. Clifton had a hell of a lot of police stations.

This wasn't really a big police station, it was just an office where some cops sat. It was next to a bank and a Coconuts. Carlos thought that was gangsta. He could drop the gun off and then go D-block the latest Akon CD. That shit was hot.

He pushed the glass door open and felt like he was entering a dentist's office. His mom used to take him to Dr. Scott's office, and it was just like this. A few metal chairs, a table, and shitty magazines scattered over it. Against the far wall was a thick glass window, behind which a cop shuffled papers.

Carlos sat down and felt the barrel of the gun press into his hip. He'd kept it there for the past two days. He'd almost forgotten it was there. And now it was fucking uncomfortable.

The cop behind the glass, a fat guy with a porno mustache and brown hair combed over, looked up at him. His hair was too long and it made him look like an asshole. He should get a shape-up. Which reminded Carlos—he had to go get a haircut himself soon.

"Can I help you?" the cop asked.

"Yeah." He stood up and walked to the glass. "I found something down by the Passaic River. I didn't want to leave it there or anything. Some kid could find that shit and hurt somebody."

"What is it?"

"It was like half buried in the mud and sticking out, so I picked it up. I ain't gonna use it or nothing. I just thought, yo, I should bring this shit to the cops."

The cop stopped shuffling his papers. "What is it?"

Carlos reached under his jersey and pulled out the gun. He

didn't hold it like he was gonna shoot it or nothing. Held it from the barrel. He didn't want the cop to wile out or nothing. So he held the gun at arm's length like a bag of dog shit.

Still, the cop's eyes widened and his hand immediately went to his own holster.

"Jesus Christ," the cop said.

At that moment, Carlos got pissed he was giving the thing back. He just scared a fuckin' cop.

Now, *that* was really gangsta.

***

Iapicca showed up at the front of the hospital as Donne was being pushed through the doors in a wheelchair. The sunlight forced him to squint and aggravated the dull roar in his head. The doctor—a very perceptive asshole in a lab coat—prescribed Tylenol. Donne could have done that. He was going to have to bill his hospital stay to Franklin Carter. It sucked being without insurance.

Iapicca sported a tie, a white-collared shirt, and sweat stains under his armpits. A line of sweat glistened on his forehead. He looked miserable.

He must have noticed Donne eyeing him up, and he said, "Yeah, it's fucking hot. I left my coat in the car. Let's go."

Donne unfolded himself from the wheelchair, thanked the nurse who'd pushed him, and followed Iapicca into the parking lot.

His car was an unmarked Chevy Caprice. It smelled like cigarettes and rotten french fries.

"I didn't even know they made these cars anymore."

"Rutherford Police Department. Only the finest." Iapicca started the car and pulled into traffic.

Checking his cell phone, Donne saw he had three voice mails. He dialed his mailbox.

"What are you doing?" Iapicca asked.

"I have a few missed calls. I was in the hospital all night. They kept my cell phone from me."

"I asked them to do that."

"Why?"

"Before we were rudely interrupted by your nurse last night, I was going to check your calls. You got lucky."

"Well, I have missed calls to check."

"You're not checking them now."

"Why not?"

He stopped for a red light.

"The only reason I agreed to drive you was so we could talk about what happened the other day."

"We have an hour drive ahead of us. I think you can wait a few minutes."

The detective started to reply, but his own cell phone rang. His ring tone was some Sinatra song. He took it out and looked at the caller ID.

"Sinatra? You're like, what? Thirty-two?"

"Thirty-three, and you don't have to be old to enjoy the Chairman."

"Thirty-three is old."

"You're an asshole. And you're only five years behind me. I have to take this, so go ahead. Check your goddamned voice mails."

The first message was Donne's sister asking him to call her back. There was a tension in her voice, something underlying that worried him. Next to Donne Iapicca was talking, but it wasn't clear what he was saying.

The next message was Susan again. She sounded even more upset. The time stamp on the message showed it was only a few seconds after the first call.

The third message she was practically screaming into the phone. Something was definitely wrong. And not hearing from Donne was adding to her stress. She was worried about him. And now he was worried about her.

Somewhere deep in the recesses of his mind, he realized that before this week he hadn't been worried about a family member in a long time.

He hung up the phone and turned to Iapicca. The cop's eyes were on the road as he flipped his own cell phone closed.

"Forget New Brunswick," Donne said. "Can you take me to Upper Mountain Road? Something's wrong with my sister."

"No can do. You're coming with me."

"What?"

"That was a call from a cop I know in Clifton. He said they have the gun."

"What gun?"

"They think it's the one that killed your aunt and uncle."

Jesus Christ.

"I have to call my sister."

"Do what you gotta do. It's ten minutes to Clifton, easy."

Iapicca reached under the seat of his car and pulled out a red light. He plugged it into the cigarette lighter and it started to flash. Then he rolled his window down and stuck the light to the roof.

He blew through the intersection.

CHAPTER 16

SUSAN OPENED HER EYES AND THE WORLD came into focus. She saw clouds, the sun shining, and felt the heat on her face. She could still hear the traffic and knew the world was still moving around her. The nurse who had helped her mother stood above Susan with a clear bottle. Susan wondered if the nurse had gone back inside to get it. How long had she been out? It couldn't have been too long. They wouldn't have just left her out in the street.

"Sit up," the nurse said. "Have a sip of water."

Susan felt her stomach give out. She turned her head and threw up. Vomit splattered on her clothes. She really felt the summer heat as she puked. Along with the embarrassment of getting sick in front of the nurse. By the time she was finished, her throat was raw and her mouth tasted sour.

The nurse gave her a sympathetic smile.

"Okay," she said. "Now try some water."

Susan took the bottle of Poland Spring the nurse offered. For the first time, Susan saw the nurse's name tag. It said, "Bernadette."

After sipping the water, feeling the cool liquid wash the taste from her mouth and moisten her throat, Susan said, "Thank you."

"You're welcome." Bernadette took Susan's hand and helped her to her feet. "Let's get you inside into the air-conditioning."

They walked along together and Bernadette said, "Are you going to be okay? I know it's hard watching your mom be sick."

"It's not only that," Susan said. She stopped and looked around at the ground. "Did you see my cell phone?"

Bernadette held it up. In two pieces.

Susan quickly took the pieces and tried to fit it back together. No luck. Jesus Christ. What if Jackson had tried to call? Or the people who had her husband?

She felt light-headed again, and Bernadette saw it. She put her arm around Susan and held her up. Kept walking.

"Come on," the nurse said. "Keep moving. Keep the blood flowing, you'll be fine. Let's just get inside."

Everything was going wrong. And Susan couldn't do anything to stop it.

✷

Getting to the Clifton Police Department wasn't very complicated. Iapicca made only one right turn once he found Valley Road. They followed Valley to Van Houten, passing a strip mall, two schools, a Charlie Brown's, some houses, and an intersection that took seven minutes to get through because of construction. The entire way, Donne kept trying Susan's phone.

No answer.

His instincts didn't like whatever that meant.

"How the hell do you know where the Clifton Police Department is?" Donne asked. "It's not even marked."

"I have some family in Clifton."

The department was located inside Clifton City Hall, a long brick building with three glass doors in the middle. They walked through the doors, and Iapicca turned toward Donne.

"The only reason you're coming along is because I'm starting to believe your story. Anything doesn't line up with what you've already said, you'll find a different way home."

"I haven't said much of anything yet."

"Keep it that way. I don't need a headache."

They followed a long dark tiled hallway through a narrow doorway into a bright white waiting room. On the walls were various framed pictures of successful Cliftonites. The high school marching band seemed to have some kind of reputation, because the picture of it filled the biggest frame. Along the far wall was a windowed counter and another doorway. Behind the counter, a uniformed cop watched them.

"Wait here," Iapicca said.

Donne took a seat on a plastic chair and looked at the brochures on the table in front of him. Most of them regarded sexually transmitted diseases. He felt more like he was in a doctor's office than anything else.

Iapicca was bullshitting with the cop behind the glass. They both laughed at some joke Donne didn't hear. He checked his watch and worried some more about Susan.

A buzzer sounded and Iapicca pushed the door next to the window open. He turned his head toward Donne.

"Come on, tough guy," he said.

Donne followed him into the back office. It looked pretty much like any office you see on TV. Brightly painted walls, and cubicles. The only difference was that the guys in the cubicles were in cop uniforms. And the box of doughnuts by the coffee machine was empty.

At the back of the office, a kid in a LeBron James jersey about six sizes too big for him, baggy jeans, and untied Timberlands sat looking pissed off. A plainclothes detective, jacket off, leaned on his desk watching him. Neither spoke until the detective noticed Donne and Iapicca.

"You look like a Rutherford cop. Greasy as hell," the detective said to Iapicca.

"And you're doing an impression of a police force in this town? Christ, do you even have a jail back here?" Iapicca shook the Clifton detective's hand. "How you doin', Krewer? This here is Jackson Donne. He's a private detective. Or at least used to be."

Iapicca gave him a look, and Donne realized he'd done a little research on him.

"A PI?" Krewer took Donne's hand. "Is that why he's all bruised?"

Cops are such cutups.

"Nice to meet you," he said.

Krewer turned from Donne and waved his hand in Carlos's direction. "And this here is Carlos. He found a gun. Didn't you, Carlos?"

"Fuck you. I ain't gotta stay for this."

Krewer smiled. "Yeah, you kinda do. Otherwise we'll talk to Juvie. You've been holding on to a gun for a few days. Not supposed to do that."

"Yo, I just found that shit three hours ago." Carlos puffed out his chest and looked at them. "Who are these fucks?"

Krewer ignored Donne and pointed toward his chauffeur for the day. "This is Detective Iapicca from Rutherford. He'd like to ask you a few questions."

"Why I gotta answer more questions? This ain't school. Take the gun. I gotta go home." Carlos folded his arms in front of him. "Fuckin' cops."

"Whoa, he's been brought up well, hasn't he?" Iapicca said, and laughed.

"Yo, fuck you," Carlos said. "This ain't your town."

Donne leaned against a desk across from the trio, deciding to watch and keep his mouth shut like Iapicca had advised. The way this kid was spouting off, the conversation that was about to happen would no doubt be entertaining.

"Make it quick," Krewer said. "I got tickets to see Brian Wilson tonight at Radio City."

"After all the shit that's gone on, you're gonna go into the city?"

"Dude, the city's the safest place to be right now. Cops are everywhere. And he's gonna do all of *Pet Sounds*. So get this over with."

"Listen, kid," Iapicca said, putting his hand on the kid's shoulder, "we just need to ask a few more and then you can go home."

Carlos shrugged violently. "Don't touch me. You ain't my father."

"All right, all right. Calm down. How'd you get the gun?"

"I already told the other one."

"Uh-huh. And now you're gonna tell me." Iapicca's voice was no longer playful. There was a tension to it, commanding. Definitely a cop's voice.

Carlos let out a long sigh, flared his nostrils, and leaned back in the chair. Completely defiant. But at the same time, he answered.

"I found it down by the Passaic River. Down by Delawanna. In that park over there."

"It was just lying there?"

"Nah, yo. Some gangsta threw it out his car window."

"Oh really?" Iapicca leaned forward. "What did this 'gangsta' look like?"

"I don't know. He was black. That's all I saw."

"What kind of car did he drive?"

Even Donne noticed Carlos's eyes light up. "Yo, that car was hot. It was like a black Cadillac Escalade, all pimped out. Shiny, and you shoulda seen the rims. Man, those shits were spinning the opposite way of the wheels. And he was thumpin' some Akon on the radio. You could hear the bass, man. That shit was hot."

"And you watched him throw the gun right out the window."

"Well, he didn't like throw it. He just kinda dropped it. I think he thought it would roll into the river, but he didn't know how muddy the ground was. Didn't even get out the car to check. Drove off like a motherfucker. Too bad, too. I wanted to hear more from the radio. I think he had on Hot Ninety-seven."

Carlos's legs were both bouncing up and down, and his eyes weren't focused. They rolled from side to side. He looked like he was about to jump up and run off.

"So then what?"

"After he drove away, I went over to see what he dropped. And it was all stuck in the mud and shit, the gun. So I picked it up and thought, you know, some kid might find it."

"Like you?"

"Nah, I ain't no kid, yo. I'm thirteen." Carlos sucked his teeth. "I mean, like a little kid."

"I see. And when was this?"

"I don't know, this morning?"

Krewer jumped in. "Right. That's why we had reports of some kid shooting in the bushes over by Rutt's Hut yesterday."

Carlos didn't say anything. If the cops were any good at their job, they both saw the answer in Carlos's eyes—Donne knew he did. But at the same time, the kid was smart. He didn't say anything that could get him in any more trouble.

"I'm just trying to do something right," Carlos said finally.

"All right, kid," Iapicca said. "Did Detective Krewer get your information?"

"Yeah. I gave him my shit."

"Good. You answered all the questions I have."

For right now, Donne thought.

"That's it? Nigga, I told him all that shit already. Waste my fucking time."

Iapicca turned to Krewer. "You tracing the gun?"

"Of course."

"Let me know."

Iapicca turned back toward Donne and signaled it was time to go. "Enjoy the concert, Krewer," he said as they exited.

✳

Franklin Carter blinked the sweat out of his eyes and felt it trickle across the cuts on his face. It burned like hell. And all he wanted to do was stand, but his arms were still strapped to the wooden chair.

Bryan Hackett stood before him, frowning, cell phone against his ear. The belt hung limply from his left hand.

After the beating, Hackett had reached above his head and clicked on a dim lightbulb. It didn't do much, but Carter could at least see more of his surroundings.

Not that there was anything to see. It looked as if the place had been emptied out. The light illuminated a slop sink with a drippy faucet catty-corner from the stairs. The rest of the basement was empty except for a few pieces of rotted wood that lay on the ground.

Somehow, the dim light was comforting. He wanted to stay near it, stay where it was.

His mind traveled back, and he remembered lyrics from one of the John Mayer tunes. Something about staying where the light was. He wished that was all he had to worry about now. Kate and her fucking poor taste in music.

Hackett put the phone down and shook his head.

"This is not good," he said.

"What?"

"Jesus. I'm surprised you're still able to talk." Hackett took a step toward him. "Your wife, she's not answering the phone."

Hackett took another step forward, this time letting the belt buckle scratch along the ground.

"Susan," Carter said.

Why isn't she answering the phone? There had to be something wrong. She loved him. Something must have happened.

"Her phone isn't even on. It's going straight to voice mail."

"I don't know. I don't know why."

"Yeah, why's not the problem here. The problem is I can't get anything accomplished if she doesn't answer her phone."

Something broke inside Franklin Carter. A well of emotion that he'd done his best to bury the past few days. Tears flowed from his eyes and a wail escaped his lips. He wasn't a strong man, and Franklin wasn't even sure if a strong man could deal with this.

"Oh, stop being a bitch," Hackett said. He picked up the cell phone. "Here, if it makes you feel better, I'll try one more time."

He started to dial.

Carter let his head hang limp. Snot bubbled from his nose and he couldn't even wipe it away. He came from one of the richest, most respected families in New Jersey and he'd been reduced to a bawling child by this mick. The thought made him cry even more.

"Susan," he said. "Susan, please pick up."

Hackett pressed the phone to Carter's ear.

"—can't get to the phone right now, so leave a—"

"Jesus Christ," Carter said.

"Yeah, this does not bode well for me," Hackett said. "Not at all."

Franklin didn't look up, but he could hear the belt cut through the air again. Felt the impact against his temple and then more searing pain.

"And," Bryan Hackett's voice was like steel, quiet and cold, "if it doesn't bode well for me, then it sure as hell isn't good news for you."

Franklin Carter squeezed his eyes shut tight as he heard the familiar whizzing sound in the air again.

ɪᴀᴘɪᴄᴄᴀ ᴅʀᴏᴘᴘᴇᴅ ᴅᴏɴɴᴇ off ɪɴ fʀᴏɴt of ʜɪs sɪs-
ter's on Upper Mountain. After knocking and ringing the doorbell to
no effect, he decided to hoof it to Carter's. It was about a fifteen-
minute walk. During the trip, he took the time to try Susan. No answer. He tried Franklin and got the same result.

Carter's must have just opened for dinner. Donne looked at his
watch and saw it was just five. The front door was propped open and
three tables were set up on the street. A busboy with glasses and
greasy hair put napkins and silverware on each table. He smiled at
Donne when he passed.

Kate didn't smile when he entered. In fact, Donne thought she
rolled her eyes. In the crook of her arm was a pile of menus. She put
them on the counter.

"What?" she asked.

Donne didn't have time to return the sarcasm.

"Is Franklin here?"

"No."

"Have you seen him at all today?"

"No," she said. "I haven't seen him since yesterday when we closed. I left and he was still doing receipts and tips."

"What about Susan?"

She must have heard the concern in his voice, because her icy exterior melted away.

"Is everything okay?" she asked.

Donne told her about the voice mails. The panic in his sister's voice.

"I haven't heard from either of them," Kate said.

The phone on the counter rang and Kate picked it up, saying, "Carter's. Fine dining. This is Kate speaking, how may I help you?"

She paused to listen, playing with the name tag on her apron.

"No," she answered. "He's not here. He hasn't been here all day. But your brother is here."

She passed Donne the phone. Donne took it and said, "Susan, are you all right?"

"Oh, Jackson. Someone called me and said they took Franklin. I don't know what to do."

"They took him?"

When Donne said that, Kate looked at him. She seemed like she wanted to ask a question, but two customers came in the door. He turned his back to them, and Kate went to seat them.

"That's what they said. I don't know what happened. I dropped my phone and haven't been able to call anyone since then."

"Where are you now?"

"I'm at Mom's. They're letting me use the phone." She was breathless. "Can you come up here?"

"I don't have a car right now."

She didn't ask why.

"All right, I'll pick you up at the restaurant. I'm leaving now."

He put the phone back in its cradle. His head throbbed. He still felt the effects of the knock on the head. When he turned around, Kate was standing directly behind him.

"Is everything okay?" she asked.

"Just peachy," he said. "Do you have any Tylenol?"

She dug in her purse and came up with a few tablets. Donne took them dry and went to sit at one of the tables on Church Street. Susan was a good twenty minutes away at this time of day.

As he sat, Donne was overcome with the urge to get up and run away. To not stay here, not help. He'd seen it too many times before. Once he was involved people got hurt, even killed. Jeanne, Tracy Boland, Beth Deegan, Omar Hassan, Gerry Figuroa. There was no escaping it. He felt like some incurable jinx. And now his family was in danger. A family that had been safe for years when he wasn't around.

Donne wanted to run.

And if not for the fact that he had no place to go, he would have.

✳

Detective Mike Iapicca stopped at Rutt's Hut for dinner. His wife was in Wisconsin visiting her brother, so it wasn't like she was going to cook tonight. So he settled on two deep-fried hot dogs with relish. Best meal he'd had in days.

When Donne had gotten involved in the case, Iapicca looked him up and saw he used to be a PI in New Brunswick. But he was involved in a shoot-out in central Jersey and was stripped of his license. Iapicca called the Morristown PD—figuring maybe they worked the case—to talk to someone down there. He wanted to know about the shoot-out. The cops who worked the case, he was told, were actually from Madison. He tried that department and left a message.

As he bit into his second hot dog, standing at the counter looking over the dirty Passaic River, his phone rang. He didn't recognize the number on the caller ID, so he picked up and identified himself.

"This is Detective Daniels from Madison," the voice said. A woman. "You called?"

"Yeah," he said. "I'm working this murder case. An old man and his wife. We had a witness to the murder, and it's somebody you know. I was looking for a little background."

"Who's the wit?"

"Jackson Donne. Used to be private."

"Christ, I remember Donne."

"Is that a bad thing?"

He heard Daniels take a deep breath.

"I actually like Donne," she said. "He's a good guy. And he saved some lives down at Jockey Hollow that day. But man, he can't keep out of trouble, can he?"

"How come he ain't licensed anymore?" Iapicca asked between bites.

"He beat the shit out of a few guys in New Brunswick. After he helped us out, my partner and I tried to get it reinstated. No luck."

Iapicca picked at an onion ring as he thought. The damn things were falling apart and staining the counter with grease, but they were still delicious.

"So you're saying I should call New Brunswick?"

"Not if you want to know the real Donne."

"What do you mean?"

"They hate him down there. He used to be a cop there, but he turned the entire Narc Division in for stealing drugs. If you want to get the real scoop on Donne, stay away from talking to the New Brunswick cops."

"So, what do you think?"

"I would trust him. He can be stubborn as hell, but he means well. He'd probably help you."

"Yeah, that was my vibe too. Thanks, Daniels."

"No problem. If you need to know anything else, don't hesitate."

Iapicca hung up. He finished his hot dogs and onion rings. Listening to Daniels had made him feel good. It was always a bonus to know your instincts about someone were right.

Iapicca picked up his phone again and called headquarters. A tail on Donne could only help solve the case quicker.

1938

Joe Tenant was tired. He should have been home sleeping, but instead he sat in his car watching a funeral. It was Maxwell Carter's funeral, and Tenant was trying to find Carter's wife.

He'd read about the funeral in the obituaries the night before at work. It was slow at work, nothing to dredge up from the river. Nothing reported missing, no boats clogged in the mud. It was easy. So when he saw the article about the funeral, he decided to find out who Carter was.

The priest was talking as rain dripped from the sky. Tenant watched through a wet windshield, wondering what he was saying. The tribute to this murdered man was probably glowing. He was someone very important in the state, no doubt. Someone everybody should be proud of, and it was unfortunate that he had to be taken from them in this way.

But he was in a better place now. Now he was with God.

A few men held umbrellas over themselves and the women standing next to them. Some of the women dabbed at their eyes with tissues. The men remained stalwart. In the center a woman sat between two young children. That must have been Carter's wife. What did the paper say her name was? Lisa. And the two children. Burt and Claudia.

Lisa held the hands of Claudia and Burt until the funeral broke up. Only then did they stand, after the crowd had dispersed, and lay three roses on the casket. If Lisa was crying, she wasn't showing it. She escorted the children into a car and it slowly drove away.

Tenant followed it. The roads were bumpy in Saddle River, but passable. No one was out in the weather and the street was empty. Tenant thought Lisa Carter might know she was being followed. Then again, it being the day of her husband's funeral, odds were that the thought of being followed was the last thing on her mind.

The car made a right turn onto Holly Avenue, where most of the cars from the funeral were parked in front of an enormous brick house. The wake was probably there. Tenant parked on the corner and waited for Lisa and the children to go inside.

He felt dirty, and knew this was the wrong thing to do. He'd even lied to his wife, telling her he had to talk to the police again. And he was wearing his suit because he wanted to look professional in front of them. He didn't know if Caroline believed him, but she hadn't argued when he left.

He thought about Lisa Carter sitting, holding the hands of her children at the cemetery and imagined Caroline doing the same thing with his own child. He had to know more about what was going on. He had to know who the Irishman was who'd threatened his life. Who'd threatened his family.

And the only way he could think of doing that was by talking to Lisa Carter. After she disappeared inside the house, he straightened his tie and counted to ten. Slowly.

When he finished, he got out of the car and approached the house. The door was open and he stepped inside. Most of the people congregated in a large, carpeted living room. The fireplace had a mantel, and on it a large portrait of Maxwell Carter. The same portrait that was a picture in yesterday's paper.

A couple of guys were sipping beer from longneck bottles and discussing whether or not Dimaggio and the Yankees could win a third straight World Series. And who would be facing them from the National League, Brooklyn or Chicago. Two women sipped wine and discussed whatever the hell was going on in Europe. He didn't see Lisa Carter.

Again, he felt wrong being here and was about to leave when he felt a tap on his shoulder. He turned around to see Lisa Carter standing in front of him.

She caught him.

"Thank you for coming. Can I get you anything?" She had long auburn hair tied in a bun. She had soft cheeks and full lips, and reminded Tenant a little bit of Rita Hayworth.

"I was looking for a beer," he said.

"Come with me."

She walked down a short hallway into the kitchen, where a chef in white sliced some sort of roasted meat and two maids in black outfits poured wine. Lisa Carter took one of the beers off the counter, popped the cap, and handed it to Tenant.

"Thank you," he said.

"I don't recognize you. Are you one of Maxwell's friends?"

Tenant took a long swig to delay the answer. Lying wouldn't work. It wouldn't be the right thing to do, not after she'd just buried her husband. So he decided on the truth.

"My name's Joe Tenant. I'm the one who found your husband."

"Oh," she said, putting her hand to her throat. She turned toward one of the maids and asked for a glass of wine. Now it was her turn for a long sip.

"I just came to offer my condolences, Mrs. Carter. I'm very sorry."

"Thank you," Lisa said. "And you may call me Lisa."

"Do you have any idea why your husband was killed?" He blurted it out. It had been on his mind for days, and it just came out. He instantly regretted it when Lisa's face turned pale.

"I imagine it had something to do with his business, but I wasn't aware of anything along those lines. I never asked my husband about his work."

"I'm sorry," he said. "It's just—I want to know who did it."

"I do too." She finished her wine and passed the glass to the maid, who refilled it. "But why is it so important to you?"

"An Irishman threatened me the night I found your husband. He put a knife to my throat and told me to stay away from the police. And now he's threatened my family."

"My God." And the wine disappeared from the glass as quickly as it had been filled.

Tenant drained his beer, not wanting to fall behind.

"I'm afraid I don't know anything about what happened to my husband. I told the police everything I knew. He got up early Tuesday morning, kissed me and went off to work. I didn't see him again."

"If you do know something, it would be best if you went to the police. Or at the very least, the newspapers."

"And in your best interest as well," she said.

Tenant took another beer and popped the cap. It was early, only one o'clock, and he would be two beers deep and still have to work.

"Why did you really come here?" Lisa asked.

"To help my family. To keep them safe."

"And you thought coming here could help that?"

"It was the only thing I could think of doing."

Lisa Carter took his hand in hers and whispered, "I wish I could help you. I wish I could whisper to my husband's soul and ask him what happened. I want to know why he was killed as well. He was a nice man. A wonderful father. It's not fair to us that he was taken. And it's not fair that you were involved in this. For that I am sorry."

"I think I'll be on my way, then."

"No," she said. "Stay. Have something to eat. You are welcome here. Without you, he may never have been found. And we wouldn't have been able to say a proper good-bye. Now, if you'll excuse me, I want to make sure my children are okay."

She walked back the way they came. Joe stood there, beer in hand, and watched her.

An hour later, he'd eaten and talked Yankees baseball. No one he spoke to had an Irish accent. No one talked to him about Maxwell Carter. And no one asked why he was there.

He left without saying good-bye. He was pretty sure he'd never see Lisa Carter again.

He strode down the street quickly, trying to avoid the steady rain but not doing a good job. Caroline was going to ask how it went with the police, and he would have to use the ride home to come up with a believable answer.

"Wait!" a voice yelled behind him.

Joe Tenant turned to see a man in a black suit and tie jogging toward him. The man was thin and tall and looked like he used a lot of Brylcreem to push his hair to the side. Tenant stopped and let the man approach. He was pretty sure he hadn't spoken to this man at the repast.

"I understand you found Maxwell's body."

Tenant nodded, his neck and arms tense.

"I also understand you've been threatened a few times."

Now Tenant balled his hands into fists.

"I wanted to talk to you, but not in there. Out here is better, where no one can hear us. You better watch your step," the man said.

"Who are you?"

The man squinted, confused at the question. "The more you know, the worse it will be for you."

"I just want my family left alone."

"Then you shouldn't be here. You should be with your family."

Joe Tenant didn't wait to respond. He swung his right arm and connected perfectly with the tall man's jaw. The man went down into a puddle, water soaking through his jacket. Joe kneeled in front of him and grabbed him by the collar.

"Tell me what's going on!" he yelled. "I don't want to be involved in this!"

The man spit blood on the ground. "You're making a big mistake."

"Who are you?"

Tenant hit the man again. His head snapped backward and bounced off the street. Tenant prepared to hit him again, but the man put his hands up.

"Don't you read the newspapers?" the man asked, his face bloody. "Don't you vote? My name is Connor O'Neill. I'm one of your New Jersey state senators."

Tenant's eyes widened and he let go of the man. Looking up, he saw a few other men rushing from the house toward them. One of them was the pale face he saw on the dock. Tenant didn't wait for them. He jumped into his car and pulled away.

The senator was right. Tenant knew it. He may have just made the biggest mistake of his life.

CHAPTER

THERE WASN'T A SPECK OF DUST IN SUSAN'S HOUSE, not a stain on the table from a glass, not an out-of-place newspaper. The Susan Donne he knew was a slob, someone who couldn't keep her dresser organized. She wouldn't even put her own laundry away.

Granted, this was twenty years ago, but he still assumed she and Franklin hired out to keep the place this clean. Few people changed their habits, and Donne couldn't picture his sister being one of them. After all, he hadn't.

He sat on the edge of an easy chair staring at the beer she gave him, still thinking of running. Probably not. And that meant people were going to die.

Susan sat across from him in a rocking chair, next to the land-line phone. She rocked back and forth, but it didn't look like the movement relaxed her. She had her arms crossed in front of her, and she stared at the phone.

"How do I deal with this, Jackson? He could be dead."

"You don't know that. If these people who took him want something, then he's not dead."

"I'll bet you weren't this calm when you were waiting to hear about Jeanne."

It was a low blow, and Donne felt a chill run through his body. Sitting back in the chair, he said, "Jeanne was sudden. I didn't have to wait. I was with her father when the phone rang."

"Jackson," she said, "I'm so sorry. I shouldn't have brought it up. But Jeanne is the core of everything with you. And you lost her. And I need to know how it felt."

Susan was torturing herself, sitting here and thinking about Franklin being dead. She wanted to know what was going to come, how it would feel, and he couldn't tell her. He didn't want to tell her.

"I don't know," he said. "Jeanne wasn't everything I thought she was."

"What do you mean?"

"Nothing," he said.

"God, if Franklin's . . . Is that why you left us, Jackson? Why we didn't speak after Jeanne died?"

This definitely wasn't the time to have a conversation about Jeanne. His fingers tingled at the thought of continuing. But he spoke anyway.

"I couldn't talk to anyone."

"So you threw away your family?"

"I threw away everyone, Susan. I don't talk to her parents anymore. Not even after Jeanne died. All I did was get drunk. I'm lucky I didn't fall back into coke."

"Why?"

"I don't know. I didn't want anyone to see me like I was, I guess."

"I don't think that's it at all," Susan said. "I think you were afraid of what could happen if you got too close to anyone else. You isolated yourself because you couldn't afford to get hurt again."

"That's not—"

"Yes. It is, Jackson."

He didn't speak. Susan was no longer staring at the phone; her eyes bored through Donne instead. At least, for the moment, her mind was off Franklin.

"Look at the people you've helped since she died. That's right, I still followed you. You were in the papers. That guy who lost his wife in 9/11. That woman who came all the way here from Fresno. People who isolated themselves as well. No ties to the world. That's what you want."

He couldn't change her mind. Keeping his mouth shut was the only option. Sit there and take it, just like when he was a kid.

"You're like Dad, you know that? Things get tough and you run off. If you weren't in the fucking papers, we wouldn't even know you were alive."

"I'm sorry, Susan."

"Don't apologize to me," she said. "Apologize to Mom. The one who might never hear you tell her you love her again. Why do you really think I 'hired' you? I don't want to know about the past. Or at least I didn't before this week. I just wanted to get you back into the family, before it was too late."

He drank his beer.

"It's like Uncle George always used to say at Thanksgiving. Do you remember? Family is the most important thing. And for God's sake, our family needs you now."

A single tear fell from her right eye. He could only imagine how much she must have cried in the past few days.

They jumped when the silence was broken by the phone ringing.

✴

The funny thing about kids, Delshawn thought, was that they couldn't keep their mouths shut. Even his own kid, Damon, fucking twelve years old and every day he'd say "snitches get stitches," a phrase warning that anyone talking to the police would be jumped. But when something really *gangsta* happened, that kid would give you up in a second.

Because they couldn't keep quiet, and they didn't even realize it. But for once, it helped Delshawn out. Even though his world kept getting more and more fucked up, you were always better off knowing about it. Then you could do something to control it.

When he'd gotten home yesterday, he'd kissed Shemiah on the mouth. His girlfriend had smiled at him as she cut the chicken. And Damon came running up to him, yelling, "Dad, Dad!"

"What's up, son?" he said, talkin' ghetto-like, not like somebody on *Leave It to Beaver*.

"I gotta tell you what happened to my friend Carlos."

Even though they lived in Paterson, Damon went to Clifton schools. They snuck his ass in because the system was better there. The teachers seemed to care.

"Tell me about it."

"Well, he was down by the river the other day, you know. He was on the run from the *police*."

Delshawn smiled. Even his son knew cops were shit.

"And he was down by the mud, and he found a gun."

Delshawn didn't react. Not on the outside, at least. "When was this?"

"I don't know. He said some Escalade pulled up and an ol' gangsta just threw it out the window."

"What did he do with the gun?"

Damon got quiet for a second, like he was thinking. Probably wondering whether or not to tell his father the truth.

"He took it to the *police*. He didn't know what else to do with it. He wanted me to come by and shoot it, but I said no. Like you said, Dad, I ain't old enough to play with guns yet."

Shit.

Delshawn smiled at his son. "You did the right thing."

Damon smiled and ran out of the kitchen.

"That Carlos a Clifton kid?" Shemiah asked.

"Yeah, I think so."

"He gave the gun back? They got good kids in Clifton."

"No shit."

So this afternoon, after his wife went off to work and Damon found a place to go play hoops, Delshawn took the Escalade out of the garage and drove to Clifton. Damon didn't know where Carlos lived, so Delshawn was gonna have to find out. He had a copy of the middle school yearbook with him, opened to a picture of Carlos Ramierez.

Things weren't good right now. That dude from the bar was alive. The gun was with the cops, and Carlos was a witness. Whether the kid knew it or not.

Delshawn had a lot of business to take care of. His girlfriend didn't know that he killed people for a living, so he was going to have to keep it all quiet. But if this hung over his head, Shemiah finding out what he did would be the least of his problems. Fuck if Hackett ever found out about this. That motherfucker had even more to lose than Delshawn.

Best to start small. Find Carlos. And then, like Damon always said: *Snitches get stitches*.

19

"SUSAN CARTER, IT'S BEEN SO LONG."

Susan held the phone tight to her ear. Wanting to squeeze her eyes shut, she instead kept them on Jackson.

"Who is this?" she asked.

Jackson edged off his seat a little more, the beer still cradled in his hand. He turned his head to the right, as if to hear better. She wouldn't dare put this on speakerphone.

"You know who this is, but I'll let you figure it out in due time." The voice on the other end was confident. And it was familiar to Susan, but it seemed to be missing something. She couldn't tell what.

"What do you want?"

"Are you alone?"

She looked at Jackson and put her finger to her lips.

"Yes," she said. "It's only me."

"Good. We've had some problems getting in touch with you since the last time we talked."

Get on with it, asshole.

"I'm sorry. My cell phone broke."

"Inconvenient for you and your husband. I had to convince Franklin he should give me your home number."

"Don't hurt him."

The voice on the other end laughed. "I'm afraid it's a little late for that."

"Oh my God." Susan's stomach tightened and she thought she'd retch. Her vision clouded and she felt light-headed. She told herself not to let her emotions take control. *Take a deep breath.*

Jackson started to approach her, but Susan held out her hand to stop him. He did.

"Is Franklin okay?"

"He's alive, if that's what you're asking."

"I want to talk to him."

"No, I don't think so. We have business to discuss, you and I."

The voice sounded so familiar.

"What do you want?"

"Money. Your husband owes me one hundred thousand dollars."

Her grip tightened on the receiver and her knees were weak. "One hundred thousand? Why?"

"That's not important to you. All you need to do is get me the money."

"How am I supposed to do that?"

"Yeah. Not my problem. All I know is if I don't get a phone call to 973-555-1980 in twenty hours, you are going to be a widow. I hope you wrote it down."

"You're insane."

Again the voice laughed. "If you call the police, Franklin is a dead man."

She heard the click of the line being disconnected. Slowly, she lowered her own phone back into the cradle. One hundred thousand dollars. Where was she going to get that? She couldn't get into Franklin's bank account without his signature.

Susan felt Jackson's hand on her own, callused and rough.

"What did they say?" he asked.

Taking another deep breath, she told him.

✳

Bryan Hackett's cell phone buzzed. Not the anonymous prepaid one he used to call Susan, not the one he used to call Delshawn, but his private phone. Only one person knew the number.

"I told you not to call me this week."

"I'm sorry," Jill said. "But I just checked the messages at home. It's your old job. They really want you to call them. Something about the explosion in New York City. I can't believe you don't have the money yet."

He hung up. Hackett hadn't expected this to be as big a deal as it was. The city had enough feds to investigate the explosion. But they wanted him to call? He was a former member of the New Jersey State Trooper Bomb Squad.

Could his employers have figured out who was actually behind the bombing?

He was going to have to take some time to think about this before he called them. At least the night to sleep on it.

CHAPTER 20

twenty HOURS

"I don't know how I'm going to get the money," Susan said.

Donne held her, and expected to feel her tears on his shoulder. There weren't any. Her voice was steady.

More proof he didn't know his sister as well as he thought.

"We have to call the police." He pushed her back from him and looked into her hazel eyes.

"No," she answered. "They'll kill him."

There were two schools of thought on kidnapping. Pay the ransom and hope for the best. Or don't pay at all. Not paying a ransom at all was a solution for major kidnappings, and it was the only way to stop them. Donne had read about kidnappings in other countries, and the governments contended that if all ransom paying stopped, then the kidnappers had nothing to gain. That was fine in the abstract, but not so convincing when a loved one's life was on the line. Their best bet was to get the money, pay up, and hope.

"You can get the money from your joint account. I'm sure he's good for it."

"It's one hundred thousand dollars, Jackson. We don't have that. Most of our money is invested. In the house, in the restaurant, in stocks. Franklin also has a private account I don't have access to."

"For what?"

"It's for the restaurant. Any money used on repairs, to pay the mortgage on the building. It's not that he doesn't trust me," she said, as if sensing Donne's skepticism, "but he insists it's easier that way. I could forge the signature."

"They would know. If you get caught . . ." Donne paused. "It's illegal."

"It's my husband, Jackson! We have to try."

"There has to be another way. The banks aren't even open."

"It's all I have."

"If the bank catches you, if they stop you and you get held up, we'll have no chance."

"I'll get the money somehow." Susan's voice was quiet. "I can't get stopped at the bank. There's some time. There has to be a way."

There was another option, but one he wasn't willing to consider. Months earlier, he'd used a woman as bait and nearly got people killed. No way was he going to put his sister and her husband in that corner. No way was he going to let anyone else in his family die.

"How long do we have?" he asked.

"Twenty hours," Susan said. "I need to figure something out."

"We," he said. "We need to figure something out."

Susan gave him a hard glare and said, "I don't have time for this shit."

She grabbed her purse and left the house.

Still without a car, Donne was stranded. Making his way back to the restaurant wouldn't help. And just sitting in the house was unproductive. What else could he do?

The sun was setting to his left as he stood on the steps. Susan needed help on this. She wasn't going to be able to access the money. And he wasn't going to willingly drag her into a firefight. Donne hesitated only a moment before dialing Iapicca.

CHAPTER

"**I NEED YOU to take me to see my mother**,"
Donne said.

"I am not your fucking car service," Iapicca responded.

"I don't have a car. Come on, you know how long it takes to get
a cab service around here. And the buses don't take you anywhere but
New York and the mall."

"Have your sister take you. It will be a nice family moment. I'm
off for the evening. I'm going to go out on my deck, drink a beer and
smoke a cigar."

"Are you sure you're in your thirties? Sinatra? Cigars?"

"Shut up."

Sitting on the steps of his sister's porch, he could understand
the appeal of staying in tonight. Since the sun had set, the air had
cooled and it was turning into a comfortable evening.

"My sister's not around."

"Why so urgent?"

"My mother has dementia. She's going to die."

"I'm sorry for that, but you'll have your car back tomorrow. The cops were even nice enough to tow it over to the shop to get it fixed for you. Go see her then."

"She knows what's going on."

Silence on the other end of the line. Cicadas buzzed behind him somewhere, and a car sped down the road across the way.

"What do you mean she knows what's going on?"

Donne told him about the visits. Iapicca didn't disrupt with questions, just went with it.

When he finished, Iapicca said, "That's a pretty thin strand to tug on."

"It's all I have."

"Get your sister's husband to talk to you. This is my job. Not my life. I need some time off too."

Donne sighed. No avoiding it now.

"Franklin's been kidnapped," Donne said. Respecting Susan's wishes was important to him, but he needed Iapicca. And what were the odds the kidnappers were listening right now? If anything, they'd be following Susan. The thought sent a ripple down his spine.

He heard glass crash to the floor on the other end of the line. "When did this happen?"

"As far as I can tell, sometime last night."

"Did you call the police?"

"No. I called you."

"Only because you needed a ride." Iapicca's voice was tense now. Angry. "Jesus Christ, Donne, you should have called us."

"I am now. I couldn't do it when Susan was around. They told her not to call."

"Are you at her place now?"

"Yeah, sitting on the front porch."

"Look down the street, the way we came."

"Uh-huh."

"See the car there, the unmarked?"

There was a Chevy half a block down the street, the last remains of sunlight reflecting off the windshield.

"You put a tail on me?"

"Come on, Jackson. I'm not an idiot. I needed to keep an eye on you."

Donne walked in the direction of the car, phone still to his ear, stride quick but casual.

"You want him to take me to my mother?"

"No. Have him take you to my house. There's no way I'm going to miss this."

Snapping the phone shut, Donne tapped on the window of the unmarked with his free hand. It rolled down slowly, revealing a blond woman.

"Made me, huh?" she asked.

"Not without Iapicca's help. I need you to do me a favor."

NINeteeN HOURS

Susan stood outside the building her mother stayed in, remembering the day they decided to bring her there. About a year and a half ago, she'd decided to take her mother in to live with her and Franklin. One of the neighbors had found Mom picking fruit in their garden in her pajamas. It was a sign that she could no longer live by herself.

With a little convincing, lots of tears, and a weeklong packing adventure, they got Mom into their house on Upper Mountain. At first everything seemed okay. Mom was adjusting nicely. She'd help with dinner or set the table, knit, or sit and watch TV. She was quiet, almost sad, but she got by. Susan would sit and talk with her when

Franklin was at the restaurant. They'd try and reminisce about the old times, but things seemed to be slipping from Mom's mind.

That was okay. Susan was happy to have her there. Occasionally, Mom would get up and forget why and Susan would have to help her. It was frustrating, but nothing she couldn't deal with. Mom would get more frustrated with it, swearing at herself, twisting her hands together in annoyance.

About two months after they'd moved her in, Franklin came home early. He was going to have dinner with them and then go back to the restaurant. He came over and kissed Susan hello first and then walked over and said hello to Mom. He had barely got into the room when Susan heard him swear. She asked what was the matter.

"Your mother just shit herself on the couch," he said, backing up into the kitchen.

"Oh, Mom," Susan said, hurrying into the room.

It was true. Her mother's pants were stained, the odor permeated the room, and the couch was stained with feces.

"Mom, come on. Let's get you cleaned up," Susan said. Her face flushed, and she was embarrassed for her mother.

Her mother, however, didn't budge from the chair, her own face red. "It's that bastard's fault!" she yelled, pointing at Franklin. "He is a curse to this family! I can't live with him."

It took half an hour to get her mother cleaned up and out of the room. The entire time, Mom swore at Franklin, cursed a blue streak. "He's an asshole," she said. "He's been stealing from me! He's been stealing from all of us! Motherfucker."

Susan cried that day. She and Franklin decided they couldn't handle Mom on their own anymore.

Now, as she stepped through the front doors, Susan was sure her mother, the one who survived being a single mother and working two jobs, who stood tall and beamed at Susan's graduation, was still inside her mind somewhere.

The receptionist smiled at Susan as she buzzed the door open.

Mom was awake, wide-eyed, smiling.

"Hi, Mom," Susan said.

"Hi."

"Mom, I need to talk to you."

"Okay."

Susan sat next to the bed and took her mother's hand. The room smelled of Lysol and the sweet flowers that someone had placed next to the bed. Her mother's hair was still wet, which meant the staff must have just bathed her.

If only they'd kept their mother's money in a bank account to save for her will. Instead, they used it to pay for the nursing home.

"Mom," she said. "I miss you."

Her mother smiled at the sound of Susan's voice, returned the squeeze of Susan's hand.

"Franklin's in a lot of trouble, Mom. I don't know what to do."

Her mother squeezed her hand tighter at the mention of Franklin's name. Susan was sure of it. Mom was in there somewhere.

"Come on, Mom. Why can't you help me anymore?"

Susan squeezed harder and waited for her mother to respond. Mom slowly turned her head and looked at her. Gazed deep into her eyes. As Susan met the glare, she was certain there was recognition in the gray orbs.

"My daddy works on the docks," Mom said.

"No. Mom, come on. I need you right now. I need you to come back to me. I need someone to talk to."

"He walks me to school in the morning when he comes home."

"Mom, your dad's been dead a long time."

Mom squeezed her eyes shut and started shaking her head. "No. No. No."

Susan stood up, letting go of her mother's hand. Putting her hands on her mother's shoulders, she gently shook her. If only there was an inheritance. If only there was money left. And her mother could just die. Tonight. And Susan would have the money.

"Mom. Franklin is gone. I can't get the money. We're in trouble. I need you to tell me it's going to be okay. Even if it isn't. I need you to be my mother. Tell me Franklin will come back."

Mom's eyes shot open. "That fucker is a liar!"

Susan stepped back. She was still shocked that her mother used such language. Her mom never swore before she got sick.

This wasn't her mother anymore. Her mother was gone. This disease had taken her mother. And left this *bitch*—this unresponsive *bitch*—in its place.

Susan imagined her hands pressed harder on her mother's shoulders.

It would have been so easy.

She remembered the woman who was no longer her mother losing complete bowel control on their couch. She saw her cursing at Franklin, letting loose all sorts of bile and hatred to a man who'd done nothing to her. She saw the frustrated woman, unable to remember why she had gotten up from her seat. The woman who couldn't even bathe herself. Who needed to be tended to like a child.

This is no longer my mother.

Susan pictured her hands wrapped around the woman's neck, starting to squeeze. The woman's eyes would bulge and her mouth would shoot open, trying to gasp for air.

"I can't take it anymore!" Susan yelled. "I want my mother back!"

The woman's head would shake back and forth, her eyes looking like they'd pop out of her head.

"How could you do this to us?" Susan screamed.

✴

Donne and Iapicca pulled into the parking lot off Berdan Avenue. It took them only twenty minutes to get to Wayne from Rutherford, the mall traffic at a relative lull for eight in the evening. They had the Yankees on the radio, and John Sterling was telling them how good Jason Giambi would be by the time the season really got under way, even though it was well past the All-Star break.

"I can get the FBI involved. It's kidnapping, Jackson," Iapicca said as they approached the front door of the nursing home. "It can only help."

"They said no police, no authorities." Donne nodded at the receptionist, who buzzed them in.

"Your sister just went in," she said.

They walked through the door only to see nurses running toward his mother's room. *We are too late*, he thought. *She's already dead*. And her secrets had gone with her.

Donne jogged toward the room, listening to an old woman scream that she hadn't gotten her ice cream yet. Through the door, he saw several nurses in a crowd watching his sister yell.

Susan hunkered over his mother, a high-pitched howl escaping from her lips. Donne stepped through the crowd and grabbed Susan by the shoulders. He had to pull once, twice just to pry her away.

"Let go of me!" Susan struggled against his grip.

She shook herself free and ran toward the door. Iapicca caught her and held her.

Donne's mother was coughing up phlegm, and tears flowed from her eyes. Her shoulders shook, and between coughs she kept saying his grandfather's name, Joe Tenant. One of the nurses stroked her hair and whispered that it would be okay.

Donne turned toward Susan, trying to push the memory of his sister's pain-filled yell out of his head.

"Sue, what happened?"

Susan sank to her knees. Her hair was ragged and sweat poured from her brow. Her entire body shook as if she were cold. She stuck a weak hand out and pointed toward the bed.

"That," she said, "is not my mother. She can't help me."

CHAPTER **23**

HACKETT DROVE IN CIRCLES. IT WAS TOO EARLY TO settle into a hotel room for the night. And he wasn't going to stay with Franklin now. Carter needed to think for a while, sit in his own filth and worry. And he didn't want to call work. Not when it was about New York.

Could they know he was the culprit? No, that wasn't possible. He'd been careful, gloves, false names, unmarked vehicles. Paid in cash for the materials. Even the research in the library was done with a false library card. No one could know it was him.

He drove along MacCarter Highway. Newark was quiet, nothing going on at the PAC Arts Center, and the Bears minor league team must have been on the road. A wino stood on the corner, panhandling. Hackett ran the red light.

As much as it pained him to admit it, the FBI was good. They would figure it out eventually. The plan was to be in the Bahamas by then. It was too soon. They shouldn't know about him.

Not knowing was driving Hackett nuts. Finally, he reached for his cell phone and dialed a number he wished he'd forgotten.

"Detective Marshall," his old boss said.

"Jason, this is Bryan Hackett."

Hackett always liked Jason Marshall, even though he was a black guy with an Irish name. *Shouldn't pretend to be Irish if you aren't,* Hackett thought.

"Hackett, how you doin'?"

"I'm all right. I was on vacation. My wife just happened to check our messages."

"Sorry to disrupt. What have you been up to these days?"

Hackett hated the small talk and wanted to know what Jason Marshall's real intentions were. He also knew, though, that forcing the issue would arouse suspicions, so he played along.

"I've been working at Ploch's Farm, helping sort shipments, test fertilizer, that sort of thing. A few months ago, I did some technical advising in the city."

"Technical advising?"

"Yeah, one of those *Law & Order* kind of shows was filming, needed a bomb expert."

"Sounds like you've been keeping yourself pretty busy."

You don't know the half of it. Or do you?

"I try."

"Well," Marshall continued, "I hate to interrupt your vacation, but we need your help."

"We?"

"The FBI called me in. You heard about the explosion on the Upper East Side?"

"I'm on vacation, sir. Not hibernating."

Marshall chuckled. "Good. Are you within driving distance?"

"I'm in Point Pleasant."

As he drove along the Passaic River, he noticed the rotten metal bridges and Harrison out across the way. Despite the attempt at gentrification, it still felt like Newark and the surrounding area were falling apart. He wished he really was staying in Point Pleasant.

His call waiting beeped and Hackett pulled the phone from his ear to see who it was. Delshawn Butler. What the hell did he want now? Hackett would call him back.

"Well, do you think you can cut it short and get up here tonight?" Marshall asked.

"Why?" Hackett's stomach tightened.

"I know we let you go. You were a hothead, Hackett, and we couldn't have that. But I always trusted your instinct. Some of the materials that were used, the clues we have . . . We think it was a cop. Someone on the inside who knew how to make us look the wrong way."

Hackett had to keep from laughing out loud.

"We want you to come in and help. See what's going on without arousing suspicion. The FBI doesn't want the regulars working it, because it could be one of them."

"You want me to help investigate the case?"

"Yes."

This was too good to be true.

"I'll be there tonight."

Marshall took a deep breath. "Good. We'll be here."

Hackett listened to the address he already knew and hung up. A drive from Point Pleasant to New York would take nearly two hours, so he had time to go back to the house and tell Franklin Carter the good news.

❉

Delshawn didn't think that much when he hit the road to find Carlos. He thought it would have been easy to find the kid. A phone book, maybe drive around the area where he dropped off the gun. He'd met Carlos before, or at least was pretty sure he had. How hard could it be to find him?

Harder than expected.

There had been a ton of Ramierezes in the phone book. And calling each one and asking if Carlos was there wouldn't have worked, because when he had called the first five, three of them had Carloses in the house. The other two hadn't spoken a fucking word of English.

Delshawn drove up and down street after fucking street with no luck.

Sometimes this job sucked. But it was a safer way to make money than dealing, which was what Shemiah thought he did. He knew people who'd make close to twenty grand a month dealing, but there was too much competition. Too many gun battles. Hell, he even heard about some guy down Central Jersey trying to take out all the competition in one shot.

Nah, killing people was easier. Bang, one shot, ten grand at least. And if you did it right, no one came after you.

Times like this, when you made a mistake, that's when it was a pain in the ass. But fuck it. Every job had its drawbacks.

His cell phone buzzed. It was Bryan Hackett finally calling him back.

"We got a problem," Delshawn said without a greeting.

"I'm having a good day. It better not be too bad."

"The cops have my gun."

"What gun?"

"The one I used the other day."

"Oh, Jesus Christ. We can't talk about this now."

"I just need to know what you want me to do."

"Well, as far as I can tell, you have something to take care of. You know who found it?"

"Yeah."

"So take care of it. Permanently."

The line disconnected. Delshawn didn't even think about not being able to talk on the phone. He didn't think about the possibility of other people listening. He'd never had this problem before. Then again, this was only his third assignment. Once he left the Bloods, he'd had to find something to do. Freelance had seemed like a great idea. It was just a matter of drumming up publicity.

Fucking up like this was not a good way to do it. Hackett was right. He was going to have to take care of the situation.

Otherwise, he'd have to get a real job.

CHAPTER 24

eichteen HOURS

"I'm so sorry," Susan said to Donne. "I just—I just couldn't take it anymore. If you knew—if you knew what I was thinking."

The nurses and aides had been kind enough to give them some space. Even Iapicca stood back, talking to a few of the nurses, assuring them that he could take care of it. That the Wayne cops didn't need to be contacted. He was calm and he was smiling, and it seemed like whatever he was saying was working.

Donne sat with Susan, his hand on her back, quietly listening.

"She's going to die anyway, Jackson. She doesn't have much time left. If it just happened a little quicker, we could end this nonsense. Franklin and I could get on with our lives. And I could see her dying in my head. I wanted it to happen."

Taking a deep breath, Donne said, "There's a lot more going on here than Mom being sick, Sue."

"I know," she said. "But it started with Mom being sick. That started all of this. Before you were even around. And now Franklin's gone. One of the restaurants is gone. Our life is ruined. And you're going to go back to New Brunswick and forget this ever happened."

He took his hand off her back.

"I'm not going anywhere right now. We're going to solve this together."

"No," she said. "You're a quitter. You probably want to leave right now."

"What I want to do has nothing to do with what I'm going to do."

Susan took her face out of her hands and looked at Donne.

"You mean that?"

"I do."

"We only have eighteen hours to go. Before they kill him."

"I know."

"I'm not going to be able to get the money."

"We'll figure things out. Just need to find out who took him."

"Do you think I can see her?" she asked.

He looked at the group Iapicca had corralled.

"Probably not tonight," Donne said. "I think the screaming freaked everyone out."

Susan nodded but didn't speak.

"Let's get you home. I'll drive."

She slowly gave him the keys to her car, but she didn't move from her seat. He walked over to Iapicca.

"I think they realize that sometimes stress gets to be too much. Next time your sister visits, though, they're going to be in there with her for everyone's sake," Iapicca said.

"Of course. Want to follow me back?" Donne asked. "I'm going to drive Susan home."

"I'm not gonna get my night off, am I?"

Donne's watch told him Susan was right. They had only eighteen hours before Franklin's kidnapper's deadline. Hopefully, Donne could find him by then.

"Not if you want to help."

Iapicca shrugged. "My wife's on vacation, so I have nothing to do anyway."

"Good. I just need to talk to my mother."

"You got time to do that?"

"She might be able to help us."

The nurses who were talking to Iapicca were moving off in different directions now, sensing they were no longer needed. And that they didn't have to worry anymore.

"How about this? I'll drive your sister home. Ask her a few questions. Maybe she'll tell me something she wouldn't tell you. And when you're done, you drive her car back."

"Sounds good," Donne said.

Susan would find out he called the cops sooner or later.

Following the scattering nurses, he walked down the darkened hall toward his mother's room, hoping she'd continue what she'd started to tell him days ago.

✳

Susan Carter sat in the passenger seat of the detective's car. It smelled like cigars and the cherry air freshener that hung from the rearview mirror.

She put her head back against the headrest and closed her eyes, then reopened them.

The detective, who on the way to the car had introduced himself as Detective Mike Iapicca, started the engine and smiled at her.

"Hell of a night," he said.

Susan met his glance but didn't say anything. Jackson had called the police. She'd trusted him and now here she was sitting next to a detective. *Son of a bitch.*

They pulled out onto Berdan Avenue.

"You know," Iapicca continued, "I remember when my mother-in-law died. She suffered from Alzheimer's for years."

Fuck this. She was not going to let him get in. She knew the tricks, and there was no way she was going to let this sob story get her to talk to him. The cops could not be involved. No story about how this guy's mother-in-law died of Alzheimer's was going to get to her.

"She wasn't that bad. Not according to my wife. I wasn't around much, was working a lot. Just went on what she said. But there was this night when Kerri had to go out. I took the night off and stayed home."

Big fucking deal.

The detective turned right onto Valley Road. Mini-malls on the left were closing, and the apartment complexes on the right were waiting for the renters to come home.

"I make dinner. Nothing fancy, I think it might have been Manhattan clam chowder, right? So we sit down to eat and I'm slurping this stuff up and my mother-in-law's not eating. She's got her mouth squeezed shut and she's shaking her head no."

That never happened with Susan's mother. Her mother was always good. Just that one time to Franklin. No, her mother didn't deserve to be in this home. Didn't deserve to have this disease eating away at her brain. Didn't deserve to have someone as awful as Susan as her daughter.

"I ask her to eat her soup. Nicely, right? 'Mom, you gotta eat.' And my mother-in-law, you know what she says?"

"Did she tell you to go fuck yourself?"

Iapicca took his eyes off the road. "Yeah, actually she did."

"Get that a lot, huh?"

The detective laughed at that one.

"Anyway," he said when he was done laughing, "I ask her again. And she crosses her arms and tells me to go fuck myself again. And now I'm pissed off. It'd been a long week, I was working this robbery case, and I was getting nowhere with it. And now this old woman is giving me shit? I get out of my chair and I'm yelling at her to eat her soup. Yelling.

"And now I'm in her face. 'Eat your soup!' Ridiculous, right? And she's still refusing, and finally, I don't even know what came over me, but I just up and slapped her. And her face was red from my hand. Her eyes teared up. So did mine, if you want to know the truth. After that, I poured her soup bowl out. I never told my wife and I don't think my mother-in-law did either, if she even remembered it.

"It wasn't too long after that she passed away."

Susan looked over at Iapicca, whose eyes were now back on the road.

"She didn't deserve that," Susan said. "You didn't have to hit her."

"I know. Sometimes you just think they'd be better off if they died. Better off if they went quick. Better off for themselves, better off for everyone. If she had a heart attack, I'd have never been pushed to that limit."

Susan put her head back.

"My husband is going to die. I can't pay. And I wanted my mother to help us."

"Yeah," Iapicca said, stepping on the gas. "Let's talk about that."

C H A P T E R **25**

something had been awakened in his mother.
Donne didn't know what doors Susan unlocked during the incident,
but his mother was a ball of energy. Two nurses were standing over
her, preparing a sedative.

"The headlights!" his mother screamed. "Oh my God!"

"Hold her down," one of the nurses said to the other.

"Wait," Donne said.

They both turned toward him, his mother still screaming about
headlights.

"Who are you?" the blond nurse asked. "You're not supposed to
be in here."

"Please, let me talk to her. I want to calm her down."

The brunette looked at the blonde. They both had bodies like they worked out. But it didn't help the bags of exhaustion under their eyes.

"Sir, you really shouldn't be in here."

"THE HEADLIGHTS! They're coming right for me."

Panic laced his mother's voice. In all his years living with her, he'd never heard fear like that.

"Mom," he said. "Mom, listen to me. It's okay."

His mother stopped screaming. For a second.

"Daddy! Help me!"

"Mom! Mom, it's me, Jackson. You need to listen to me."

She paused again. She turned her head in his direction, and again he noticed the dark, heavy wrinkles around her face. The skin hung from her skull. She was no longer human, her soul barely holding to her body. He needed to talk to her before it left her completely.

"Jackson," she said. There was a speck of her left. "My dad. My dad wanted to hurt me. He put me in front of the headlights. I was going to die. I don't want to die."

The force of her words cut through his skin. *She didn't want to die.* He didn't want her to either. The realization gave him pause for a moment. Susan did. Donne clenched his fists. How could she imagine killing her own mother? How could he then promise to help her? Susan was crazy.

He gathered himself and stepped through the two nurses and took his mother's hand. He gave it a squeeze and felt her return the pressure.

"Mom, you're not going to die."

Yes, she is. Don't lie to your mother.

"But you have to tell me what you're talking about."

"Cars. It's so loud."

"Mom," I said. "Mom. Come on, Mom."

"Oh my God! HELP ME!"

There was nothing more to say. She wasn't responding to his voice. He turned to the nurses.

"Give her the sedative."

"Connor O'Neill says hello," his mother screamed. Then she

looked directly at Jackson. "We never wanted to tell you he was arrested. And it was Daddy's fault."

The blonde nodded, slowly, as if she was commiserating with him. As if she knew what he was feeling. His mother knew something, he was sure of it.

But he doubted if he would ever know what it was.

The blond nurse injected her with something and the screaming stopped immediately. The brunette shushed her, cooed her.

✳

What it came down to was listening to your son. Delshawn Butler thought he was a good father. He'd listened to Damon tell stories of chillin' with Carlos down by Rutt's Hut.

After hanging up with Hackett, all this had come rushing back to Delshawn. It made sense; he was nervous and worried about fucking up, and he always worked best under pressure.

Delshawn took the Escalade down Delawanna Avenue toward River Road. It was only about a mile from where he had dumped the gun a few days earlier. Delshawn was pissed he didn't think of it sooner.

After ten minutes of circling the area, he thought he recognized a kid waiting to cross the street. Delshawn pulled the Escalade to the curb in front of the kid. The boy looked like a fake. Shape-up, long white tee, baggy-ass jeans, and untied Tims.

"Yo, Mister Butler, what the fuck?" the kid said, holding his hand out toward the window.

Delshawn grabbed it, gave it a shake, then a fist bump.

"Carlos?" he asked.

"Yeah, yo. This is a nice ride."

"Uh-huh."

"Yeah. I saw one the other day, just like this. I was tellin' your son about it."

Damon. Delshawn hadn't thought how this would affect his own kid. Having a friend die so young. It'd fuck him up and there was no way around it. And hell no, he wasn't gonna pay for no therapist.

Carlos still went on. "Dude dropped this motherfuckin' nine out the window and it got caught in the mud. So like I brought it to the cops and shit."

"Yeah," Delshawn said. Maybe he should let Carlos go. He was just a kid. It was a fucking mistake. He even thought he was doing the right thing. Just let the kid walk away.

"Man, that fuckin' car looked just like this. It was hot. And the black dude who was hanging out the window. He had on a white do-rag. Yo, it was just like—"

Shit, Delshawn thought, realizing he had the do-rag on still.

"Yo," Carlos shouted, holding the word out. "That shit was you, wasn't it? Oh man, that is fuckin' hot!"

Delshawn reached into his console and wrapped his hand around his newest gun. A Glock nine, newer than the one Carlos found. New silencer and everything. Shiny as hell.

Just shut up and I'll let you go. Delshawn found himself rooting for the kid.

"Man, wait until I tell everybody. Your son is gonna think this is so fuckin' cool. Motherfuck, yo, I know a stone-cold killah. You gangsta, Mister Butler. You gangsta."

Delshawn nearly rolled his eyes.

He felt bad for Damon. He was going to lose a friend. But it would also teach him a lesson. Don't fuck around with this crowd. Don't fuck around with guns. Go to college. Get a job.

He leveled the gun at Carlos.

"Yo," Carlos said. "You got another one. This one is even—"

Delshawn pulled the trigger twice.

1938

Joe Tenant and Mikey Sops sat in the rowboat, letting the current take them back to the dock. There was no need to do anything other than an occasional stroke to specify their direction. Tenant's eyes were heavy and he just wanted to get home and get to sleep. He'd been going nonstop since Maxwell Carter's funeral.

But as he tied the boat to the dock, he knew he wasn't going to get the sleep his body craved. A man stood on the dock watching them. He was thin and tall, dressed in slacks and a thick jacket. The wind was cold coming off the river. The man folded his arms, relaxed and confident.

"You know this guy?" Sops whispered.

"No, but I think I'm gonna find out who he is."

Sops nodded, finishing the knot. Tenant stepped out of the boat and walked toward the man, realizing that as tall as the guy looked from the boat, Joe still had him beat.

"Mr. Tenant?"

It was the man from the car that first night, the same Irish brogue. His face was pale, with thick lips and icy green eyes. His hair was parted to the side, like the senator's, but it was blond and held less Brylcreem.

"You know it's me."

"Right, boyo. Well, I'm here just to give you some information. After your little stunt with Mr. O'Neill yesterday, we wanted to send a message."

Tenant's muscles tensed. He waited for a weapon and knew Sops was at his back.

"How is Isabelle?" the Irishman asked.

Now his muscles went limp and his nerves tingled. Everything was suddenly cold, like he'd just stepped outside for the first time on a winter morning.

"What did you do to my daughter?"

The Irishman winked. "I didn't do anything to her. Last time I saw her—" He gestured to the large metal bridge off in the distance. "She was wandering on the Pulaski Skyway. Not a good place for a kid to walk by herself."

Joe Tenant didn't even bother to fight this time. Didn't stick around to hear the rest of what the Irishman had to say. He ran to his car only to find Mikey Sops right beside him.

When Joe started the car, he turned to tell Sops to leave him alone.

Sops just put a hand on Tenant's shoulder.

"Let's go get her," Sops said.

✳

They pulled onto the skyway ten minutes later, Tenant hoping it wasn't too late. Cars were traveling slowly. The headlights moving in their direction kept blinking. But Joe didn't see any ambulances and traffic wasn't stopped.

The skyway was a long metal bridge that towered over Jersey City and Newark, with barely a shoulder. It had opened five or six years before, and Tenant thanked God that they had kept the promise of arresting any truck driver who took the skyway.

When it was windy, like it was tonight, the cars on the

skyway rattled back and forth, and even at the slow crawl of traffic, he felt his clunker shimmy.

After five minutes of crawling forward, his stomach couldn't take it anymore. He stopped the car, jumped out, Sops yelling after him. Horns blared and he heard people swearing at him.

To hell with them.

His legs pumped hard up the hill, staying in between traffic, on the white-dotted lines. He could hear the sound of train wheels clanking against the metal tracks, their whistles cutting through the night air, and water sloshing. Off in the distance a foghorn blew. Tenant didn't like noticing these things. He wanted to ignore everything but getting to the top of the bridge.

Ignore the fact that his legs ached.

Ignore his lungs begging for more air.

Focus on the process of running, like when he used to box. He could do six miles up hills.

Focus on Isabelle. He pleaded with God to keep her alive.

The hill crested and he could see ahead. The right lane was clear. It was clouded in shadow, the sun rising behind him reflecting off the iron girders. He couldn't see Isabelle.

He kept pumping his legs. After each step his thighs tightened a little more. They felt as if they weighed a hundred pounds each. He struggled to lift them.

She wasn't there. He was closer and he couldn't see her.

Tenant's mind flashed to four years ago. Isabelle had fallen. She was playing in the backyard while he washed the car. Every few minutes, he'd look up and give her a reassuring smile. She'd wave back at him. At one point, between rinses, she started balancing on the wall between their house and the Simpsons. She lost her balance, fell, and cried as if the sky was falling. Tenant dropped the hose and rushed toward her. When he got to her, he kissed her knee, reminded her how the bear reacted when he scraped his knee in the book they'd read together the day before. She nodded, wiping the tears from her eyes. She would be okay, she said.

Now she could be gone. Dead. His own daughter.

No! He wouldn't give up that quickly. Still he ran, everything getting closer, everything more in focus. His body pleaded to stop, the muscles in his legs almost too tight to go on. His calves cramped and loosened each time his feet pounded the pavement.

And then he saw her outline. A small girl clinging to the barrier overlooking the city. The body was motionless.

Another ten feet and he'd be there.

"Isabelle!" he screamed.

The head of the body looked up, peeling itself away from the barrier. She was alive!

He covered the last few feet in seconds.

Isabelle recognized him and yelled, "Daddy!"

Wrapping her up in his arms, he peeled her away from the girder. He hugged her. His baby was alive.

"Oh, Daddy," the girl said. "I'm so scared."

"It's okay, baby. You're okay."

He lifted her off the ground and began to carry her back to the car. He'd promised himself, that day she was born, he'd be there for her. That he'd be her hero, never be weak in front of her.

But he couldn't fight it. Tears rolled down his cheeks.

"Daddy?"

"It's okay, baby. We're going home now."

"They told me to tell you something."

Horns honked. People applauded. He was her hero.

"What did they say?"

"They said to tell you 'Connor O'Neill says hello.'"

part three

BRYAN HACKETT

26

seventeen hours

Franklin Carter was barely conscious. And with the lights off in the basement, he wasn't even sure if his eyes were open. He could smell his own piss. He had to let it out about an hour ago, felt the warmth run down his leg. And now he sat in it, soaking in his own waste.

Christ, he hoped he didn't have to shit.

The funny thing was, as miserable as this all was—the piss, the pain his face was in, being unable to move in the chair—it meant he was alive. And if he was alive, there was still a chance he could talk Hackett into letting him go.

"Hackett!" he yelled, and not for the first time since his last beating. "Hackett!"

But there wasn't an answer. Nothing. No sounds except for some ambient noises in the basement. He listened to water trickle. He was pretty sure he heard something scurry across the ground.

At one point—his mind wasn't working well with chronology—at one point he had struggled against his bindings, only to feel the ropes dig into his wrists. Blood from that wound now congealed on his fingertips.

Franklin could talk Hackett out of this shit. He knew it. Just like he knew this all could have been avoided years ago. But now he was going to have to rely on his ability to negotiate. He had to rely on Hackett being logical. Franklin knew logic would work. He'd seen it work before.

If only the man would come back downstairs and talk.

"*Hackett!*"

Nothing.

He started rubbing his arms up and down, trying to get some friction from the chair against his binds. Skin seemed to peel away from his wrists as he did. Blood dripped down along his fingertips, crusting at his nails. He gritted his teeth and kept going. The ropes were getting looser. He was sure of it.

Carter kept scraping. No one else was in the building. If there was a time to get out, this was it.

Things were going to break his way. He knew it.

The John Mayer songs were finally out of his head.

The first ropes gave way on his left side. Franklin pulled his arm away from the chair and flexed the muscles to loosen them. His eyes had long adjusted to the dark, and he could see the scratches and cuts along his wrists. Blood still dripped from them. And his wrist hurt like hell.

But that was okay. He was almost free now.

He rubbed his right arm up and down with even more force now. Just a matter of time.

Franklin Carter was going to get the hell out of here.

✳

Donne pulled up to his sister's house and saw Iapicca's car parked in the driveway. When he got out of the car, he felt his neck and back crack simultaneously, the muscles straining against his skin.

Inside, he smelled coffee brewing and heard Susan talking to herself in the kitchen. It brought back memories. Whenever Susan had a difficult exam ahead in high school, she'd lock herself in her room. Mom and he would always hear her talking to herself. The thought that his mother couldn't remember those moments anymore slowed his step.

Iapicca stood in the living room holding a mug. He caught Donne's eye and crooked his neck toward the glass sliding door that led to the backyard. Donne followed him silently.

When Donne shut the door, Iapicca said, "Get anything from your mother?"

"She was talking about headlights. I have no idea what she meant. Who's Connor O'Neill?"

Iapicca shrugged. "Sounds familiar. Why?"

"My mother said he was arrested because of my grandfather."

Iapicca nodded and was quiet for a moment.

"Your sister and I talked too," he said.

Somewhere a cricket chirped in the huge backyard. Donne leaned against the deck railing, smelling the freshly cut grass and feeling a bit of condensation on his skin, as if the humidity was becoming liquid as they spoke.

"What did she tell you?" he asked.

"Not too much. She said whoever called her to tell her about Franklin's ransom had a very familiar voice. She was certain she'd heard it before, but she couldn't place it. She said it sounded like the voice was missing something, like an accent."

Something tickled at the back of Donne's brain too when Iapicca said that. Some lost memory trying to fight its way back to the surface. Again he wondered if this was how Mom felt anytime someone visited. That feeling like something was on the tip of her tongue, that she *should* know it but couldn't place it.

"She didn't want me to tell you," Iapicca said.

"Why not?"

"Because she thinks she's grasping at straws, some kind of hope that isn't there. She's about to give up, Jackson. She doesn't want any false hope."

"I don't think she's grasping at straws."

"Why not?"

"I don't know, déjà vu? Something about the accent struck a chord with me. I can't put my finger on it. Connor O'Neill too."

Iapicca nodded. "It'll come."

"I know. We don't have time to wait for it, though."

Iapicca looked at his watch. "Less than seventeen."

"Shit."

"I'm calling in the cops, the feds, whoever. You need help on this."

"No."

"It's the right thing to do. They're professionals. They'll help. They'll bring Franklin home."

"Whoever this is finds out there's a cop involved and Franklin's dead."

"You ever work a kidnapping when you were a cop? No, you were Narcotics. Franklin stays alive. Without Franklin, this guy has no collateral."

"He'll kill him."

"Jackson, I could lose my job. I have to do this."

"Eight hours. Just give me eight hours."

"You trying to make up for something?"

Donne didn't say anything. He'd abandoned his family. Just like his father had.

Iapicca nodded. "Eight hours. Because I like your sister. Then I call it in. Things get too heavy before that, I call it in."

Behind them the door slid open. Donne turned as Susan stepped through the doorway. She handed him a cup of coffee. Cream and sugar. She remembered. Not that it was hard to remember, but somehow it meant something. Like she'd thought of him. The feeling surprised him, and he wondered why he suddenly cared.

Perhaps he was making too much of things.

"Did Mom say anything?" Susan asked.

"She talked about headlights."

"How was she?"

He thought about lying to her. Just tell Susan everything was okay, relieve her conscience. But he didn't.

"She was scared, Sue. Terrified." Donne took a sip of coffee to let his words sink in. Then he swung low. "She was screaming. They gave her a sedative. You scared the hell out of her."

Susan's face flushed just for a second. Her lips quivered and she squinted hard, and he expected her to cry. Composing herself, she walked back into the house.

"You didn't have to do that," Iapicca said. "She's been through a lot."

"So, what do we do now?" Donne asked.

He looked up at the stars. There weren't many; the lights from New York, just ten miles away, blurred most of them out. But you could still see the North Star and part of the Big Dipper.

"We get her husband back," Iapicca said. "Eight hours. I stay with you the whole time."

Donne nodded. Like it was that easy.

Iapicca reached into his pocket and pulled out his cell phone. Apparently, it was vibrating. He didn't say much, just a few yeses and uh-huhs. He snapped the phone shut without saying good-bye.

He held out his phone. "That was Krewer. The kid who brought the gun in? Carlos? They just found him shot dead in Clifton."

CHAPTER 27

BRYAN HACKETT CONSIDERED HIMSELF A TRAIN GUY when it came to the city. He hated to drive the grid, and preferred to park in Hoboken, catch the PATH, and then hop the subway cars until he got to where he wanted to be. Hell, the other night driving the Ryder truck in was the first time he'd driven in the city in ten years. And even then he had to take the bridge in, where security was the lightest.

Tonight he parked in Hoboken, caught the path to Fourteenth Street, and then the 6 train to Lexington and Seventy-seventh. When he ascended the stairs to the street, he realized the night felt exactly the same as a few nights earlier. The warm air, the shine of the street-lights off the railing, there was a cleanliness to the Upper East Side. The rush of adrenaline he'd gotten driving the Ryder truck flowed back to him. The streets were empty, save for one woman walking her dog. A few of the bars were open, but most places were closed even though it was only midnight. He assumed the closed businesses were because of all the police activity around the area.

The city that never sleeps. Unless shit blows up.

The local bar owners didn't know the cops as well as they probably thought they did. Nothing a cop wants more than to drown his sorrows after working a long shift of digging through building rubble.

As he came around the corner, he found the former location of Carter's. It was a hole in the wall, literally. Most of the debris looked like it had been swept up, and all that was left was police tape and crumbled walls.

He could see the remains of the restaurant through the broken walls. The entire bar was gone, and mirrors were cracked and charred against the far—still standing—wall. Wires hung from the walls, but the electricity must have been shut down, so there were no sparks.

Jason Marshall, a tall guy with close-cropped black hair and a neat dark suit on, caught Hackett's eye. Hackett felt underdressed in his polo shirt, shorts, and sandals. But he was supposed to be coming directly from the beach, they'd understand.

"Hackett. Over here," Marshall said.

Spotlights, illuminating the crime scene, reflected off the agent's skin. What did Jill call the color? Oh yeah, café latte.

Hackett stepped under the yellow tape and gave Marshall a firm handshake.

"Want to go sit?" Marshall asked.

Hackett nodded. He'd rather go to one of the open bars. But this was going to be a long night. And he still had to get back to Franklin Carter.

Just throw them off long enough to get the money.

They crossed the street and entered a Starbucks that was being kept open for the benefit of the cops. Sitting at the small table, Hackett didn't place an order. He wasn't a coffee guy and found the fact that everyone drank it maddening. People were lemmings, following social expectations. No one really liked coffee, they just watched everyone else doing it. Marshall drank tea with lemon. Maybe he was his own man.

"Fertilizer bomb," Marshall said. "Diesel fuel, paper, cotton. Just a ton of that shit. A small patch of C4 connected to the battery port of a cell phone. Dial the number and ka-boom."

Hackett's stomach turned. Marshall said the bomb was something only an inside man could do. He regretted mentioning he worked at Ploch's now.

"Anyone could get that stuff," Hackett said. "I thought you said it was an inside job."

"Remember the name Michael Garibell?"

This was a bad idea. Hackett had been off the force. There wasn't any reason for him to be here. Just say no.

"No," Hackett said. "No idea what you're talking about."

"One of our most popular undercover names. Generic, but not Smith or Jones. Could pass for anyone, whatever we needed it to."

"Uh-huh," Hackett said. Had to sound like you were listening and learning new things. Make sure it didn't look like this information rang any bells.

"Nothing?" Marshall asked. "Well, the Ryder truck, we found its license plate. It was registered to a Michael Garibell out of New Jersey."

"I'm sure there are a lot of Michael Garibells out there."

Marshall nodded. "We're looking into that."

"But you think it's an inside job?"

"Well, the thing is, we think the bomb was set off with a remote."

"You think?"

"There's no evidence supporting that yet. Just the blast radius meant it couldn't be on a fuse. We don't think the guy could have gotten far enough away if he set up a burning fuse."

"So?"

"How many normal people you know can get a remote to set off a bomb?"

"Terrorists were going to use Gatorade, shampoo, and cell phones."

Marshall nodded but didn't speak. He swirled his cup of tea.

They have more evidence, Hackett thought. But they weren't ready to share it with him yet. No way. Marshall was out to get him.

"I'm sick of this fucking Starbucks," Marshall said. "Been in it six times today."

"Should have gone to a bar."

Marshall laughed. "I wish. You going to help?"

Say no. Go home, fuck with Carter for another seventeen hours, get your money, and get the hell out of Dodge.

But there was an opportunity here. Getting fired by these assholes was the reason this whole thing started. He needed the money. Jill needed the money.

Now was a chance to fuck with them right back.

"Yeah," he said.

✳

Iapicca and Donne met with Krewer on Delawanna Avenue. There were three police cars, lights flashing, cordoning off the street. Traffic backed up toward Route 3 and down toward the river. Spectators lined the streets to get a look at the sheet that covered a child's body. They'd parked on one of the side streets and walked three blocks to get to the scene. Trying to avoid the traffic and the spectators behind it, an ambulance sounded its siren and pulled into the oncoming lane.

"I'd just gotten out of the city," Krewer said. "My boss called me and asked what the kid I interviewed looked like."

"It's Carlos, huh?" Iapicca asked.

"Yeah." Krewer lit a cigarette. "Fucking what—fifteen years old?"

Iapicca pressed his fingers against both sides of his nose and let out a deep breath.

"What happened?" Donne asked.

Krewer and Iapicca turned toward Donne. It was like they'd forgotten he was there. Or didn't want him there.

"Far as we can tell, Carlos was standing along the curb and a car pulled up and somebody shot him."

"That's it?"

"What the hell else do you want to know?" Krewer sucked his cigarette.

"Come on. Go easy. He's just trying to help," Iapicca said.

Krewer glared at Donne, then turned his back and started walking toward the crime scene.

As they followed, Krewer spoke. "We think Carlos knew whoever shot him. He walked right up to the person and was shot in the forehead. We think the killer was in an SUV, because the angle of the shot came from above Carlos, as if he were looking up. There are tire marks on the road, but no footprints. Carlos was facing whoever shot him and fell backward after the impact of the bullet."

Against the curb, thirty feet to their left, the sheet covering the body fluttered a bit in the breeze. Yellow crime-scene tape formed a perimeter around him. A few CSI guys took pictures.

"The first shot killed him, most likely. The second was just to make sure," Krewer said.

They stood at the police tape, unwilling to cross that line into the official crime scene. Krewer probably didn't want them to fuck up anything. Across the tape, two guys in white shirts and khaki pants dug through the grass with rubber gloves on.

The EMS stood over the body, waiting for the okay to take it away. The detectives had gotten what they could at the scene, but would be taking the body back for an autopsy very soon.

"Any ideas?" Krewer asked.

Iapicca said, "No."

"Kid found a gun. Could it be the owner coming to get it back?"

"Was Carlos in a gang?"

Krewer nodded, but his eyes were far away. "It could be just a gang initiation. We get a lot of that around here, near Paterson. Not that we have a lot of murders, but when we do, usually gangbangers just fucking around. The double tap bothers me, though. Too professional."

Krewer said to Iapicca, "Come talk to me for a second."

Donne started to follow the two as they walked toward the curb. Krewer held up his hand.

"Not you."

Donne stopped. The lights from the police cruisers flashed, reflecting off the backs of Krewer and Iapicca. Krewer rested his hand on Iapicca's shoulder and whispered in his ear. To Donne's left, Carlos's body was still covered by a sheet and on the ground. Donne put his hands in his pockets and turned away.

Stupid kid.

Iapicca tapped Donne on the shoulder.

"Time to go," he said.

They started off for his car.

"I'll send the evidence we got from the Rutherford shooting over to you," Iapicca said to Krewer. "Maybe we'll find a match."

"Sure." Krewer shook his head. "Fuck. Such a good night, too. He even closed with 'Love and Mercy.'"

1 9 3 8

"She was where?"

Caroline dropped a glass and it shattered against the kitchen floor. Shards littered the ground, and Joe Tenant had to watch where he stepped as he tried to get closer to his wife.

An hour earlier, he'd brought Isabelle in and quietly put her to bed. He didn't want Caroline—who was still sleeping—to know she'd been gone. Isabelle had calmed down a bit on the ride home, Uncle Sops helping out with a five-dollar bill and the promise of a lollipop the next time he saw her. As soon as they were home, Tenant got the girl under the covers and poured himself a shot of scotch.

And waited for Caroline to wake up.

When she came down, dressed in a robe and a calm smile, he let her take a glass for her orange juice and told her flat out.

"The men who are after me came in last night and took Isabelle. They left her on the Pulaski Skyway."

The glass crashed and Caroline yelled. Tenant closed his eyes and let the heartbreak, fear, and shame wash over him.

"Is she okay? They were in our house? Oh my God, Joe. I was asleep."

All Tenant could do was nod.

"Where is she? Where is my daughter?"

"Upstairs."

Caroline ran out of the room. Joe Tenant drank some more scotch and listened to the sound of footsteps go up the stairs and into Isabelle's room. Caroline's voice carried to the kitchen. Soon, Tenant was sure he heard crying.

He downed the rest of the scotch and walked to Isabelle's room. As he climbed the stairs, he stopped for a minute to look at the family portrait they had taken after Caroline and Isabelle were allowed to leave the hospital. In the photo, he stood behind a chair, his hand on Caroline's shoulder. She was sitting, Isabelle in her arms, smiling. He remembered the picture was originally supposed to be taken outside, but it had rained that day.

Tenant turned into Isabelle's room and found Caroline crying and cradling the girl in her arms. Isabelle was awake and had wrapped her small arms as far around her mother as she could.

He stood in the doorway until Caroline turned toward him. He'd never seen such hate in her eyes.

He took a step forward.

"Get out," Caroline said.

Without another word, Joe Tenant went back downstairs. He sat in his easy chair and waited. Not knowing what was going to happen next was the worst part. He wanted another drink, but at the same time, he wanted to be clearheaded when Caroline decided to talk to him.

The minutes ticked by. No sound came from upstairs anymore. Isabelle would not be going to school today. She was late already. Joe Tenant just listened to the ticking of the old grandfather clock he'd inherited from his father, and waited.

Ten minutes later, Caroline appeared. She stood at the foot of the stairs and didn't speak.

Joe held her gaze for a long time, waiting. Nothing.

"You have to go to your mother's," he said, not being able to take the silence anymore. "It's not safe here."

"When she wakes up," Caroline said.

"Good."

He wanted to say something to make it all okay. There had to be a way to fix this. But as he sat there, Joe Tenant realized he wasn't smart enough to come up with a solution.

Caroline, however, seemed to figure one out.

"How could you bring this into our family, Joe? How could you do this?"

Now was the time to apologize, but nothing came.

"It's not safe being with you," she said. "I love you, but it's not safe."

Joe Tenant balled his hands into fists. Knowing what was coming didn't make it any better.

"I want you to pack up your things and be out of here by breakfast. You just have to leave."

"Caroline, please—"

"No, Joe. You put our daughter in danger. You put me in danger."

"It's not—"

"They were in our home! Do you understand that? They took our girl! They tried to kill her! They told you to stay away, and you can't do that. Not even for your own family."

The bell in the grandfather clock began to chime. It was eight in the morning. He'd always remember what time it was.

"I can't be with you anymore."

"I—I'm—"

Anything he could say wouldn't stop this from happening. And even while he tried, no words would come. He never wanted this.

"We're leaving, Joe. And when we come back from my mother's, you'd better be gone."

It took Caroline an hour to pack her a suitcase. Then she woke up Isabelle. Five minutes later, she pulled out of the driveway. Caroline didn't even let Isabelle say good-bye.

Joe went upstairs and sat on Isabelle's bed. Across from him was her bookcase. He reached out and pulled the tattered book from four years ago. The one about the bear with the skinned knee. He stared at the cover—bear fur peaking out from behind a bandage—for a long time.

CHAPTER 28

SIXTEEN HOURS

When the rope finally snapped free, Franklin Carter's right arm swung so far in front of him, he thought he might hit himself in the head. Blood from his wrist splattered against his forehead. But that didn't matter; he was loose.

He tried to stand, but both legs had fallen asleep. He stretched them out in front of him, letting the blood flow. He couldn't afford to be slowed down.

Finally, the feeling subsided. Standing was an odd sensation, like balancing on a tightrope. He felt as though each step might cause him to fall over. Instead, he hit his head on the ceiling. He blinked, trying to force the sharp pain from his skull.

He could barely see, but he was afraid to turn the light on. Who knew who he might alert. Across the room was a table with nothing on top of it. Other than the chair, it was the only furniture in the basement. He heard skittering again and decided it was time to go up the stairs and get the hell out of there. He hardly noticed he was holding his breath.

Stepping through the puddles, Carter reached the stairs. The wood creaked with each step, bending but not breaking. The sound was deafening, like when he used to sneak home to his parents' after a night of drinking in high school. Ten minutes, that's what he gave himself. Ten minutes to get the hell out of this place, get to the police, and tell them all he knew. Ten minutes before they came back. He didn't know why, but he was sure of it.

Finally reaching the landing, Carter allowed himself to exhale. He was so damned close to getting free. And that meant getting his life back. Explaining everything to Susan, telling Donne to fuck off, and rebuilding the restaurant.

He grabbed the metal doorknob. At first, the sensation was just like his legs waking up, pins and needles. But suddenly the feeling was wrong—a wave pulsed through his skin. Carter smelled something burning and a current coursed through his body. He pulled his hand back, screaming.

As the electric current caused some of his muscles to spasm, he tumbled backward. He reached out for the railing, but the decaying wood snapped in his grasp.

Each step stretched and warped beneath his body. He reached out one more time but couldn't break his fall. The pain was enormous, rising through his back and shooting down his legs. Every muscle constricted and felt like softballs beneath his skin. His arms scraped against the wood as he clawed for a handhold.

He was still tumbling when the room went black.

✳

Donne sat in the car with Iapicca as he drove aimlessly through Clifton. They went around the Allwood Circle and crawled up past

Mt. Prospect toward Broad Street. Donne read the street signs as they went, trying to familiarize himself with the area. At Broad, they turned onto the road and passed a place called Ploch's, which sold gardening items.

"Where are we going?" Donne asked. "What did Krewer say to you?"

Iapicca turned left at a fire station onto Van Houten Avenue. Alongside the road were houses, a school, and several small restaurants. Clifton seemed to try to pack everything into one small space—living, eating, learning, and faith. All you needed in walking distance.

"One eighty-seven Harris Street. Paterson," Iapicca said.

"What's there?"

"Delshawn Butler."

"Who's that?"

Iapicca turned right on Valley Road. Condos lined the left side of the street. To his right Donne could see the New York skyline.

"Krewer tracked the gun. It belongs to a Delshawn Butler, one eighty-seven Harris Street," Iapicca said.

"You think he'll be there?"

"What kind of guy is this? He's driving around killing people in his Escalade, and he has his gun registered under his own name and address? I don't know if it's really him."

"Maybe he's the dumbest killer ever. Maybe we're going to get lucky."

Iapicca shrugged. "Maybe it's a fake name."

"Could be that, too."

They stayed on Valley Road, passed over Route 80, and then went past St. Joseph's Hospital. He hated to admit it, but Donne could tell they were in Paterson by the condition of the streets. Garbage littered the side of the road, a stray dog was pissing on a fire hydrant, and all the houses could use a paint job.

Paterson used to be a hub for the Industrial Revolution, one of the North's most important cities. Factories pumped out all kinds of different products, spewing steam and smog into the air but keeping the nation's economy going. Over the years, however, it had fallen apart. Age had taken its toll. The buildings began to deteriorate and closed, and people moved out.

Now it was a haven for gangs, drugs, and the poor. While downtown was the center of the county, holding the courthouse and a few state buildings, most of the city was decrepit. Recently, it was most famous for a school in need of such help that a principal had to come in, chain the doors shut, and carry a bat and megaphone. The story had been made into an uplifting movie. But no one liked the principal. He was fired, and last Donne had heard he was a warden of a prison somewhere. Maybe the two jobs weren't that much different.

"Paterson's really done well for itself, huh?" Donne asked.

Iapicca looked at him and laughed. "Yeah, they really cleaned it up nice. Safest city in New Jersey."

"You know where we're going?"

"Yup."

"Krewer didn't send anyone over there?"

"I promised you eight hours. I'm calling in every last favor I have."

"You got a gun, just in case it's not a fake name?"

"Yup."

"I don't."

"Well, technically you shouldn't even be in the car, but since I'm off duty and you're not even a licensed PI, we'll just write it off as two buddies stopping by an old friend's house."

The mention of his revoked license hit home. Iapicca had really done his research on Donne. He wondered who Iapicca talked to. The fact that he seemed to trust him led Donne to believe it wasn't his ex-partner.

"And you're armed."

They stopped at a red light. Some deep instinct in Donne wanted Iapicca to run it.

"Did you kill Faye and George?" Iapicca looked at him, his face unreadable.

Maybe he did talk to the New Brunswick cops.

"No," Donne said, meeting his eyes. "I told you I didn't."

"I believe you."

"Well, that's good."

The light turned green and Iapicca made a left. Donne missed the street sign. Maybe there wasn't one. Spaced between the decaying houses were a few boarded-up warehouses, dive bars, and strip clubs with blinking neon signs. He could only imagine you needed to make sure you had a complete supply of antibiotics ready when you left one of them.

"Yeah, it is good. For you and me," Iapicca said.

"Why's that?"

"I have a spare gun in my trunk. I'm gonna let you hold on to it." Iapicca kept his eyes on the road. "You know, just in case this isn't as friendly a meeting as I would hope."

CHAPTER

DeLSHAWN BUTLER COULDN'T GO HOME JUST yet.
His body was pumping with adrenaline. He was wired like he'd drunk three cups of coffee. Now would be the perfect time to find that guy he beat the shit out of in the bar. Kill two birds with one stone.

Literally.

He turned up the radio, letting Akon scream through the speakers. He had no idea where the guy was. He wasn't at Mountainside this morning. No dice.

Now he had no idea where to look.

He called Hackett.

"What?" the motherfucker said when he answered.

Jesus Christ, if he wanted things done, he was going to have to hear about it.

"I took care of the kid."

"Don't tell me about that now. Is that why you're calling? I'm fucking busy over here."

"No."

"Get on with it, then."

This time of night, there was no one on the road. Delshawn pushed the gas to go as fast as he wanted. No one was going to pull him over.

"That guy I beat up in the bar—"

"Jesus Christ, I told you—"

"I think he knows that Carter family you been messing with."

"Uh-huh. His name is Jackson Donne. He's part of the family."

There, Delshawn had his attention.

"Where they live? He might be there? I could, you know, take care of him then."

Hackett sighed, then said, "Six ninety-seven Upper Mountain Road. Montclair. Don't hurt the girl."

Delshawn hung up the phone.

Montclair? Shit, that was right around the corner.

✳

One eighty-seven Harris Street wasn't as bad as Donne expected. The lawn was clean, minus one stray Crunch Bar wrapper. The bags of trash were in trash cans, and tidy along the driveway. The house itself wasn't falling apart and even had aluminum siding instead of peeling paint.

Before they approached it, Iapicca handed Donne his backup weapon. It had been months since he held a gun, and when he hefted it, it was lighter than he expected.

"Let's hope we don't have to use these," he said. Then he shook his head. "I am getting fired tomorrow. I know it."

Donne nodded, remembering his days on the force. Something must have convinced Iapicca Donne was trustworthy. At the same time, Donne wasn't even sure how much he trusted Iapicca. Something happened when Iapicca and Susan talked, and now he seemed more dedicated to solving this situation than Donne did.

Something nagged at Donne. The police never really wanted to help. They just wanted their cut.

On the porch, Iapicca took the lead. He pulled the screen door open and pounded on the inner door with his fist. He held his badge, but not his gun. Donne had tucked the gun in the waistband of his jeans and made sure his shirttail covered it.

After a few minutes of banging, the door opened and a short black woman, hair in braids, and wearing white pajama pants and a pink tank top, stared at them.

"Who the hell are you, knockin' down my door at one in the morning?"

Donne hadn't realized how late it was. That made it sixteen hours until Franklin's zero hour. They needed a big break.

Iapicca held out his badge, then quickly pocketed it. "Police, ma'am. We're looking for Delshawn Butler."

"Oh, hell no. What do you want him for?"

"Just want to ask him a few questions."

"Usual police bullshit," she said, and started to close the door.

Iapicca put his hand flat against the door and held it open.

"This would be a lot easier for both of us if you'd just cooperate. I really don't want to have to go wake up a judge and get a search warrant. And I'm sure you don't want me knocking this door down and tearing up all your possessions looking for anything that I can arrest you with."

Iapicca was bluffing. A Bergen County cop had no jurisdiction in Passaic County. He would catch shit if Donne fired his weapon. He could also catch a ton of shit if anyone found out he was here tonight.

The woman hesitated.

"Delshawn ain't here."

Iapicca nodded. "Any idea where he is?"

"Nah. He out working."

"And what does he do for a living?"

"Takes care of people on the streets."

"Any place in particular?"

"All over. He don't tell me."

"Okay. What's your name, ma'am?"

"Shemiah."

"Last name?"

"Washington."

Shemiah Washington yawned.

"How are you related to Mr. Butler?" Iapicca asked.

"He my man."

"You two married?"

"Hell no. We don't believe in that shit."

"Well, thank you, Ms. Washington. You can go back to sleep now."

"When he comes home, you want me to tell him you looking for him?"

"No," Iapicca said. "He'll turn up. No need to bother him."

Shemiah shut the door, and Iapicca turned toward Donne.

"Working the streets, huh? He's not a prostitute, so that leaves drugs," Donne said.

"Yeah. She thinks he's a drug dealer."

"You don't?"

Iapicca shook his head. "Dealers don't kill a couple of senior citizens in my town for no reason. I think he's a hit man."

"And he used a gun registered under his own name and address?"

"I didn't say he was a good one."

"What now?" Donne asked.

"Would you recognize Delshawn if you saw him?"

"Yeah."

"Feel like cruising the streets of Paterson?"

"Not really, but I don't think we have much choice."

Iapicca looked at his watch. "Fifteen and a half hours. Yeah, not much else we can do."

✳

Franklin Carter felt his cheek saturated in water and realized he'd fallen the entire stairway. He was on his stomach and couldn't get his arms under him to push himself up. Sharp pain shot through his elbow as he tried to move his left arm. It had to be broken.

He gritted his teeth and used his right arm to push himself over onto his back. Now he felt the puddle soak through his hair.

The last of his adrenaline coursed through his veins and allowed him to turn over. Once he did, Carter took a second to catch his breath. Some of the muscles in his legs and right arm spasmed.

Motherfucker electrified the doorknob somehow.

He'd known Hackett for years, but he never thought he was this sick. He'd never thought it would go this far.

Should have paid up years ago.

For the first time, Carter realized this was his fault.

Carter had always gone with his instincts. And the one time they were wrong, everything fell apart. There was no way out now. It was too late to pay. Hackett was going to win.

And, lying on the cold floor, Carter knew he was going to die.

fіfteeɴ ʜours

Bryan Hackett stood next to Jason Marshall, staring at the gaping hole in the building. Answering Delshawn's call earlier had given him a moment to think about what was going on here. Marshall let him talk, thinking it was Hackett's wife. The best part was Delshawn was an idiot and Hackett was pretty sure he wouldn't be able to actually kill Donne, but he'd probably cause some more chaos, keep him off Hackett's trail.

Marshall jammed his hands in his suit pocket, looking relaxed and unaffected. Hackett stood straight, trying to show confidence, but not liking the situation he'd gotten himself into. They watched an FBI agent break away from a crowd of investigators and walk their way.

The agent was clean-cut, gelled hair pushed to the side, clean-shaven. Hackett wondered how long the guy had been on the scene. Couldn't have been long. Unlike Marshall, this guy looked like he'd gotten some sleep.

"This the guy?" the agent said to Marshall.

"Special Agent Sam Draxton, meet Bryan Hackett."

They shook hands.

"Let me get this straight. You want me to tell you which guys I used to work with who might have done this?"

Draxton nodded. "That would be very helpful. I assume Detective Marshall explained everything to you?"

"I'm not sure I'm comfortable giving up that information. I mean, these guys were my colleagues."

They knew. Somehow, they knew Hackett was involved. Nothing added up. Why was Marshall—a New Jersey state trooper—on a crime scene in New York? Where were the New York cops? They had to have one of the best bomb squads, crime-scene guys, and police in the country, but they weren't here. The FBI was here, even though it had been decided it wasn't a terrorist attack. They knew Michael Garibell was Bryan Hackett.

Hackett wondered how far he could get if he took Marshall's gun and killed them both. Not very. His best bet was to beg out of here, finish the job with Carter, and get the hell out of the country with Jill. Start over.

"We're talking here about something on a par with a terrorist attack, Mr. Hackett. Anything you could do to help, we'd really appreciate it."

This is how they'd get one of their own. They'd come smiling, asking for help, and then you're in the back of the car, cuffed. Hackett was not going to let them have their way.

"I'm going to need some time to think about it."

Draxton shrugged.

"Not too much time," he said.

Hackett turned around and started walking. The subway station, only a block away, was his destination. *Act like you've been there before. They won't stop you.*

"Hackett." Marshall's voice echoed off the canyon of buildings. Hackett didn't realize until that moment how empty that area of New York was. How one act of violence could shut the whole damn thing down. He hated to admit it, but the feeling of power was amazing. Probably like Oswald felt that day in Dallas. He could do anything and no one could stop him. He clenched his hands into fists and forced himself not to smile.

"Yes, sir?"

"Do the right thing here."

"Yes, sir."

He made his way down the stairs, finding the number 6 train pulling up to the station. Timing was everything.

✳

The house on Upper Mountain Road was high-class shit, that was for sure. Delshawn Butler pulled his Escalade up across the street in front of another huge brick house. The street was filled with them.

Back when he dealt, he knew a couple of guys from Montclair, but there was no way they lived up in this area. Maybe down on the other side where those apartment buildings were. Butler felt more comfortable there. Here he stuck out like a black man at a Klan meeting. Some Neighborhood Watch asshole might see the truck and try to be a hero.

Butler would have to make things happen quickly. Hacket said not to mess with the girl, which meant he couldn't go inside. She'd see him. Get the guy out into the open, take him down with one shot, and get the fuck out of here. Assuming he was inside.

Delshawn Butler got out of the car and walked across the street toward the house. He felt his gun, heavy, at his side.

Susan Carter found the bills and began to pore through them. Looking for numbers, loopholes, anything that showed her husband had a lot of money she could access. Thus far, she had no idea what she was looking for. Deep down, she hoped she'd come across a piece of paper that read, "FREE ONE HUNDRED THOUSAND DOLLARS HERE."

The coffeemaker percolated in the otherwise quiet kitchen. The pale light above the wooden table felt as bright as the sun on the beach at noon. She squinted and kept flipping papers.

Nothing.

She stretched and walked to the living room, wondering when Jackson and the detective would come back. She found herself liking Iapicca, even though she knew the police shouldn't be involved. They related well to each other, and he'd been through the same things she had.

She peeked through the front window and froze. Parked in front of the house was a black Cadillac Escalade.

Donne's phone rang, shattering the silence in the car. Save for a few homeless people, they hadn't seen anyone on the streets. It was too late at night, even for criminals.

He looked at the caller ID and put it on speaker.

Susan said, "Maybe I'm just being paranoid, but there's a car parked outside my house. Well, not a car, a truck. I've never seen it on this block before."

Iapicca glanced over at him.

"What kind of truck?" Donne asked.

"Like a Cadillac. One of those Escalades you see on MTV."

Donne clutched the cell phone a little tighter. She wasn't being paranoid.

"Don't go outside. Lock the doors. We'll be there in twenty minutes."

"We're catching a break," Iapicca said.

"Looks like it," Donne said. "As long as he doesn't get to her first."

1938

A month had passed, and Joe Tenant was living in a motel. He made enough money for food and the room. The rest he sent to Caroline and Isabelle. He never heard from them. He didn't hear from anyone except when he worked with Sops.

He walked to work, two miles every night, because he'd left Caroline with the car. No phone, no contact. Nothing. Joe was afraid that if the Irishman couldn't find him, then he'd go after Isabelle and Caroline. He asked Sops to check up on them, and he reported they were fine.

Two weeks ago, he'd written Lisa Carter a letter and told her he wanted a response. Gave the address of the hotel so she could write back. It was a Tuesday morning when she replied. It wasn't in the form of a letter.

He'd been asleep for the better part of two hours when he was awoken by a knock at the door. Joe Tenant got out of bed, dressed in only boxer shorts, lifted the fire poker off the table, and peeked through the peephole. Lisa Carter stood by herself, looking over her shoulder, as if she was waiting to be spotted.

He pulled the door open and let her in, embarrassed he was nearly naked. Joe watched Lisa Carter scan his body.

She smiled and looked at the fire poker on the table.

"You don't have a fireplace in this room," Lisa Carter said.

"No."

"What's it for?"

"Protection. I brought it here from work."

"I got your letter."

She crossed the room and sat on the edge of the bed. She wore a long skirt and white blouse. She peeled the long black gloves off, placed them on her lap. Her dark hair was pulled back in a bun. She looked like she was going to a funeral. Maybe she was still in mourning.

Joe found a pair of slacks and pulled them on. Then he sat at the desk across from her.

"Why was Connor O'Neill at your husband's funeral?"

"You don't make small talk, do you?"

Joe Tenant shook his head. "Not when my family is threatened."

"My husband used to donate to O'Neill's campaigns. O'Neill came to offer his condolences."

"Used to?"

Lisa nodded. "I don't get into my husband's affairs, but Connor was a friend of the family. I know my husband and he went out on fishing trips, out for dinner. We'd even been to the O'Neills' home for holiday parties. But in the last year that all stopped."

"Why?"

"I don't know."

"Did O'Neill say anything to you at the funeral?"

"Just that he was sorry for my loss."

Joe Tenant walked over to the bed. He wasn't sure why. He was drawn there somehow.

"Is it an election year for O'Neill?"

Joe didn't follow local politics unless he was going to lose his job because of one of the president's plans to jump-start the economy.

"Yes," she said.

"Did your husband donate to a campaign?"

"He didn't tell me. He was very secretive about it this year."

"You need to go to the press with this. Say he did. Say it's what got him killed."

"I can't do that. I would be lying."

"That doesn't matter. You just need to get their attention."

"And if they come after me?"

"They won't. I'll take care of it."

Joe nodded. Things were making sense. He was glad she came.

"I'm sorry about what happened at your home last month. I was worried about my family."

Lisa Carter stood and placed her hands on his shoulders.

"You're a very interesting person, Joe Tenant. Your wife kicks you out of your home, and yet you're still protecting her."

She knew more than he'd told her. Lisa Carter had looked into his life.

"Not being able to protect her is what got me kicked out. It's why I'm here. I don't want to be. I love my family."

She ran her hands down his bare chest. What was she doing? And why was he letting her do it?

"I miss my husband."

Because it felt good, that's why.

"We've only met once," she said. "I don't know why I'm here."

"You want to help."

She shook her head.

"No. It's more than that."

She stood on her toes, angled her head, and kissed him on the lips. The kiss was soft, and the message behind it was evident.

He didn't want this. He wanted to be back with Caroline. But Lisa was attractive. He wondered if she missed her husband like he missed Caroline. He wondered if she was making this happen for the same reasons he was going to let it happen.

They kissed again, her mouth opening. Her hands ran across his stomach, then found the button of his pants.

He pushed her away.

"I can't," he said.

Her eyes met his. "Your wife?"

"And daughter."

She nodded. "I like you, Joe. You seem like a good man."

"I'm trying," he said.

CHAPTER 31

BRYAN HACKETT DIDN'T get off the train in Hoboken. He took the PATH to Exchange Place, then caught the Light Rail into Bayonne. While it wasn't the safest time of night to make this journey, he thought he could risk it. He wanted to take one last look before he and Jill ran off.

The feds wouldn't be after him this quickly. Not if they wanted him to think they needed his help.

He walked down Avenue A, the air still warm even at three in the morning. A homeless guy sauntered across the street, pushing a shopping cart. Otherwise, the street was empty and silent. Hackett tried to look like he belonged.

He reached the end of the road, the Starting Point bar on the corner, a left turn to nowhere the only option. The Bayonne Bridge to

Staten Island, lit up in red, white, and blue, hovered in the distance. To Hackett's right was a grassy marsh area. A quarter mile beyond that a train carried freight toward Port Newark. He could smell the dead fish, shit, and sewage from the Hudson and Hackensack Rivers. It smelled like the world's biggest toilet.

Texaco used to own this land. A new ethanol company was supposed to be moving in.

Hackett's anger made his hand shake. This whole area was bullshit, unused and untouched. Soon, the government would have its control of this area, trying to slow the ethanol company down.

But that didn't matter.

It should have been his.

✳

Delshawn Butler did a lap around the house, checking for open doors, easy entry, and any way to escape. Everything was locked. Butler saw the woman sitting in the kitchen, poring over papers. Damn, it was late, her husband wasn't home, and she was up paying the motherfucking bills. His target wasn't around.

For now.

He sat back, pressed against the brick house, waiting. He needed a plan, a way to get his target here. What did Hackett say his name was? Donne? Yeah, that was it. Part of the fucking family.

He thought for a while. Hackett told him not to hurt the girl. But he didn't say not to scare her. Or use her as bait.

Butler could go in there, scare the girl into calling Donne. Get him here. Kill him.

He could leave the girl alive.

No, shit, that wouldn't work. Because then the girl would recognize him. Shit, shit, shit.

A car rolled down Upper Mountain slow. Butler tensed and watched as it passed. Nothing to worry about.

But, watching the car, he realized his plan would work. He could kill Donne, let Hackett finish whatever he had to do with the girl, and then Butler could come back and kill her.

A hit man just starting out needed practice.

"I'm going to call it in," Iapicca said.

"No. Don't. I want to handle this."

"Bullshit. This is someone's life. Your sister's life."

"You gave me eight hours."

"Unless things got fucked up. Which they are now."

"What are you going to do? Call your Rutherford buddies? And fuck up your career?"

Iapicca hesitated before answering. "No, I'll call Montclair."

"And say what? There's a suspicious SUV sitting outside a house on North Mountain? It'll take fifteen minutes for them to get there. We'll be there by then."

"Fuck."

"You've come this far with me."

Iapicca didn't respond. He didn't radio anyone, either.

The car sped up. Donne appreciated what Iapicca was doing, breaking a lot of rules to do what was right. He wondered if he would have done the same thing when he was a cop. Probably not. He turned in his own partners. What did he care about some random guy?

No, Iapicca wasn't like him.

"I don't like this," Iapicca said.

Donne blinked and turned toward him.

"You can't call it in. I need to handle it. We've come this far."

Iapicca said slowly, "We're ten minutes out."

"I know. Thanks for all of this."

Iapicca shook his head. "I just want the good guys to win."

Delshawn Butler followed the house around to the back deck. Before climbing the deck, he checked the kitchen window and saw that the sister had left the room. Where the hell had she gone?

The way he thought it, he'd get into the house by getting her to answer the tapping at the sliding door, and take her there. But if she wasn't in the kitchen, she might have decided to go to sleep. Odds were she wouldn't even hear a tapping at the glass door.

Tugging at the handle confirmed that the door was locked. Shit, he wished people still left their doors open. He was going to have to do this the hard way.

Butler pulled his gun, holding it by the barrel. He brought it down like a hammer, watching the glass shatter when he made contact.

The screaming started before he was able to step through the door.

CHAPTER **32**

fourteen hours

They pulled up to the house, and Donne was out of the car before Iapicca was able to shut the engine off. His instinct was to rush the house, get to Susan, and get her the hell out.

Good thing Iapicca came along.

"Wait," he said.

Donne froze at the edge of the grass.

Holding a finger up, Iapicca walked to the SUV. He placed his free hand on the hood.

"Been here awhile," he said. "And he's not in the car. He could be anywhere."

"You knew that hood would be cold." It had to be cold. Susan had called twenty minutes ago.

"Of course." Iapicca grinned. "I just didn't want you running up the hill and getting your head shot off."

Asshole.

"So, what do we do?" Donne asked.

Looking at the house, they saw nothing out of the ordinary. Just like every other gigantic house on the block. All the lights were out at four in the morning, most everyone probably asleep. Cicadas hummed in the distance.

"You go left, I go right. Check the windows, check the doors, but be careful and be slow. Don't go inside yet and we'll meet at the back."

Donne nodded and stepped across the grass. It smelled like it had just been cut. Looking through the first darkened window, he could see nothing except his own reflection. With the lights out, the room was black, and he couldn't even make out outlines of furniture. He moved on to the next one, pressing himself close against the wall. The edges of the bricks tugged at the fabric of his clothes.

The next window was less dark, the illumination of the moon curling around the neighbor's house. He could see the kitchen, the silhouette of the table, and the counter. But no people. Nothing out of place.

He pushed on, feeling the weight of Iapicca's spare gun on his hip. He wanted to hold it at the ready, but was afraid he'd fire it accidentally and attract more attention than he needed. His nerves were making his hands shake. He wasn't going to pull the gun unless he needed to.

Turning the corner of the house, Donne saw Iapicca standing alone on the deck they'd shared coffee on only hours earlier. He didn't move, and his face looked pale. Donne hoped it was just the moonlight.

Stepping closer, climbing the wooden stairs, which needed to be stained, he saw that it wasn't the moonlight. Mike Iapicca stared at the shattered glass all over the inside carpet.

When Donne reached him, Iapicca said, "He's inside."

"What do you want to do now?"

"Your call."

"Let's go in."

Iapicca nodded and stepped through the broken window. Donne pulled out the gun.

✳

Delshawn Butler followed the screaming all the way through the darkened house. He wanted to move quickly, before a neighbor heard them and called the cops, but he kept tripping over furniture. Sure as hell there were going to be bruises on his fucking shins. He even almost dropped the gun once.

The screaming was coming from upstairs. He took the staircase quickly, counting the steps as he went. Twelve. He wasn't sure why, but that seemed to be an important number to remember. Maybe his hit man instincts were getting better. Maybe all the practice was finally kicking in, like playing basketball against better opponents.

Eventually, you get good too.

The screaming was coming from a bedroom across the hall. Delshawn barreled down the hall and slammed into the door, and it came flying off its hinges.

As soon as Delshawn was inside, the screaming stopped. The girl lay on the bed. She went silent, and he could see the tears in her eyes. He trained his gun on her and felt around the wall for the light switch. He made the room dark.

"Call your brother, yo. Jackson Donne." He tried to say the name in a whisper, all stone-cold killer.

She moved ever so slightly in the dark, and it seemed like she was confused.

"I already did," she said.

"So he's on his way?"

"No. I saw your car and told him to get the hell out of here. I don't want my brother hurt."

Fuck.

"Get him here."

"No."

He stepped up to the bed and pushed the gun's barrel into her stomach. She inched back, but tried not to. Bitch was trying to be brave.

"Call the motherfucker or I will shoot you."

"You can't."

He pressed the gun harder against her. "And why the fuck not?"

"Because your boss needs me alive to pay for my husband."

And the words Hackett said swam back to Delshawn Butler. He was going to break his promise in order to get Donne here.

✳

The stairway was dark as they climbed. Iapicca went first, trying to keep the stairs from creaking. They were lucky. This was a million-dollar house.

Stairs don't creak.

✳

Delshawn Butler held the woman down as long as he could. She did not resist.

What should he do? Call Hackett.

He felt around for his cell phone, then remembered he'd left it in the Escalade.

"Stay here," he said.

He stepped off the bed and over to the front window, wanting to know how far the Cadillac was parked from the house. Could he make it before the girl ran?

Peeling apart the blinds, Delshawn saw his Cadillac. Hell yeah, he could make it. This bitch couldn't escape if he went downstairs. He'd see her. Just before he backed away, he saw the car parked out front. It looked like an unmarked.

Shit.

The cops were here.

There were twelve steps. Iapicca must've missed the last one. He lost his balance and fell forward into the hallway. He grunted as he fell forward. In the silent hallway it sounded like thunder.

Then the gunfire started.

The hallway exploded with flashes of light. Bullets whizzed in their direction from his sister's room. Donne went down, pressing his body against the stairway, trying to avoid a ricochet. He looked up and saw Iapicca jerk across the stairway from the impact of bullets. He was firing back, but Donne couldn't tell if he was hitting anything.

Like Butler.

Or Susan.

Donne grabbed Iapicca by the ankle and hauled him back down the stairs, sliding him gently out of the line of fire. The gunfire stopped, probably so Delshawn Butler could reload.

"Susan?" Donne called, against his better judgment. Delshawn would know he was alive, but Donne needed to know if Susan was okay.

"I'm okay," she called back.

"Shut the fuck up." The voice must have belonged to Butler.

Donne found Iapicca's throat and pressed his fingers against it to find a pulse. It was faint. Iapicca's breathing was shallow, and if he could speak, he wasn't trying to.

Pulling the gun from his waistband, Donne pressed himself against the closest wall. Across from him, as his eyes adjusted to the dark, he saw framed pictures on the wall. One was of Franklin and Susan's wedding. Another was a collage of pictures of children. The wall was a veritable hall of memories.

Footsteps tapped against the floor above him. Someone was coming this way. He held the gun tighter, ready to shoot. He had to be alert, however. Delshawn could have sent Susan ahead of him.

The footsteps got louder, heavier. Trying to judge the weight, Donne guessed it was Delshawn. He aimed the gun and waited.

The steps paused.

The outline of a huge, thick body spun around the corner. Donne's guess on the weight of the footsteps was correct. It was a man.

He pumped three bullets into his chest.

✳

Delshawn Butler felt the impact: one, two, three. They were quick, and hard, and hurt like hell.

As he fell backward, he knew he'd made a mistake.

Maybe he hadn't learned anything after all.

✳

Donne called Susan's name. She answered by turning on all the lights and rushing into the hallway.

"Oh my God," she said.

"Call nine-one-one and check on Iapicca."

He pushed himself to his feet and they switched places. Kneeling next to Delshawn, Donne felt for another pulse. His was even more faint.

Donne looked Delshawn over as Susan yelled instructions into the phone. His eyes were glassy, but he was talking. Air wheezed in and out of his mouth, and blood pumped from his chest. It was all over Donne's hands.

"Shoulda called Hackett," Delshawn said. And then the breathing stopped. The pulse was no longer there.

Susan must have heard what was said too as she put the phone down. They made eye contact, and she nodded.

"Jesus Christ," Donne said.

CHAPTER

thirteen HOURS

Pain woke Franklin Carter. Something was on top of his broken arm. The pain shot up his arm through his shoulder, across his neck. He screamed, squeezed his eyes shut, and really let it out. The rest of his body convulsed, his cheek splashing back into the puddle he'd passed out in.

Then he realized it wasn't *something* on his arm, but some*one*.

He tried to roll over to see who it was, but he didn't have to. He knew.

"Found the door, Carter?" Hackett said, even more menace in his voice than earlier in the evening.

All Franklin could do was grit his teeth and hope no sound

escaped. He couldn't afford to scream again. Any sign of weakness was an advantage to Hackett. And Franklin thought his adversary had all the advantages he needed.

The pain lessened, Carter feeling some pressure taken off his arm. Hackett must have removed his foot.

"Don't worry, Carter. Only thirteen more hours. Then I'll be a rich man and you'll be in a hospital. Or I'll be in jail, and you'll be dead."

The thought of death was welcoming to Franklin. He had no idea how long he'd been down here. Hackett's use of hours didn't help him focus on time. All he wanted was the pain to go away.

The room went hazy and a flash of light came through the window. It was warm and comforting, like a thick blanket. He wanted to go toward the light. Was this what death was like?

Hackett stepped on his arm again, and the shock woke Franklin from his hallucination.

"You listening to me?" Hackett asked. "You seemed to zone out there for a minute. Maybe it's the shock. Maybe I should give you something to eat. Order a pizza. On second thought, nah."

He pressed harder.

"You should have paid me when you had the chance. This is your fault."

"You're delusional." Somehow he found the words. They came from deep within him.

The pain was so strong this time, Franklin couldn't control the scream.

"Don't you dare speak that way to me. I've done the research. I know what should be mine. What should be my family's. You fucked it up. You and your father and your grandfather took it away. And your wife's too. This has been a long time coming."

Hackett lifted his foot and Franklin Carter was able to breathe again.

"Only thirteen more hours," Hackett said, and disappeared.

The police flooded the house, along with EMS and a few firefighters. Donne never understood that. You could be as specific as possible on the phone and still the ambulance, the police, and the fire department came.

Susan was crying on the couch. He sat on an easy chair, fighting against the exhaustion that came after an adrenaline rush ended. Delshawn Butler had been carried out nearly fifteen minutes ago, a sheet over his face. And Mike Iapicca was being worked on by two more doctors.

The cops were giving them a few minutes to compose themselves. Mostly they were waiting to see if the paramedics needed help getting Iapicca down the stairs. They knew he was a cop and they were concerned.

Donne was too.

As he got up, his eyes wouldn't leave Susan. He couldn't remember the last time he'd seen her cry this hard. He walked across the room, sat next to her on the couch, and put his arm around her. She put her head on his shoulder. This week had been hell on her.

Donne was going to be there for her this time. Like she tried to be when he lost Jeanne. He hoped Susan wouldn't push him away like he did to her.

"The police are going to want to talk to us," Donne said.

Her chin dug into his shoulder, a short nod.

"We're going to have to tell them about Franklin," he said.

"We can't."

Donne pulled her tighter.

"We have to," he said. "You aren't going to get the money. We have less than fifteen hours. Iapicca isn't going to be able to help us anymore. We need help."

"He said—"

"I know what he said."

"Is it really Hackett?"

People began yelling and rushing around, calling for something, but Donne wasn't sure what. Their words weren't making sense. Something was happening, but at the moment it was all white noise.

They watched the activity through the door leading to the hallway. Two more EMS came through the front door and rushed up the stairs.

"Is it really Bryan Hackett?" Susan asked again.

"It sounds like him," he said. "I want to find out for sure."

As he sat with Susan, focusing on what he was going to do next, Mike Iapicca died in her stairway from three gunshot wounds to the chest and face. A cop came in and told them a few minutes later. Susan wept harder.

Donne could faintly taste beer on his tongue, the craving taking over. A drink would make this all go away. The warm arms of alcohol would have let him forget all of this.

His instinct was right. Anytime he got involved, people got killed.

The cop was telling them they needed to separate and be interviewed. Donne didn't want to do that.

He should be asleep.

He should be drinking beers at the Olde Towne Tavern, listening to Artie tell stories about Vietnam.

He should be working a job as a security guard at a storage center.

Hell, he should be getting ready to go back to college. Getting ready to start a new life.

"Franklin's next," Susan said as she started to get up. "Don't let him die."

Again Donne wanted to run. The muscles in his arms contracted and he wanted to curl up into a ball. A drink would be perfect right now. But Susan was right.

He didn't answer her. Instead, he went and stood on her deck.

<hr />

✳

The sun wasn't up yet, but the dark blue of the sky was beginning to lighten into a pale shade of purple. Donne had felt the cold chill in his spine before. The tensing of the muscles, the desire to run.

It struck Donne how much he'd isolated himself from everyone since Jeanne died. Artie, the bartender at the Olde Towne Tavern, was the closest he had to a friend. Artie had always been there. Even when

Donne was trying to clean up. When he was about to go into rehab. Just before Donne left, Artie had come to his apartment.

"What's up, Artie?"

"Just checking in, making sure you were okay."

"I don't know."

"Why not?"

"Scared?"

"I just turned in four corrupt cops, left my job, and am going to try and clean up my act, so I can get my girlfriend back. What do you think?"

There was a long pause before he spoke again.

"I've told you about my days in 'Nam, right?"

"Artie," Donne said, "you barely say a word about those days."

"I was a helicopter pilot. It took a hell of a lot of training. There was a lot of shit you had to know. One day, right when training was ending, I asked my superior a question. I asked him what you do when the bullets are flying and all hell is breaking loose and you're scared.

"He didn't smile. He didn't laugh and he didn't read something off a fortune cookie. All he said was, 'You fly the helicopter.'"

Artie didn't say anything else that day. The next day, Donne went into rehab. A few weeks later, he called Jeanne and won her back. No matter how briefly.

Through Susan's sliding door he could see the EMS taking Mike Iapicca's body out on a stretcher. Donne wondered about his wife, how she was going to take the news.

Susan pulled the door open.

"The police want to talk to you."

"I need you to run interference for me. Give me some time to get out of here."

"What? Why?"

"I'm going to find Franklin and get him back."

Donne was going to fly the helicopter.

tweLve HOURS

Susan Carter slipped Jackson the keys to her car and went back inside. The police were waiting for her. Two plainclothes who weren't polite enough to give their names. They sat waiting, one with legs crossed and hands crossed on his knee, the other legs spread and notepad in hand.

"Ma'am, where is your—" The cop with the notebook looked at it. "Brother?"

"He'll be in in a minute."

"Why don't you tell us what happened?"

Susan took a seat in an easy chair across from the two cops.

One of them had a scar at the corner of his lip. She wondered how he got it. The other cop, the one asking the questions, was plain, boring.

"I already told you."

So far it was just a home invasion, while her brother happened to show up with one of his buddies. The guy was probably a drug addict, and a shoot-out had occurred.

"I don't think you're being honest with us. So maybe you should tell us again." The plain one smiled without much warmth behind it. He didn't buy her story, that was for sure. But she had to keep Franklin out of it.

And get the police out of here before the kidnapper—Hackett?— called again.

She opened her mouth to speak again, but one of the crime-scene guys peeked into the room.

"Hey, Johnson," he said.

The plain cop turned around. How fitting the plain cop was named Johnson. The only way it could be better would be if his name was Smith.

"I don't know if you talked to everybody yet, but a car just pulled out of the driveway and headed down the street."

The cop looked at Susan, then back toward the crime-scene guy.

"Son of a bitch!" he said.

❋

Donne drove to Rutherford doing the speed limit. Pulling up in front of his aunt and uncle's home, he realized that he was probably the last family member who'd been there. The cops had definitely been in and out of there gathering evidence, following up clues, and searching for a reason why a gangbanger would kill two senior citizens in their home. But at six in the morning, the sun finally starting to pierce the horizon, there was no one there.

He parked his sister's Audi on the curb, stepped out, and

glanced toward the corner. Nothing. He'd driven carefully, making sure he wasn't followed, but it never hurt to be careful.

The front door was locked. His sister probably had a key; she visited them often enough. But if she did, it wasn't on the same key ring as the car's. Checking over his shoulder again, the coast clear, he kicked the door with the sole of his shoe. It splintered quietly and he pushed it open. The smell of bleach hit him.

It seemed the cops had cleaned up a bit. Because Lord knows he hadn't. And as far as he knew, his sister didn't have the time to get over here. His aunt and uncle didn't have children. He wondered who would take care of their funeral. Both bodies were probably still locked away in the morgue cooler.

He took the narrow wooden stairway to the second floor, ignoring the bathroom and the bedroom. He found his uncle's office where he kept tax forms, paperwork, and other important pieces of information.

The same Thanksgiving when Uncle George told Donne how important family was, he'd brought Donne up here to show him his lockbox—and his plans for the rest of his and his wife's lives. That day Donne sat in the old leather chair that he stood next to now, the smell of it filling his nostrils the same now as it did then. The thick stench of leather always brought Donne back to this room.

Donne remembered George pulling out his old metal lockbox from underneath the desk, sliding a small key into the lock, and popping the lid. In it were plans for adoption. He wanted Donne to see it before he told Mom and Susan. He wanted Donne to know he believed in family so much that he was going to adopt. He was going to help right a wrong by bringing someone new into their lives. Family was important. He'd say it again and again.

The boy was an Irish boy whose parents had emigrated back to Ireland from the United States. And then were killed, but Donne couldn't remember how.

He found his uncle's metal lockbox in the exact spot he'd remembered it, tucked under the corner of his desk. He slid it out, a cloud of dust coming with it. The lock on it was rusted now. George must not have cared too much about the security of the box as he aged; otherwise he would have gotten a new one. Donne popped the lock off after two swift kicks.

Inside were manila folders filled with old receipts, a car title, birth certificates, his aunt's college diploma, George's military discharge papers. Donne flipped through the folders, searching each one. After the seventh folder, he found what he was looking for: the adoption papers.

According to the paperwork, they adopted a boy named Bryan Hackett. Beneath the papers was a school photo from his first days here. He was almost a middle school student, his reddish-blond hair hanging over his eyes, ruddy freckles across his cheeks.

Underneath all the paperwork was a sloppy handwritten note. It was dated two months ago. It read, "I'm sorry for what's about to happen. I know you tried. I know you wanted to help. But you all have to pay. The entire family. For me to live, you can't exist. But you need to know I'm sorry. BH."

Jesus Christ.

He folded the documents and put them in his jeans pocket. He didn't know if it could help him track down Hackett, but taking the stuff with him couldn't hurt. It wasn't like the police were using it. They hadn't done a decent enough crime-scene search to come up with it. Probably wasn't something Iapicca was looking for. The last time he'd been here, he was still under the impression it was a gangland murder.

And now he was in the morgue as well.

Donne shook the image from his head and took the steps two at a time. As he headed for the front door, he tried to figure out his next move. There had to be ways to track Hackett. Was he married? Did he have a job?

As Donne put his hand on the doorknob, the door swung open, knocking him on his ass. He sat there realizing that as careful as he'd been on his way here, he should have been just as careful leaving. He hadn't even noticed the red and blue flashing lights through the front window until now, as they streamed through the open venetian blinds on the front window.

Two tall figures he'd never seen before burst through the door, guns trained on him.

"Hands in the air!" one yelled. "FBI!"

The feds? This kept getting better and better.

1938

Joe Tenant got Sops to pick him up the next day. He worked an overnight, got in for a nap, and Sops met him around lunchtime.

"Where are we going, Tug?" Sops asked.

"To talk to a senator."

Sops shook his head.

Lisa Carter had given him the address before she left. She also called the local paper and set up an appointment to talk to a reporter.

Then she'd paused at the door to Tenant's motel room and turned back to him one last time.

"When this is over, will I hear from you?"

He'd nodded. It didn't feel like a promise if he didn't say anything. He wanted to see her again. But it was going to be platonic. Otherwise, he'd never get Caroline back.

Sitting in the passenger seat, he couldn't get the image of his wife out of his head. The hurt on her face when he told her what happened to their daughter. He envisioned the moment her heart broke. But that wasn't what scared him the most.

No matter how hard he tried, he couldn't see Isabelle's face.

What kind of father was he?

Connor O'Neill lived three streets away from the Carter house. The senator's was just as big, with a long front yard littered with foliage and trees. From one of the small trees a tire, attached by a thick brown rope, swung in the breeze.

Sops pulled the car to the curb across the street, the engine idling. Tenant took a deep breath, feeling the driver's eyes on him.

"What do you want me to do?" Sops asked.

"Leave the car running and wait here."

"You don't want backup?" Sops smiled as if he was joking, but they both knew he wasn't.

"You are backup. You see me come running out that front door, get ready to roll."

"Jesus Christ, Tug, what the hell are you into?"

Joe Tenant reached across the console and put his hand on Sops's shoulder.

"Thanks."

He got out of the car before Sops could say anything else.

Tenant spent the walk across the street steeling himself for what he planned on doing. No longer the time to be nice, Joe clenched his fists and inhaled through his nose. The lead ball in his stomach made him want to turn around, but he'd come too far.

"He'll be alone," Lisa had said. "He told me at the funeral his wife would be on vacation this week. That I should stop by and say hello."

Tenant pounded on the door with his fist. As he did, he wondered if Lisa would try to sleep with Connor O'Neill as well.

The door opened and Connor O'Neill stood before him. He was dressed down in light pants and a sweater. He wore fucking slippers. It was now or never.

Before recognition formed on O'Neill's face, Tenant hit him flush in the nose. O'Neill grunted, stumbled back, and then fell over. Tenant stepped in the door and swung it shut behind him.

"What in the world?" O'Neill screamed. He didn't curse, and that surprised Tenant. He was still trying to be a senator. Even with a busted nose, you had to put on a performance.

Tenant kicked him once, twice, in the ribs. He hoped he cracked one. O'Neill rolled over onto his side and brought his knees up to his chest to deflect more blows.

"Get up!" Tenant yelled.

O'Neill didn't move, just lay in his protected position. He kept trying to say something, but with his face covered by his arms, Tenant couldn't understand him.

"What did you say?"

Tenant crouched before the senator and pulled one hand away from his face. He slapped the exposed cheek.

"Say it again!" he ordered.

"You don't know who you're dealing with."

Tenant allowed himself to smile.

"I don't? You're Connor O'Neill the senator. You've had monetary backing from Maxwell Carter for several years. He stopped backing you and suddenly he's dead. I know more about who I'm dealing with than you think."

Connor O'Neill didn't speak, but his face paled, and Tenant knew he'd struck a chord. Tenant put his hands around O'Neill's throat.

And squeezed.

O'Neill's eyes bulged and his face flushed, his skin changing from pale white to red. The senator's mouth opened and closed and fought for air. Tenant released his grip.

O'Neill coughed, spit flying from his mouth as he tried to catch his breath.

"You have it wrong," he managed.

"Then tell me what's right," Tenant said. "Tell my why an Irishman has been threatening my family. Tell me what is going on."

"I can't."

He punched O'Neill in the face, the old boxing instincts returning. He didn't just try to punch the face, he tried to punch through the face. O'Neill's head snapped back and bounced off the wooden floors. When it came back up, Tenant caught it with a left cross.

Connor O'Neill, the powerful New Jersey state senator, screamed in pain. He yelled for Tenant, the lowly overnight longshoreman, to stop. He begged for mercy.

"Tell me what's going on!" Tenant screamed. "My daughter almost died. My wife is gone. My life is falling apart because of what I saw. I need to know the truth!"

"I never wanted Maxwell Carter dead. He was a good friend of mine."

"But he wasn't supporting you anymore."

"I know."

"Why did he stop?"

"Willy Hackett."

"Who?"

"This Irishman. I grew up with him in Newark. He's crazy."

Tenant didn't even realize he'd grabbed O'Neill by the lapels and pulled him close to his face, listening to every detail of his words.

"Why did you have Maxwell killed?"

"I didn't!"

"Did Hackett?"

"Please don't make me say it!"

Tenant hit him again. And again. He was screaming at O'Neill to talk. To tell him more. But if O'Neill knew any more, he wasn't talking. Even with a broken nose and *bruises swelling in his cheeks, O'Neill kept the secrets close to the vest.*

"Please," the senator finally begged. "I can't tell you any more."

"You'd better."

"You're nothing compared to Hackett."

The words actually made Tenant step back. Even when he was in the ring, very few fighters were able to withstand the kind of beating he'd just given the senator. They would have done anything to have him stop. Given up their first child, sold government secrets, anything.

"Please, just stop hitting me," O'Neill pleaded. "All I have left is my job. Hackett—he's taken everything else from me."

"You still have your wife. And, if you tell me what I want to know, you'll see her again."

"No, I don't," O'Neill said. "After I talked to you at the funeral, Hackett was afraid I'd turn him in. He killed my wife. I have nothing left except this."

CHAPTER **35**

"**WHO the HeLL aRe you?**"

Donne held his hands over his head, a natural instinct. The feds were pointing weapons at him, and though he'd had guns pointed at him before, it made him want to shit his pants.

"My name is Jackson Donne. I'm a relative."

Thank God Iapicca's gun had been confiscated at his sister's.

"A relative of who?"

"The residents of this house. George and Faye Tenant."

"Where are they?"

"They were murdered two days ago."

The black fed looked at the white one. There was a moment's hesitation in both their faces, as if they were unsure of what to do next.

"Are you armed?" the white guy asked.

"No," Donne said, and got frisked.

Satisfied with his search of Donne, the white guy held out his ID. Special Agent Draxton. The black guy was state police, Jason Marshall.

"Why are you here?" Marshall asked.

This was tricky, as usual. Donne wanted to handle this on his own, find Hackett, talk to him, see if he really had taken Franklin. And Donne wanted to know why. But cops catch up with you when you lie. Always.

"I'm trying to find out about my aunt and uncle's foster son."

"Oh really. Who's that?"

Bastards. They knew exactly where this was going. Donne wasn't sure how they knew, but they knew.

"Bryan Hackett," he said.

At the mention of the name, Draxton's eyes darkened. Jason Marshall just nodded.

"I used to work with him," Marshall said. "He was bomb squad."

"Is that why you're here?" Donne asked. His mind flashed through the scenes on the TV in the nursing home.

Draxton finally holstered his gun, and took a deep breath. Jason Marshall stalked past Donne into the kitchen. Draxton followed him, and Donne followed Draxton. By the time he entered, Marshall was sitting at the kitchen table. Draxton leaned against the counter where the sink was. Dishes were still in the sink, and Donne was pretty sure he could see bloodstains on the tiles.

"Tell us what's going on," Draxton said.

"Why should I?" Donne asked.

This wasn't making sense. Donne couldn't figure out why the feds were here. How much did they know about Hackett? Obviously, enough if they had tracked Hackett's interests here.

"We know who you are, Mr. Donne," Marshall said. "We've done extensive background checks on Bryan Hackett and his family. We understand you are a private investigator and are an adopted cousin of his. We've read the news articles on some of your cases."

"Former private investigator," Donne said, as if he scored some kind of point on their outdated research. The comment fell flat.

"Listen, if you're here looking into things about Hackett, then you have an idea why we're here."

He thought about telling them he was here to check on his dead relatives' interests, but at this hour of the morning, he didn't think they'd buy it. Stick with the truth.

"The bombing in the city."

Draxton nodded but still didn't speak. This was clearly Marshall's show, though Donne wondered why a federal agent would step aside for a state cop.

"We need to know what's going on."

"I'm not sure," Donne said. "My brother-in-law has been kidnapped, and I think Hackett had something to do with it."

"Franklin Carter is your brother-in-law, correct?"

Donne nodded. "It was his restaurant."

"What the fuck is going on here?" Draxton said.

Donne didn't know. And he told them as much, but he also told them everything else he knew, from Delshawn Butler to Carlos to Mike Iapicca. Marshall and Draxton didn't speak much, listening intently. A few times they asked some questions to clarify what he was saying. He found he mumbled his words a lot, but he guessed that was from the onset of exhaustion. He'd been up for almost twenty-four hours straight. And there was still time before Hackett's imposed deadline.

When Donne finished, neither officer said anything. He couldn't shake being in the kitchen where his aunt and uncle had died. There was a heaviness in the air, and a stale aroma, the mix of bleach and death that he tried not to notice. The memories of times as a child playing with Bryan Hackett, sharing toys, getting in trouble, doing stupid kid bullshit. It was such a brief period of time, and one he hadn't thought of in years, but now that it had been brought up again, the images were incredibly vivid.

Finally, Marshall stood up.

"Let's go talk to your sister," he said.

✳

Marshall wanted to drive the car. Donne let him. Draxton followed them. Marshall was comfortable to sit with. Without Draxton's evil eye, Donne felt able to talk more.

"Hackett came to my aunt and uncle when he was about ten years old. A little younger than me. They were older when they adopted and wanted an older kid. He stayed with them for three years. Finally, they had to send him off to a private school. I wasn't sure why. My uncle and aunt never spoke about it."

"Hackett had anger issues," Marshall said. "It's what got him kicked out of the force."

"Anger issues?"

"Yeah," he said. "He tried to blow up our office."

✳

Bryan Hackett was sure they didn't understand him. Not Franklin Carter, not his foster parents, and especially not Jason Marshall.

He still sat in the darkened room, the glow of the digital clock the only light. The sun would be up soon and the end would be near. He'd talked to Jill only minutes earlier, the tickets to the Caribbean purchased via her parents' credit card. They'd leave tonight, the last flight out of Newark. They could relax.

No one would understand why he'd lived his life the way he had. And he wasn't about to explain himself to them. But here in the dark, sitting and waiting and watching time pass, he couldn't help thinking about those times.

People had always been against him. Trying to keep him from getting what was his, what was his family's. After what had happened with his great-grandfather, his grandfather tried to make it work. And so did his father. He was fifteen and went out and got a job and met his mother and did what he could. And people still remembered, it was in the news all the time. And Hackett's father couldn't take it. The constant scrutiny. So he went back to Ireland.

Eventually, Bryan Hackett was born to the poor Hacketts in Ireland. His entire time there was bullshit. The first ten years of his life in Irish schools learning nothing, watching his parents argue over him, over money, over whether or not they could survive. Eventually, they came to the decision to put him up for adoption. Fucking sell him off.

Ten years old and he had no say. No say in the direction his life was going to take.

His parents had some sort of connection in the States. In New Jersey. John Hackett called all the people he knew and looked for a family that was willing to buy a ten-year-old, legal or not. And he found them, George and Faye Tenant in Rutherford.

They were nice enough people. They tried to be loving, George always talking about the importance of family. Inviting the cousins Jackson and Susan over all the time. But it all seemed like such fake Norman Rockwell crap to Hackett. If family was so important, why did his parents send him away?

School wasn't any better. The kids made fun of his accent. Every day, the way he said "arse" and "shite" and all that crap. It drove him nuts. He was in fights all the time, suspended, kept for detention. When he was home, he'd practice talking into a tape recorder, playing it back until he was sure his voice sounded like every other kid. Hard, tough, and Jersey.

He remembered the day he walked into class and answered a question from his teacher. They were reading "Rikki-Tikki-Tavi," and Mr. Hokenberg asked about what a mongoose was. Hackett raised his hand and said, "A tough motherfucking animal that's gonna kick that snake's ass."

The class ate it up, and it was the one detention he was proud of. He didn't have problems in school after that. Not with classmates—they loved him.

He grew up, went to college, and got recruited to be a state cop. He liked the idea, wearing a uniform, pulling speeders over on the Parkway, so he went to the academy and found he had a talent for bombs. Cool and collected under pressure, he loved to play with the wires, find the right way to defuse or detonate bombs. Loved studying all of it.

And that business with headquarters, years later, that was all bull too. If his partner was worth anything, it wouldn't have happened. Just a prank. An accident. But his partner was stupid and just let it blow up. Instead, he ended up working at Ploch's farm carting fertilizer.

And there was so much he could blame all this on. It was amazing how it all tied back to something he wasn't even alive for. He'd done all the research, he knew the stories. He knew about Joe Tenant and his great-grandfather Willy. Willy—it seemed to Hackett—was a stupid man, one who had a temper and let it lead him. He didn't plan ahead, and when things didn't work out, he let his temper go and he'd do something rash.

That wouldn't happen with Bryan Hackett. Yeah, he had a temper too, but he also thought logically. He'd waited until the time was right to enact this plan. To take out Franklin and Susan Carter. And Jackson Donne.

He was owed this. This plan had to work out. If life was based on karma, it was finally his fucking turn.

Time to turn his life around.

He wanted to know if Delshawn had created enough chaos to let his plan continue. All Delshawn had to do was distract Donne until Hackett was ready to take care of him. And now he was ready.

Hackett got up from the seat and went to visit Franklin Carter. Carter was going to give Hackett Donne's phone number.

And then he and his adopted cousin were going to have a nice conversation.

part four

JACKSON DONNE

1938

Connor O'Neill wasn't a man, as far as Joe Tenant was concerned. His wife was dead and he still wasn't willing to go to the police. Tenant even gave the battered man Detective Lacey's address. They could talk, he said, no pressure.

But O'Neill would have none of it, lying on the floor crying. He wasn't willing to give up his run for the Senate and his advisers were telling him to cover up his wife's murder for as long as possible. They were deciding whether or not it could be used for sympathy in the upcoming election.

Tenant left the house disgusted with the senator. It seemed he was like everyone else in office, unable to do what was right because sometimes what was right was hard. Tenant was not about to let that stop him.

Now he sat in Sops's car, a mile or two away from O'Neill's home. They were pulled over to the side of the road, trying to figure out what to do next.

"You beat up a senator?" Sops gripped the steering wheel like he was going to tear it off.

Tenant said nothing.

"I mean, you can't just walk into Connor O'Neill's house and beat the hell out of him, man. Have you lost your mind?

I know you're worried about your family, but come on. We're going to catch a lot of shit. I want to help, but I can't—"

"Shut up," Tenant said. "I need to think."

Sops closed his mouth and looked out the front window. Tenant tried to figure out what he was looking at. There wasn't much. The road was barren, trees on each side, a few puddles and thick mud. Occasionally, another car rattled past them from the opposite direction.

"We need to find Willy Hackett," Tenant said finally.

"I don't know, Tug. I mean, there's a lot of shit going down here. I can't be involved."

"It's too late," Tenant said, his voice even. "You don't think someone saw me getting into your car? They're going to come for us. And if you get out now, you're going to be an easy target."

"What are you talking about?"

"Our only chance is to find Willy Hackett and get him to talk about what's going on."

"How does that make sense, Joe? They haven't come after you or your family in weeks. They gave up after trying to kill Isabelle, because you stopped going after them."

"Lisa's going to the papers. Sometimes doing the right thing also means doing the hard thing."

"Tug, what the hell are you talking about?"

"Let's think about the people I've been dealing with here," Tenant said. "People with money. There's hardly any money out there right now, but the Carters and O'Neill have what money there is."

"So what? This is ridiculous."

Tenant wanted to tell Sops to shut up again. But he didn't. He was onto something.

"Who could this Willy Hackett guy be? Someone who needs money. Someone who's latched himself on to O'Neill's horse. Someone who has something to gain. Where does someone acquire a lot of money these days?"

It was there in front of him, if only he could get to the part of his brain that was holding the information. Tenant closed his eyes, tried to will himself to relax. He couldn't picture it, though. He couldn't get the answer. All he could see was Connor O'Neill's bloody face. Bloodied by his hands.

"Buy land. It's the only thing they're not making any more of," Sops said.

Tenant opened his eyes.

Sops was pointing out the car window toward the trees on the side of the road. A sign made of paper and wooden stilts was stuck into the dirt. It read: SOLD GIANT REAL ESTATE. Land development.

"Something my father used to say," Sops said. "Land was going to be big."

"You think Willy Hackett's getting a land deal from the senator?"

Sops shrugged.

Tenant smiled and put his hand on Sops's shoulder.

"I like the way you think. Stop the car. I'm going back to Connor."

"You're going to walk?" Sops said, braking.

"Yeah. You don't need to be involved anymore. This is almost over."

"What will you do after that?"

"I'll find my own way home. And then I'm going to talk to Willy Hackett."

"But you need to take something with you if you're going to follow this through."

"What?"

"It's not much, but you never know."

Sops reached across the car to the glove compartment and fished out a Swiss Army knife. He handed it to Tenant.

"If you're really going to go through with it, jam this in his throat."

CHAPTER 36

eLeveN HOURS

"Something's bothering you," Jason Marshall said.

Donne didn't answer at first. The sun rose behind them as they drove along Route 3 back toward Montclair. The highway headed east was backed up, a distinct difference from a few days ago. Once the news confirmed that the explosion at Carter's hadn't been terrorism, tourists, employees, and everyone else flocked back to the city unafraid.

"Donne?" Marshall asked.

Of course something was bothering him. His mother was dying. He had two murdered relatives and one who'd been kidnapped. There was a massacre at his sister's home. He'd shared all that with Marshall already, but the state cop had good instincts. He knew there was something else.

And there was.

"I never really knew Bryan Hackett," Donne said. "He was a part of our extended family, but I never felt like he was really involved."

Marshall got off on Valley Road.

"What does that mean?" he asked.

"When he came over from Ireland, he was polite but withdrawn. He didn't want to talk to us. He would only say 'please' and 'thank you' at the dinner table. Hellos and good-byes and that sort of thing. But even when we were around, he'd disappear into his room and only come out to eat.

"Then for whatever reason we didn't see each other for a few months. The next time I saw him, he'd lost the accent and become a bit of a prick. A bit crazy. The smallest comments bothered him and he'd fly off the handle."

Donne's cell phone buzzed in his pocket. He expected it to be Susan, calling to tell him the coast was clear, the police had left her home. Or the exact opposite, to stay away. But it was a restricted number.

He looked at Jason Marshall, whose eyes were on the road. He wouldn't mind Donne taking the call.

He picked up and announced himself.

"Ah, Jackson. It's been a long time."

"Who is this?" he asked, though deep down he knew.

"You're still alive, I see."

"Hackett? What the hell are you doing?"

He laughed. "I thought it was time you and I talked. Susan was boring me."

"Why are you doing this?"

"Settling old scores, I guess you'd say." Donne could still hear a trace of the left-behind Irish accent.

"Is Franklin alive?"

"If he wasn't, I wouldn't have any leverage, would I? Yeah, he's alive. Though I wouldn't say he's doing too well."

"Let me talk to him."

"No."

Marshall kept glancing toward him.

"Why are you doing this, Hackett?" Donne asked. It was useless to argue about talking to Franklin. If he was dead, there was nothing Donne could do about it. And if he was still alive, then Hackett would have to keep him that way until they got the money for him. Money they weren't going to be able to get.

"Your family has been screwing mine over for decades. Nearly seventy years, asshole. And it's time someone did something about it."

"My family?"

"Yours, the Carters'. Your grandfather and Lisa Carter. Your parents and Lisa's kids. Your sister and Franklin were childhood friends, high school sweethearts. Your families have been intwined for years. But no one remembered mine."

"Faye and George did. They tried to make you part of the family. They wanted to fix whatever was wrong."

"They didn't do a good enough job."

"Tell me what's going on. Why are you doing this?"

"Been keeping my eye on you for a few years, Jackson," Hackett continued. "Known all about you. You haven't seen your family in a few years. Not since you've been a PI. And now you're back."

"What do you want?"

"Your sister's what inspired this, you know. Started this whole thing, or at least my role in it."

"What are you talking about?"

"Your sister was a bitch. She told me she would make sure I was never a true member of the family. She was seventeen or eighteen, and I was eleven. And she wouldn't accept me. And neither would you. So I ran off."

"What are you talking about?"

"She provoked me. You were a part of it too. That day Susan told me I wasn't a part of the family? And I pushed her?"

"I have no idea what you're talking about," Donne said.

"You came outside and threw a rock at me. I still have the fucking scar on my forehead. You blamed me for your sister crying, when it was her fault. Neither of you cared. You both hated me!"

"You're insane. This is because you didn't get enough love as a kid?"

"This is because your family has always been fucking with mine!" Hackett said. "Eleven hours to get me the money. Or Franklin's body will sink into the swamps."

"Why is the money so important?"

"It's nowhere near what I'm owed. What my family is owed."

"Bryan," Donne said. "Be reasonable."

"Reasonable? You know what? I hope the money never shows. Because then I can kill Franklin. And your sister."

"Hackett—"

"And then *you*."

He disconnected the line.

"What did he say?"

"We have to find him. In a hurry."

Eleven hours had never felt like such a short amount of time.

✳

Bryan Hackett hung up the phone and put his head in his hands. They should have the money by now. It shouldn't be taking this long. They were stalling. Donne was looking for him. And if Hackett wasn't careful, Donne would probably find him.

Maybe he should just kill Carter now.

No, that wasn't the way to do it. Killing Carter would drop all the leverage out from under him. Holding on to Carter, and the hope that the money would come to him, was the only thing he could do.

He wanted Donne and Susan Carter and Franklin Carter dead. The money was one way to get settled, but their deaths was another. He wanted both.

Hackett still had his tools in his car, whatever was left over from New York. He knew he should have gotten rid of them—they were evidence, after all—but he kept them in case of emergency, and it was a good thing he did. Because now he'd find another way to get rid of the evidence, get revenge, and get the hell out of Dodge.

He popped the trunk and was hit with a quick smell of fertilizer. He dragged the bag out of the trunk and carried it back inside, down the stairs. He'd tied Carter back up earlier, listening to the little bitch scream as Hackett pulled the broken arm behind him. It was a highlight of the past few days.

But now Hackett didn't say anything to Carter. He just slowly and methodically went about his work.

"What are you doing?" he heard Carter mumble.

Wouldn't you like to know? Hackett continued working.

Soon, this would all be over.

teN HOURS

Susan was out the front door, down the steps, and at the window of the car before Marshall shut the engine. She tapped on the glass, looking panicked. Donne expected the worst. Maybe it was about Franklin. Maybe Hackett had killed him.

He got out of the car. Behind him, Donne heard Draxton's car pulling into the driveway.

"What is it?" Donne asked, grabbing Susan by the shoulders.

"I can't take this anymore. We have to get the money."

"There is no money, Susan. You weren't going to be able to get it."

Jason Marshall got out of the car and leaned on the roof. He didn't say anything, and when Donne looked at him, his expression didn't change. He knew he wasn't a part of the conversation, but at the same time, he and Draxton weren't about to be left out of it.

"What are we going to do?" Susan asked.

He gave Draxton and Marshall a moment to offer input. They didn't.

"We're going to go inside and figure this out."

And they did. Sitting in the living room where Delshawn Butler had grabbed his sister, Donne spread out all his aunt and uncle's information about Bryan Hackett.

There wasn't much. A few pictures of family, his adoption paperwork, and an article about Bayonne, New Jersey, which seemed out of place. He didn't read it, and he was about to take it off the table when Jason Marshall stopped him. Sam Draxton had been uncomfortably quiet since they'd gotten here.

"That's important," Marshall said, holding the newspaper article.

"How?"

"When we did a background check on Mr. Hackett, we found a link to an old case involving a New Jersey senator. Ever hear of Connor O'Neill?"

"My mother mentioned him. Susan jarred it loose the other day." He glanced at Susan, whose face flushed. "It sounds so familiar, but I can't place it."

"He was a popular senator here during the Great Depression. He really helped settle some of the few areas around New Jersey that hadn't been built up. He helped with some of Roosevelt's New Deal proposals around here. Should be a legendary senator, but he's not. Turns out he was in cahoots with a local Irish gangster."

"How is that linked to Bryan?" Susan asked.

Donne didn't say anything. He wanted to let Jason Marshall talk. This seemed like the most he was going to get out of him, and he was afraid asking questions would get Marshall to clam up and realize he was only talking to civilians.

But Susan's question didn't rile him.

"The Irish gangster's name was Willy Hackett. When we hired

Bryan, we asked him about it. He told us he didn't know anything about it. On a lie detector. But we researched it and things got really fuzzy. But it appears there was land in Bayonne that Connor O'Neill wanted to help sell."

Susan leaned over and put her chin in her hands. Draxton stepped forward. "Why didn't you tell me about this?"

Marshall waved him off. "You didn't ask, and it didn't seem important."

Draxton leaned against the wall and shook his head.

"The purchase of the land came down to two buyers. Willy Hackett and Maxwell Carter."

Donne thought of his mother the other day, calling out Maxwell Carter's name. She did know something about what was going on. She was trying to tell them about it.

"Maxwell Carter was Franklin's great-grandfather," Susan said. "He was murdered. Franklin's talked about it a lot."

Some of the pieces were falling into place.

"So all this is about some deep-seated revenge?" Donne said.

Marshall shrugged. "I don't know. Hackett didn't know about all of this when we asked him about it."

"Who owns the land in Bayonne now?" Draxton said.

"Texaco, but it's going to become government land. Right now it's basically an abandoned swamp."

"Are there buildings there?" Donne asked.

Marshall shrugged. "Probably. Abandoned, I'd imagine. There was a story on it in the *Star-Ledger* a few months ago. About how the new ethanol factory was going in there. And the old buildings were going to be demolished, starting in November."

"Do you think—" Susan started to say.

They all did. They all thought it at the same time.

Donne vocalized it.

"That's where he's hiding Franklin. He told me—" Donne looked at Susan and decided to say it anyway. "He told me that if we didn't get him the money, we'd find Franklin's body in the swamps."

"He could be talking about the Meadowlands," Marshall said.

Susan put her face in her hands.

"We're running out of time," Donne said. "I'm willing to take a shot."

✳

Bryan Hackett made the trip to St. Phillip's Church in Clifton. It took about forty minutes in rush-hour traffic. Bayonne was one of those places it seemed you could get to only by helicopter. Either a person could go to Staten Island—and who the hell really wanted to go there?—or take the Route 78/Turnpike extension back to civilization. Then he followed the Turnpike to exit 16W and then Route 3 to Valley Road.

Now he knelt in a pew in the last row. Hands clasped together, he pressed his forehead against them.

Our Father, who art in heaven, hallowed be Thy name. He forced his way through the prayer in his mind, willed the words to God. Hackett hadn't prayed much since he'd moved to America. It seemed a much more Irish thing to do. But today he needed it. It was going to be a hellish day, whether or not he got the money, and Hackett wanted to make sure God was on his side.

Bryan Hackett finished the Lord's Prayer and started a Hail Mary when he felt a tap on his shoulder. There was someone else he needed on his side, and when he turned and saw Jill, he knew she was still pushing for his success.

Her blond hair fell over her eyes and caressed her shoulders. Her thin red lips were pressed together, covering a slightly crooked front tooth. Hackett's heart sped up. He stood up and pulled her toward him in a hug. They hadn't seen each other in three days, the longest they'd been apart since they met.

"Are you okay?" she asked.

"Were you followed?"

"No," she said, pushing herself out of his grasp. "Don't you trust me?"

He met her gaze and said, "I love you."

Jill nodded as if he'd answered the question, and they shared a small kiss. Warmth spread through his body, and he wanted more.

"I don't know if we're going to get the money."

Now she stepped away from him. Hackett's eyes moved from her face to the wall at the back of the church. A sign hung from it reading, "God gives us all He has. All He asks of us is to tithe." If the plan worked out, he was going to leave ten percent of that money in the cash box at the entrance.

"What do you mean?" Jill asked. She stepped farther away from him.

"There have been complications. Jason Marshall got involved in investigating the bombing. I think he's onto me. Susan might not be able to get the money."

"But it seemed like everything was working."

"We have ten hours. Maybe it will work out."

"You have to get the money."

Hackett put his hand on her shoulder. "There are other things that have to happen too."

"No. There isn't. The money is what matters. That's what this is about."

"No," Hackett said. "I have to do this."

Jill slapped him. His left cheek burned more than the blood pumping through his veins.

"This is about revenge, isn't it? This is about you getting yours."

"We might get the money still. There is time." Hackett rubbed his cheek.

Jill looked to her left, toward the altar. "Is that why you're here?"

Hackett nodded. "And to see you. No one would think to look for us here. No matter what, you have the plane tickets, right?"

Jill nodded this time.

"It ends this afternoon. Whether or not we get the money, we need to be on that plane."

She kissed him. It was deeper this time, almost passionate. He gripped her arms tight, pulling her toward him. She started to part her lips for his tongue, but the Catholic in him wouldn't let anything more happen. He felt guilty as he felt himself get hard. He broke the kiss.

"We start over tomorrow. No more shitty jobs. No more rainy days. We'll be in the sun, we'll be safe, and we'll be together. Just a few more hours."

"I know. But what if we don't get the money? How can we start over?"

"We can get jobs down there. Anything just to keep us working and blending in with the locals. We can work at the beach and enjoy ourselves. It'll be perfect. The money won't matter." He thought of Donne, Susan, and Franklin dead. Hackett would do it now, but he had to hold out for the chance the money was coming. "All the scores will be settled and we'll start over."

"If that's what you think, you're an idiot."

The words didn't sting. He'd heard them before.

"Go back to your mother's and get ready to leave. I'll meet you at Newark. Terminal C."

"I love you, Bryan. Do what's right for us."

Jill kissed him one more time and walked out of the building.

He wanted the money, the revenge, everything, even more now. Not for him, but for her.

For their life together. She deserved it.

1938

Connor O'Neill opened the door. His face was red and puffy. He was holding a steak to his eye.

"Go away." His entire body shook as he spoke.

"I don't want to hit you again."

"Then go away." O'Neill started to close the door, but Tenant pushed him backward into the hallway and stepped into the house.

"I don't want to, but I will. We need to talk some more."

Tenant could see bloodstains on the wooden floors from the earlier beating. It wouldn't happen again. Not blood, anyway. This time he'd just break bones if he didn't get what he wanted.

He could use the knife Sops had given him, but he wanted to save the clean blade for Hackett.

"What's the best way to make a lot of money these days, Connor?"

"In these times? There is no good way, you know that. No one has any money."

"Tell me the truth. Tell me and I won't hurt you."

Connor seemed to break at that. His hands shook and he dropped the steak. It clattered against the wood, still frozen.

"It's land, isn't it, Connor? You get a good piece of land and you're set. Maxwell Carter had land. And he wanted more."

"Please. Please, I can't talk to you about Bayonne." O'Neill froze. He'd said too much.

"Just tell me. Let me go back to my life. You can go back to whatever's left of yours."

O'Neill sat on the floor. "But Hackett will kill me."

"We've come to this point and you still don't believe me?"

Their eyes met. Tenant held his gaze firm. He'd start by breaking bones. He'd kill him if he had to. O'Neill tore his eyes away and stared out the open door.

"Bayonne. There's land on the water. I owned it and was going to sell it. Help push my campaign funds higher than they'd ever been. And could you imagine acquiring that? Right near New York City? You'd be set for life. Your kids. Hell, your grandkids if things worked out right. Do you hear what I'm saying?"

Tenant didn't respond.

"Hackett wanted the land. Max wanted the land. And Max was funding my campaign, he was a friend. Hackett's a gangster, he couldn't offer as much money. The Depression had hit him hard and he was desperate. So he was trying to put pressure on me. He threatened my wife when all this started. And I gave in. Promised to make the deal with him."

O'Neill's entire body shook. But he wasn't crying, there were no tears.

"Max pulled the money he was giving to my campaign. There was no way I could run. So I wavered. I saw my entire campaign disappear. I saw my life ruined. I got scared. So Hackett talked to one of my bodyguards. A childhood friend of Hackett's and mine. Apparently, he owed both of us favors. They killed Max."

"And told you about it."

"He had me in his pocket. I had to give him the land."

Tenant crouched next to O'Neill. "It's too bad I saw it."

O'Neill nodded.

"Where's your telephone?"

Connor O'Neill lifted a shaking hand and pointed toward the kitchen. Tenant stood up. Five minutes later, he'd told Lisa Carter exactly what to tell the newspapers.

CHAPTER 38

NINE HOURS

"You need to get the money," Jason Marshall said to Susan.

Draxton turned toward him. "What? We don't negotiate with these people. We don't give them what they want. You know that."

Marshall shook his head, still looking at Susan. "The stats don't lie, ma'am. When victims of a kidnapping pay the ransom, they get their loved one back the majority of the time. You need to find a way."

"I can't. I can't access Franklin's money," she said.

Susan bit her nails. Donne looked away out the large front window, down the grassy hill onto Upper Mountain Road. An older man walked his dog, moving stiffly. The dog stopped to sniff at every bush.

"How am I supposed to get the money?" Susan asked.

The dog squatted and took a shit on the curb. The old man bent to pick it up in a plastic bag.

"What about through the restaurant account?" Marshall asked.

"I can't get to it. It's not under my name."

"Do you know the account numbers?"

Susan shook her head. "But I can find them. Franklin did all the banking. He keeps that stuff in his office."

"We need to go on the offensive," Donne said.

Marshall turned toward him, and Donne met his gaze.

"What do you mean?" Marshall asked.

"We need to find Hackett in the next few hours. We think he's in Bayonne, right?"

"Don't be an asshole, Donne," Draxton said. "Who the hell are you? You're a civilian. Some jerk who had a PI badge and lost it. That's all. You're not in on this."

Donne shook his head. "We have to do something. Too many people have died. No more."

"Bullshit, Donne. You've come this far. You've helped. Let the professionals handle it now."

Draxton stepped away from the wall he'd been leaning against for the past half hour. An aggressive move, it reeked of *don't fuck with me*. Donne didn't care if Draxton wanted him out. He was willing to fight him to stay in.

"I've been doing this sort of thing for years," Donne said. "It's what's right. It's what I do. Professionally or not, this is my family."

Marshall stepped in front of Donne and put his hand on his shoulder.

"Relax," he whispered. But behind the words was a tone letting Donne know he wouldn't be forgotten in all this.

During his argument with Draxton, he hadn't even realized Susan had left the room. She entered the kitchen with papers in her hand.

"The accounts," she said, then looked at Donne. "We're out of time. There's no other way."

Marshall watched her and waited.

"I can forge his signature. Do you think it'll work?" She looked around the room and could sense the tension. "What happened?"

"Forging a signature is illegal," Draxton said, and returned to his lean. "I don't like this."

Donne balled and unballed his fists, taking deep breaths to calm down. Jason Marshall hardly flinched.

"She's right. We're out of time. It's worth a shot," he said.

"If she gets stopped at the bank . . ." Draxton said.

"My thoughts exactly," Donne said.

Marshall ignored them. "Do they know your husband's face at the bank?"

"Probably," Susan said. Her shoulders sagged a bit. "I'm going to be taking a lot of money out."

Marshall nodded.

Donne had to get the hell out of here. If he could get to Hackett first, this wouldn't be a problem. There were a few errands he would have to run first, but he was willing to search through Bayonne to find this abandoned area Hackett felt he was owed.

Susan tried another approach. "What if I type up a letter giving myself permission to access the account and sign it with Franklin's name? It could work, couldn't it?"

Again Marshall said, "Worth a shot."

"We'd be accessories," Draxton said.

"What other choice does she have?" Marshall said.

"We know where he is," Donne said. "We go get Franklin back."

"We try our luck with the money," Marshall said.

"Don't be an idiot," Donne said.

It wasn't going to work. There was too much money involved. A preemptive strike was their only chance.

Donne started toward the door, Mike Iapicca's car keys still in his pocket.

"Where the fuck do you think you're going?" Draxton said.

"I'm going to visit my mother," he said.

Hackett fixed the last wire and stepped back. Behind him Franklin Carter moaned. Hackett wanted to hit the bastard again. Instead, he decided to have a chat with him.

He leaned in close to Carter, so close he could smell his breath. It was rotten-as-fuck, like a man who hadn't brushed his teeth in a month. In reality, it was only a few days.

"You think this is all about some land deal, don't you?"

Carter didn't say anything. He barely had his eyes open.

"Do you want to know what it's really about?"

Carter's head rolled on his shoulders, like he was about to pass out. Hackett grabbed Carter's broken arm and tugged on it. Carter's scream echoed off the basement walls.

"Look at me when I'm fucking talking to you."

He raised his eyes to Hackett's.

"I'm going to kill you and I'm going to kill your family. I'm going to take your money and I'm going to give myself a better life. The life I deserved. The life my parents and my grandparents deserved. The life you and your wife's families kept fucking up for us. I'm doing what my father wouldn't do. What my grandfather fucked up."

Franklin Carter still didn't speak. But now Hackett didn't care. All he cared about was Carter knowing. Knowing that this was the end.

"You know what? I didn't even expect Jackson to be involved in this so soon. I thought I was going to have to drag the prick up here myself. How'd you get him involved for me?" he said.

Franklin Carter drooled a little bit. And said, "The mother. Started talking about her dad. Wanted to know what she knew."

Hackett laughed. "The mom's been talking? Shit. I went to see good old Isabelle Donne. Since I was going to fucking take out the whole family, I wanted to know if I was going to have to waste my time coming up with a plan to off her. But she was completely gone."

Hackett looked at his watch.

"By five o'clock you, your wife, and her brother will all be dead."

Hackett grabbed Carter's arm one more time. Again Carter screamed. It would have made Hackett's ears hurt if the idea behind it wasn't so pleasant.

"Feel that? The bone is sticking through your skin. Do you feel it?"

Carter said nothing.

"Answer me!"

"Yes." The word sounded as if it was torn from him.

Hackett smiled. "Enjoy it. Cherish that feeling. Because it's going to feel like heaven by the end of the day."

CHAPTER 39

eIGHt HOURS

Donne's first stop was New Brunswick. Traffic was light for mid-morning and he made the trip down the Parkway, Turnpike, and Route 18 in forty minutes. His apartment smelled musty, and he cracked the window open. He planned on staying only a few minutes, and it felt strange being there at all. Like when he was a kid and they'd get home from a vacation unexpectedly early.

Like he'd left something unfinished.

Which he had.

He'd come back to get something he'd need to finish the job.

He found the shoe box in the back corner of the bedroom closet.

The gun he kept in there, a Browning automatic, was the proof that investigating would always be a part of his life. The job was in his blood.

As was violence, no matter how much he didn't want to admit it. And most likely it would take that violence to get Franklin Carter back.

Donne took the gun out of the shoe box and checked to make sure it was properly cleaned and oiled. It was an old, unbreakable habit. Donne cleaned the gun weekly. He tucked it, loaded, into his jeans and headed back out the door. He locked it, unsure if he'd see the inside of the apartment again.

✺

Donne spent most of the drive to the nursing home thinking about the last time he had planned an ambush. He'd had an advantage then. He knew the layout of the land. He had a long-range weapon, cover, and backup on the way in the shape of his ex-partner.

And he still ended up beaten to shit.

This time he had no backup, no idea what the outlook was, just sheer determination. He didn't like his odds.

✺

His mother was awake, but little else seemed to have improved. She lay motionless. The nurse in the hallway assured Donne that was normal and to take nothing from it, good or bad. Deep down, however, Donne knew his mother was going to be dead soon.

He wondered if the shock of his sister's screaming fit had jarred her spirits as well. As much as his sister had been through, as much as Franklin and he had been through, his mother had been through it too. The fact that she had little memory of it didn't make it right. It somehow made it worse.

"Hi, Mom," he said.

She didn't speak. She looked at him and her mouth curved. It may have been a smile, but was it recognition? Donne couldn't be sure.

The other day, he believed her soul was still inside her, that she knew what was going on, but that feeling went back and forth in his gut.

Donne took her hand in his and squeezed it. She didn't squeeze back.

"Mom, I don't know what you know. But some bad things have been going on in our family. People are probably going to die. Franklin has been kidnapped by Bryan Hackett. Do you remember Bryan, Mom? Your brother and sister-in-law adopted him. He's pissed, and I'm not sure why."

"Daddy," she whispered. "Daddy saved me."

That didn't make any sense, but he didn't expect it to.

Donne squeezed her hand again, almost as if he were keeping tempo, using it as a rest while he collected his thoughts.

"I'm going to go get Franklin back, Mom. I have to."

Maybe he expected a reaction then, but still he got nothing. She gazed off into the distance, as if something was buried deep underneath the floral wallpaper that lined her room and she had to find it.

"I don't know why I have to keep doing this, Mom. But I feel like it all falls on me. Remember when Hackett pushed Susan? I've always had to protect her."

The words seemed to fade into the air. Maybe he was being overdramatic, but it had to be said. Donne needed to say it for himself. Like therapy almost, and better than a drink.

"I might die today, Mom. A lot of us might." He let the words sink in. Sweat had formed on his palm as he continued to hold her hand. "And I need you to know I love you. And I hope you still love me."

Taking a deep breath, he sat listening to the beep of a medical machine somewhere down the hall. Elsewhere a television showed the morning news.

After a few minutes, he let go of her hand and left the room.

✳

Like always, Jackson had run off. He said he was going to visit Mom, but Susan was sure he was running away from their problems again.

She had just finished writing the letter on Franklin's behalf when the phone rang. She practiced Franklin's signature one last time before answering. This version of the signature would fool the tellers for sure. When she lined the signatures up, they were exact.

"Do you have the money?" Bryan Hackett said after she picked up the phone.

Jason Marshall and Sam Draxton were in the living room still, while she sat in the kitchen. She glanced down the hallway. Both detectives were stirring in their seats, as if they were deciding whether or not to make their way to listen.

"I can access it."

"Good. You need to put the cash in a bank account."

"What do you mean?"

"After all the bullshit, I'm guessing you had to borrow cash from your friends? Put it in one of your bank accounts. When you do that, call this number: 973-555-6777. Don't try to trace it, it's a pay phone."

"The money's already in a bank account. We had that much in the restaurant account." She liked that the words dripped from her mouth condescendingly.

"You guys are very well off, aren't you?" Hackett laughed. "Ah, not for much longer."

"I just want Franklin back."

"You'll get him. Though I have to warn you, he's a little worse for wear."

"What did you do to him?"

The tension in her voice was enough to get the detectives moving. Draxton came through the door first, Marshall close behind. Both were silent, and when they made eye contact, it seemed like they communicated something to each other. Something Susan couldn't understand.

"I didn't do much to him. But you see, he tried to escape and ended up falling down the stairs. I think his arm is broken. And it will probably get infected. So let's get this over with, okay?"

"You bastard. I can't believe—"

"Cut the shit, Susan. This is your family's fault. And frankly, you're getting off easy. No one's going to die. And you certainly might take a hit in the wallet, but you won't be so poor you have to leave the country. That's what happened to my family, you bitch, and I want retribution."

Like he was some sort of remainder of a slave family. None of this could be changed, as much as she would have liked to, and now she was paying for it. If she had just kept her mouth shut years ago. If Franklin's grandfather wasn't involved with his family. And if only her family . . .

And suddenly she remembered the story of her grandfather Joe Tenant. Her mother had told it to her when she was young. Susan realized her family had as much to do with this as Franklin's and Hackett's. Three families intertwined by time.

All she could do now was pay up and pray it was over.

"What do I need to do?"

"I'm going to give you a bank account number. I want you to transfer the hundred grand into that account. Once the money is in my account, I'll call you and tell you where to pick up your husband."

"I have your word?"

There was a long pause on the other end. Then: "You do. Here's the number."

Susan Carter took a deep breath and wrote the number down. It was almost over.

The line went dead.

"What did he say?" Marshall asked.

She told him.

"You don't have to get the money in cash?"

Susan shook her head behind her hands. She repeated the instructions word for word.

Marshall put his hands on his hips. "He's smarter than I thought. For sure, we expected him to go the old-fashioned route of cash in a dark parking lot."

Draxton didn't say anything. It appeared to Susan he was thinking, letting the situation play out in front of him.

Finally, he said, "This might help us. We can track the money a lot easier."

"No, this fucks everything up," Marshall said. "He might not access it until long after he's gone."

"It doesn't matter," Susan said. "I'm transferring the money like he said. Then I'm getting my husband back."

Draxton nodded. He seemed pleased by this information. Marshall, however, looked tight and uncomfortable, sweat forming along his bald head.

"I'm afraid I can't let you transfer that money."

"What are you talking about?" Draxton turned toward Marshall.

The tall state trooper pulled a gun from his holster and shot Special Agent Sam Draxton. Draxton fell backward, spilling over a kitchen chair and splaying out against the wall. Dark red blood streamed from his chest.

Marshall trained the gun on Susan.

"I need you to get the cash. And you're not giving it to Bryan Hackett."

1 9 3 8

Joe Tenant had contacts down on the docks. Most of the guys he worked with had some sort of connection to organized crime through the unions. Tenant had even had to ask for a favor once or twice, only to repay it in the weeks ahead by looking the other way when some questionable items were off-loaded from ships.

He made a few phone calls and talked to a few friends. Three of his friends knew of Willy Hackett, and the fourth knew he lived in a small apartment in North Bergen.

The next day, as the newspapers ran the story, Tenant stood outside the apartment building, hands shaking, ready to end this ordeal. Crossing the street was easy, walking through the front door of the building was easy, but pressing the button to call the elevator, that was hard. Stepping through the double doors, he thought about the step he was taking. He wanted to know why, but after that he wanted this over.

Even if it meant taking a step no man should ever have to take.

The elevator dinged on the fourth floor and Joe Tenant stepped into the carpeted hallway. Willy Hackett's apartment was the fifth door on the left. Banging his fist on the door, he hoped the man was actually home.

"Who the hell is it?" The familiar Irish voice came from inside.

"Open the door."

"Who the—"

The door swung open and Willy Hackett stood in front of Joe Tenant. Tenant thought about taking the approach he'd taken with Connor O'Neill, but something different now coursed through Tenant's veins.

Fear.

"You son of a bitch. I thought you fell off the face of the earth. Finally, I might add, my boy."

"Why?" Joe asked. "I just want to know why."

Before Joe could say anything else, Willy Hackett had him in a headlock and was dragging him into the apartment. The smell of fried fish struck Joe's nose. His eyes watered as he struggled against Hackett's grip. His heels slipped against a wood-tiled floor. His hands slipped off the fabric of Hackett's shirt. The next thing he knew, he was sprawled out on the floor.

"You want to know why?" Hackett bellowed. The Irish brogue was thick in his voice, phlegmy.

Hackett lifted his boot and pressed it into Tenant's throat. Struggling for air, Joe pawed at the boot, then tugged at Hackett's pants leg. The apartment seemed to tumble in front of Joe's eyes. The room was barren, one couch, a bookshelf, and an uncurtained window.

"You ruined me! Bayonne could have been mine. Carter was out of the way. But then you had to see it all, didn't you? You brought this on yourself."

Hackett pressed his heel down harder. Tenant was sure his windpipe was going to burst.

"I warned you to stay quiet. I warned you, and you

sent that Carter bitch to the newspapers anyway. Now you're a dead man."

Tenant pressed his hands against the boot, and then he remembered the knife in his pocket. The Swiss Army knife Sops had given him.

"I'm going to kill you! My family! You're destroying my family! My wife is bleeding what little money we have left. My kids barely have food on the dinner table. Buying this land was the last hope. And with Carter out of the way—I can't take it anymore."

The world started to go black before his eyes. But his hand fumbled the knife and he was able to flick it open with his thumb. Running on adrenaline and instinct, Tenant thrust the blade into Hackett's calf.

The Irishman screamed in pain and released his grip. Tenant rolled over into a seated position, massaging his neck and gasping for air. He coughed, but his boxing training helped him through it. Relax and the air will come. He saw Caroline, imagined her smile. And he realized he hadn't seen his daughter in weeks.

Joe Tenant would see both of them again.

He got to his knees, the air coming a little easier now. The coughing slowing. Hackett was still writhing on the floor. Tenant crawled across the apartment. He stopped only to lean over Hackett.

He wheezed, "I don't scare easily."

He wrapped his fist around the handle of the knife and yanked it loose. Hackett screamed again, blood pouring all over the floor. Tenant pressed the blade against Hackett's jugular.

"Do you remember the night I found the body? When you pressed a knife into my throat? You warned me off? No, all you did was piss me off. And then you tried to kill my child."

Hackett's eyes were closed and he wasn't struggling anymore.

"No one fucks with my family."

Joe Tenant pressed the knife into Hackett's skin, slashed open the jugular. Hackett didn't make another sound.

Tenant backed away as blood geysered out of Hackett's neck. It splattered against the wall and window. At first Hackett's body twisted and slipped against the hardwood floor. His hands pressed at the wound, but as time went on, he stopped fighting. Tenant watched the Irishman's chest rise and fall, slower every second. And when it all stopped, Joe Tenant knew he was finally safe.

That his family would be safe forever.

C H A P T E R

SEVEN HOURS

Bayonne is a shithole, Donne thought. *It smells, it's dirty, and their traffic lights all change at the same time.* A relative of Donne's used to say Bayonne was a town you could get to only by helicopter. There was only one way in off the Turnpike and one way out into Staten Island. But he figured that was an advantage.

If Bryan Hackett had really taken Franklin here, there weren't many places to hide.

The area Jason Marshall and Donne had speculated about was close to the Staten Island side. He drove along Broadway, hitting every red light. It was nearly one in the afternoon now, and a few kids straggled along the streets. They window-shopped and enjoyed the hot temperature and clear skies. Deep inside, he wished he had summer break.

Even more, Donne wished he was drunk.

He cleared Broadway and swung around down to Avenue A. It curved to the left, and he saw a grassy marsh area spread out toward the bridge. In the distance, a freight train meandered along on tracks. The bridge stood, a beacon over the marsh. He smelled trash and methane gas.

He parked and entered a bar across the street, feeling misled. There wasn't an empty warehouse or dislocated house within view. In fact, he couldn't see the appeal of the abandoned land. He supposed if the government was buying the land to put in ethanol factories like Marshall said, it would be valuable, but it would take a hell of a lot of work and a huge investment to build real estate.

Then again, land was land.

He sat at the bar and ordered a beer. It would make him feel looser, take the edge off. He would be able to think. The bartender put a Yuengling down in front of Donne. This early in the afternoon, he was surprised at how crowded the bar was.

"You're not a regular here, are you?" the bartender said.

Donne looked down at the ketchup-stained bar, not wanting to be bothered. "I've never been here before."

"Didn't think so," he said, nodding at the people around him. They were blue collar, guys in flannel and jeans, with dirty nails and dry knuckles. Apparently, he didn't fit that crowd.

An idea struck him.

"Hey," Donne said, "anyone else who wasn't a regular come in here recently?"

The bartender arched his eyes. Donne described Hackett.

"Ah," the bartender said. "He's kind of a regular. Hasn't been here in a while, though."

The bartender turned and walked away.

"Hey! Wait a second."

Ignoring Donne, he headed back into the kitchen. Looking

around, it seemed all the regulars were ignoring him. If he made a scene, at least they didn't seem to care.

The jukebox came on, Johnny Cash. Donne vaguely recalled Artie mentioning how there were only a few artists you'd hear at a bar. And most of those artists you'd also hear on the radio. Johnny Cash was the exception. You could hear him on TV.

The bartender came back, stroking his beard. His eyes were dark and Donne couldn't read them. He looked like most of the people who sat drinking. He was holding what looked like receipt tape.

"Our mutual friend is kind of a dick, isn't he?" His free hand was tight in a fist on the bar, and his nostrils flared. Donne had mentioned Hackett's name when he described him, but the bartender wouldn't even say it.

Donne nodded. "You don't know the half of it."

"You ever see him around anymore?"

"No. I'm actually looking for him now. Thought I might find him here."

"Used to be a real quiet guy. Weird, though. Come in, have a beer or three, leave and just stand outside for an hour or so staring at the bridge. You know anything about that?"

"I have a few guesses," Donne said.

"Thought so. Then you probably know him pretty well."

Donne shook his head.

The bartender nodded toward the regulars. "Better than any of them."

He put the piece of receipt tape in front of Donne. "You see, he stormed out of here a few weeks ago. He still hasn't paid his tab. Maybe you could help out with that."

Donne finished his beer and closed his eyes. For a minute, he actually thought the bartender was going to give him some much-needed help finding Hackett. He took out his wallet.

"Yeah, I think I can help."

The bartender's face flushed. Donne thought he was probably surprised this seemed like it was actually going to work.

"If you help me out first," Donne said.

"I can give you a refill."

"You said our friend was a dick. Why?"

"Last time he was here, he almost got my liquor license pulled. He was always quiet, so I don't know what the fuck happened. But he had a couple of shots with his beers this time and started talking to Eddie. He'll be in later. And the next thing I know, they're in each other's faces arguing. Eddie's saying you can't even see the scar. And our friend, he tells him the scar ruined his life. Eddie tells him not to worry about it. And our friend breaks his nose. Don and Ralph try to pull our friend off Eddie, and our friend puts Don through a table. Then he jams a dart in Ralph's cheek."

"Jesus," Donne said.

"Yeah. So he leans over Ralph and tells him now he'll have a scar too. And then he walks over to Eddie, and according to Eddie, he whispers to him, 'This scar shows me I am alive.' I don't know for sure, I was on the phone with nine-one-one at that point."

Donne looked at the receipt and paid the tab. "I'm pretty sure that's what he said."

"How would you know?"

"He's said it before. To me."

"Weird fucking guy. He was definitely a dick."

Donne didn't answer. He got off the barstool and headed toward the door, as Johnny Cash gave way to Bruce.

Outside, Donne tried to call his sister. He wanted to ask her about what Hackett had said in the bar. *I am alive*. There seemed to be a clue there, something that would lead to Hackett's location. The phone rang until the voice mail picked up. Maybe they'd gone for the money.

✳

"What are you doing?"

This didn't make any sense to Susan. A cop wasn't supposed to be pointing a gun at her. And the look in his eyes was one of pure anger.

"We have to go to the bank," Marshall said, his finger wrapped around the trigger.

"Please, put the gun down," Susan said. "Please."

This was the second time a gun had been pointed at her in less than twenty-four hours. Jackson must have been through it a thousand times. Did it always feel this way? The lead ball in her stomach weighing her down. Every muscle in her body tensed, begging her to run. But if she got up to run she was dead, shot in the back. Sitting here wasn't a better option; death still seemed certain.

"We have to go to the bank and get the money."

The words were haunting and hypnotizing. Susan felt compelled to get out of the chair and follow this man anywhere he wanted her to go. She had no choice.

Oh my God, this isn't supposed to be happening to me.

She clenched her fists, gritted her teeth, and willed the fear out of her. She was going to figure a way out of this.

The phone in the living room rang.

"Leave it," Marshall said. "We have to go. Now."

"No."

Marshall pointed the gun at Draxton's body and put another bullet in it. The gunshot echoed off the kitchen tiles. Sharp stabbing pain shot through Susan's ears. She couldn't believe how loud a single shot could be. When the guns went off before, she was on the ground, covering her ears; it sounded like a thunderstorm. Now it sounded like standing next to an airplane taking off.

"Go. Now," Marshall said.

Susan Carter went.

SIX HOURS

Bryan Hackett stared at his computer. The money should have been in his account by now.

Water dripped behind him and the smell struck him again. He couldn't wait to get out of this hellhole. He refreshed the web page displaying his bank account. Still no transfer.

Sitting back, closing his eyes, Hackett pictured the islands. The sun beat down on his face as the waves lapped along the shore. Jill held his hand. They were finally happy. His parents were there, his mother smiling at the coast. His father put his hand on Hackett's shoulder.

"I'm proud of you, son," he said. "The fire was beautiful."

Hackett smiled back at his father.

"It was, wasn't it?" he said. Surprisingly, his Irish accent was back. The one he'd worked so hard to hide. But now that it was all over, it was okay. Everything was acceptable now.

It was the way it should be.

"Ma," he said. "I'm so sorry you had to suffer. But I did it."

His mother opened her mouth, but no sound came out. It was okay, though; he knew she was happy.

"Lad," his father said. "This is what I'd always hoped of you. We never wanted to give you up."

Hackett opened his eyes with a start. Checking the clock, he saw he'd been asleep an hour. Time was ticking away. He pressed refresh once again. Still no money.

What the fuck?

This wasn't the way it should be working out. The two of them, Donne and Susan, should have paid by now and be making their way down the stairs. Creeping toward Carter. Donne would be watching his back—he was smart. But their goal would be Franklin and only Franklin. Hackett would be across the street counting the seconds. And then finally, when he knew they were downstairs, he'd type the number into his cell phone and . . . BOOM.

Just like his father said.

The fire would be beautiful.

But where was the money?

✴

Only one beer. Donne had stayed for only one beer. But his body wanted another six or seven. He wouldn't allow it. Maybe he was growing up. Maybe the last few months of his life weren't worth getting drunk over anymore. Or maybe he just wanted to save his brother-in-law's life.

He crossed the bridge on Route 78 heading back toward the Turnpike. The conversation with the bartender still tickled something at the back of his mind. He tried to remember when Hackett had said those words to him before.

Donne turned up the radio. "Walking on Sunshine" played. He sang along, trying to give his subconscious a chance to work.

They'd found themselves down along the Passaic River. It was a hike from his aunt and uncle's, but the weather was nice and his uncle had sent the two boys off in the hopes that they'd bond. Donne was trying to connect with his cousin. Hackett was having none of it.

As Hackett walked along the Passaic River, he was yelling out his name to hear the echo off the river. He walked ten feet ahead of Donne, ignoring him. Donne would try to catch up and Hackett would run ahead. The kid was a prick.

Hackett yelled, "I AM ALIVE!"

It was completely ridiculous. Donne was embarrassed, but he still tried to talk to Hackett. Every time Donne tried, Hackett would ignore him and scream he was alive again.

They trudged along the muddy banks of the river, looking at the houses up on the street. Most of them were empty or decrepit, but some were kept up nicely. One or two of them had kayaks in their yard.

After about twenty minutes—Donne wasn't even sure if they were in Rutherford anymore—they stumbled on a small concrete building. It was abandoned, and the bricks were crumbling. Hackett, now finding a use for his bundled energy, charged the door.

"We have to go inside," he said.

Donne made a show of looking at his watch.

"Yeah, I really think it's time we start going back."

"No. Let me go in here. This is the perfect hiding place. I want to see the inside."

He tugged on the door and it gave way. Without waiting for a response, Hackett went inside.

By the time Donne followed him in, the smell of must and mold making him wince, Hackett had disappeared. The room was pretty much empty and dark. Some old papers and a lot of dust. And another doorway. Through it was the basement, old wooden steps that looked like they were about to shatter if you stepped on them. Donne wasn't about to try and go down there.

"This is so cool!" Hackett yelled from the bottom. "I am alive!"

Donne had turned around and left. He didn't need this. This kid was a freak.

And as the song ended on the radio, he stepped on the gas, swerving into the left lane and passing a line of traffic. He knew exactly where Bryan Hackett was keeping Franklin Carter.

CHAPTER

five HOURS

Franklin Carter knew only pain. His face throbbed, his cheeks swollen so thick his eyes were pressed shut. He was pretty sure his nose was broken, and he'd been having trouble breathing. But that was nothing compared to the screaming pain in his arm.

He'd tried to compartmentalize it, take the pain and press to the outermost reaches of his brain. But that didn't seem to work; it was all-encompassing, all he could think about. He just wanted to go numb.

That didn't work. Numbness never came. In fact, he had to fight through the pain just to sort through what had brought things to this point. It made sense now. Isabelle had started the decline about two months ago. She'd started talking about her father all the time, talking about whatever it was he'd been through.

Hackett's visit must have spurred her on. Snapped those memories to the forefront of her mind, no matter how shattered that mind was. And how creepy was that? He'd visited her to decide whether or not he needed her out of the way.

That was why he'd killed Faye and George, Carter thought. But now he was out in the open. He was that confident. Or that insane.

And what the hell had he been doing behind Franklin? What had he been making?

Whatever it was, Carter wasn't about to find out. The pain had taken hold again.

Here we go, he thought, and gritted his teeth against it.

✳

Donne got off Route 3 at the aptly named River Road. The Passaic River flowed smoothly, any sign of the vast pollution and sludge invisible from the street. As he drove, he saw the familiar kayaks and worn-down houses. The area hadn't changed much since his teenage years.

He didn't know exactly where the building was. As he drove, he hoped it would jump out at him. The houses were in need of a makeover, new paint jobs or new aluminum siding. Some areas had construction fences up, and it looked like that would happen. But for now, the area still felt like it had a decade ago. Donne drove slowly, the cars behind him beeping or passing illegally.

As he crested a hill, the building came up on his left. It was one of the areas designated for construction, a portable john and a large Dumpster set up outside it. The cinder-block walls had crumbled at the corners and the wall facing the road had a large hole in it. The building hadn't aged well. Donne was surprised it had lasted this long.

On his way here from Wayne, he had placed the Browning on the passenger seat, and now the sun glinted off it. All morning, he'd been preparing his mind to use it again. Shooting Delshawn Butler that morning was spur-of-the-moment and he hadn't given himself a chance to even think about it. But since then, he'd decided that if he saw Hackett he'd shoot him, no questions asked.

No way would he let Susan suffer through what he had suffered with Jeanne.

He pulled the car to the curb and took a deep breath.

Jeanne.

The thought of her name caused him to shudder. His fingers were tight around the steering wheel. In spite of himself, in spite of trying to park, Donne closed his eyes. He let out a long, slow breath. He wished he didn't freeze every time he thought of her.

Before he picked up the gun, he tried his sister. Again there was no answer. When the machine picked up, he said, "Susan, don't go to the bank yet. I've found him. I'm going to get him back."

He hung up, and hefted the gun.

Closing his eyes, he thought, *Here we go.*

✳

Bryan Hackett had just finished refreshing the computer screen when he heard the car door. The best thing about this building was the acoustics. You could hear every car that drove by, every closed door, every husband-and-wife argument within a block and a half.

After seeing that the money hadn't transferred yet, he closed the laptop and got up to peek out the window. Donne was jogging across the street bent at the waist, like he was trying to stay out of sight. All it did was make him look funny, like he had back pain.

So this was how they were going to play it. *Fuck the money.* A little sooner than planned, but this was what he'd wanted. Revenge.

He might not get the money, but at least he'd be able to take one of them out. And Susan could always be tracked down this afternoon. It's not like she'd stray far from the mansion in Montclair anyway.

Bryan Hackett grabbed his cell phone and retreated out the back window. He had to hunch his back and lift his legs over the windowsill. When his foot hit mud, he knew he was home free. Donne wasn't inside yet, and Hackett hadn't been shot at either.

Ten more minutes and the plan would be complete. The building from his childhood would be in flames and his family would be avenged. Not getting the money would be a problem, but he could start over with Jill.

Once he was out the window, Hackett made his way toward the riverbed. His feet squished in the mud, the smell of litter and dead fish hitting his nose. Twenty feet down the river, he stopped running and listened.

He heard the door to the building open and close.

He took a deep breath. In through the nose, out through the mouth. The air was sour, but it relaxed his muscles.

Here we go.

CHAPTER 43

four hours

They sat in the car outside the bank on Bloomfield Avenue. Susan could see her husband's restaurant north of her on the corner of Church. There were people sitting at small tables on the sidewalk. It looked like business was good.

Maybe that would help them rebound from what she was being forced to do.

Jason Marshall had the gun jammed in her ribs from the passenger seat. "You're going to go in, get the money, and come right out. All you have to do is hand them the letter. They're going to give you a rough time, but you're not going to give in. Your husband is out of town and you need the money for a family matter."

252

"They're going to want to talk to him."

"Then you call me. I'll pretend I'm Franklin."

"I'm sure they have his number on file."

"Talk your way out of it. I don't care if you have to threaten to blow the place up, you're going to come out of there with the money." Marshall pressed the gun harder against her. "If you don't, you're fucking dead. Just like Franklin."

Anger flushed her face. The gall of this guy to mention her husband. It was going to be his fault if Franklin died. There was no hope. Fucking Jackson had to skip town.

"Now go."

She stepped out of the car and felt the heat on her shoulders. It was one of those summer afternoons where the humidity was unbearable. The air hung thickly and people walked slowly toward their destination. The thirty-foot walk from the car to the bank was enough to make her break a sweat.

She stepped through the glass door and felt the air-conditioning wash over her. The line was short, only one person being helped.

The teller smiled as Susan stepped up to the nearest open window and slid the letter under the tray. The teller took it and opened it. Her blond locks fell over her eyes as she looked down. The woman was pretty—small, thin, with high cheekbones.

"My husband is out of town on business. But he asked me to cash out the money."

The teller read the letter and looked at the signature.

"I don't know if I can do this."

"Please," Susan said. "You have to. We're—we're trying to buy a car and we want to pay cash. He was called out of town. I just need the money."

In the back of her head, she knew she sounded panicked. But could she be blamed for that? There was a man outside waiting for her with a gun.

"I'm going to have to get my manager to sign off on this," the teller said, and dashed off.

This wasn't going to work. In a minute, the manager would

come back and say there was no possible way this could get done, it was just too much money.

The teller came back with a curt smile on her face. A tall man wearing a pin-striped suit followed her. The manager's name was Paul, and Susan had spoken with him before. He was always polite and did well with their money. Franklin had taken him out to lunch once or twice.

Paul shook Susan's hand.

"I read your husband's letter. How is he?"

"Fine," she lied. *He's probably dead by now.*

"Are you okay?" He arched his eyebrows. "You look like you're about to pass out."

"I'm all right. It's just hot outside."

"Okay." He looked at the letter again. "This shouldn't be a problem. If you'll just wait a few minutes while we cash it out. It will take us a while to count up the cash. How would you like the money?"

"Hundreds would be fine."

Susan grinned and felt relief settle through her blood. It felt better than the air-conditioning.

"We'll get right on it. Good luck with the car. Nancy, would you start the process?"

The teller strode toward the back of the bank. For the first time in what felt like days, luck turned Susan Carter's way.

Paul stepped around the counter and stalked over to Susan. He took long, purposeful strides. His suit was neatly pressed and he gave off an aura of power and professionalism. He furrowed his brow as he approached.

Taking Susan by the arm, he walked her toward an empty corner of the bank.

Whispering, Paul said, "I've seen the news, Mrs. Carter. We are all very sorry about your husband's loss. I understand if you want to keep this hush-hush, but I know this has to be about the explosion in New York. I'm breaking all sorts of rules giving you this money, but I consider your husband a valuable client."

Susan had nearly forgotten about the explosion. Everything

else was so much more immediate. It seemed so far away from them, dreamlike. Her only concern was getting Franklin back alive.

"I just want you to know that anything your husband needs," Paul said, "we will be there for him."

"Thank you," Susan said.

Ten minutes later, Susan lugged a duffel bag toward her car and a smiling Jason Marshall.

✳

Donne held the gun tight against his thigh, pointing the barrel downward as he crossed the street. Moving quickly, he kept in a crouch behind a car, peeking over the hood. The building was a little worse for wear than he remembered, but it still stood. The gray stone building was less than a story high, and some of the stones had tumbled from the top right corner and were scattered across the grass. The river rushed past about one hundred yards behind it.

Between Donne and the building was probably about one hundred feet of open space. If Hackett was watching, he'd be a sitting duck. But what other choice was there? He moved quickly across the ground, trying to vary his movements, taking sharp angles and changing directions as he moved. Nothing happened, and within seconds, he pressed against the cracked wooden door.

Hearing nothing through the door, he tried the knob and it turned easily. He went into the dark room gun-first. The building held the heat like a brick oven. He felt an extra sheen of sweat on his skin. Donne blinked his eyes to adjust them to the darkness. He pressed himself against the wall, staying low, and looked around.

A lone empty table with one plastic chair decorated the room. Garbage, food wrappers, and small pieces of concrete from the walls of the building were strewn around the rest of the room. No one was there.

Across from him was the doorway he remembered so well. The one Bryan Hackett went through without hesitation years ago. The door itself was thick and solid-looking, as if it had been recently replaced. It led to the basement. Next to it, an exposed wire lay on the floor. Staying clear in case it was live, he opened the door to the basement. He paused a moment when it opened easily. He'd expected it to be locked.

He pointed the gun toward the doorway, trying to listen for any sounds of movement. Nothing in front of him. And if Bryan Hackett was going to sneak up on Donne from behind, he was stealthy as hell.

His eyes would have to adjust again, because the basement was even darker. The unlocked door worried him, however, and he didn't want to stand there waiting to be able to see better.

The first step creaked beneath his foot. The stairs were old and wooden and steep. He felt a sense of vertigo, especially since he couldn't see three feet in front of him. Each step was a slow and cautious affair, and he stopped at each one to listen for any sign of life. When he got to the third step from the bottom, the thick smell of wet wood and shit filled his nose. A thin stream of light poked through a hole in the ceiling on the other side of the room. He saw the outline of a body in a chair, as his eyes continued to adjust to the darkness.

He aimed the gun at the body and for the second time in a day broke a cardinal rule.

"Hello?"

No response. No movement. Donne stepped closer. The body didn't move, but now he could see more than just an outline. Bruised, battered, and basically looking like hell was Franklin Carter.

Donne rushed up to him and checked his pulse. It was surprisingly strong. His arm was bent awkwardly and looked like it was broken. His breathing was shallow and forced. And he looked like he'd been hit with a wooden pole several times. Donne shook him gently by the shoulder.

"Franklin? Franklin, wake up."

He coughed and stirred.

"Franklin, it's me, Jackson. I'm going to get you out of here."

Franklin grunted and lifted his head.

"You're going to be okay," Donne said.

"Not safe," he mumbled. "Hackett did something."

Donne stepped back and raised his gun. What did Hackett do? The smell of shit was thick in his nose. His eyes were watering. And it was then he realized that it wasn't shit he smelled. Not exactly.

It was fertilizer.

Just like Marshall said was in the bomb at the restaurant in New York City.

Donne put the gun back in his waistband and went to work on Franklin's knots.

As he worked, Donne prayed hard the room wouldn't blow up.

✳

Hackett waited five minutes. Jackson Donne was good and would take his time sweeping the building. He would make sure it was safe. Then he would have to untie Franklin and get him out of the chair. Plenty of time.

At the three hundredth second, Hackett gripped his cell phone tight. The number was already dialed in. All he had to do was hit send.

He did.

It was all a matter of seconds now.

And then Jackson Donne, Franklin Carter, and half of Hackett's past would be up in flames.

He began to trudge along the riverbed away from the house.

CHAPTER **44**

THEY DROVE BACK TOWARD SUSAN'S HOUSE. SHE didn't know why. She gassed through the lights and made a right turn onto Upper Mountain. The money rested on the backseat in the duffel bag.

"You're going to kill me," she said.

The curbs of Upper Mountain were lined with thick oak trees. Their branches and leaves hung above the road, making it seem like they were driving through a tunnel.

"Don't be ridiculous. Too many people have died already." Marshall had lowered the gun to his lap.

But it didn't make sense. He'd been willing to kill Draxton. What would keep him from shooting Susan as soon as they got back? Marshall would have the money, and all he would need to do is get rid of her body. One pull of the trigger and it would all be over.

Her life would end. And it was all out of her control. She couldn't have that. She needed some semblance of a say in what happened to her. It was her life. She wasn't going to let some greedy asshole end it.

She checked the traffic in her rearview mirror. It was clear. In the oncoming lane as well.

Susan stepped hard on the gas. The car jerked forward, accelerating from twenty-five miles per hour to forty-five. She pushed down harder. Fifty, sixty, sixty-five.

"What the hell are you doing?" Marshall yelled.

Out of the corner of her eye, Susan saw Marshall fumble for his gun. The engine roared. Just as Marshall wrapped his hand around the gun, Susan slammed on the brakes and cut the wheel left across the oncoming lane. The wheels screeched and Marshall crossed his arms in front of his face.

The rest of the event moved in slow motion for Susan Carter. She heard his gun thunk against the floor of the car, and felt the duffel bag hit the back of her seat. The giant oak tree she'd aimed for got larger and larger in the windshield. Out of the corner of her eye, she saw Marshall's arms rise in front of his face to brace himself.

Impact.

The hood of the car crumpled in front of her, the bark of the tree rushing up toward them. The air bag blew up as her body went forward, her vision flooded with white plastic. She heard Marshall's scream stop suddenly, the sound of glass and bending metal filling her ears. Her seat belt locked and pulled against her skin.

Then everything went black.

✸

Donne didn't know how much time they had. He could see the glint of a cell phone lying on a thick clay-like block through the stream of light. He undid the rest of Franklin's bonds, yanked him from the chair, and they hustled to the stairs.

After three steps, Franklin started to drag. He couldn't keep up. Donne hefted Franklin over his shoulders in a fireman's carry.

"Hurry," Franklin said.

"No shit," Donne said.

A cell phone rang. It wasn't even an entire ring, just a bit of noise suddenly cut off.

That couldn't be good.

There wasn't time to take the steps. He knew that with the weight on his shoulders he'd never get up them in time. The whole place was going to blow up. They needed cover. Behind the stairs was a small hole where they could both crouch. He hurried across the room, and dropped Franklin. He pushed hard, and Franklin slid inward. Then Donne pulled himself inside.

Then the room went white and yellow and loud. Donne felt the heat on his skin. He closed his eyes and gritted his teeth.

And he prayed.

CHAPTER 45

THICK DARKNESS WAS ALL HE COULD SEE AT FIRST,
to the point where he couldn't tell if his eyes were open or closed. As
his vision cleared, he could see flames licking the sides of the walls
around him. Then the pain settled in. His face stung and burned as if
splinters had embedded themselves in his cheeks. His arms throbbed
as if he'd just curled hundred-pound weights.

But pain was good. It told Donne he was alive.

Donne tried to call out Franklin's name, but nothing came out.
He tried to scream it. Still nothing. He couldn't talk.

No, that wasn't right. It wasn't that he couldn't talk, because he
could feel his vocal cords vibrate in his throat.

I can't hear.

A loud rumble ran through his ears. It was constant, like rushing water. It clouded everything else. He tried shaking his head, but all that caused was more pain, like a migraine.

A long piece of wood rested across his stomach, but his arms and legs were free. Angling his arms beneath him, he pressed his hands against the two-by-four. And pushed, hard. It gave way, but dust and debris shifted onto him instead.

The room was thick with smoke hanging above him and smelled like a fireplace the morning after the fire went out. Only stronger—the smell wasn't faint, it encompassed everything. Donne decided to breathe through his mouth instead.

Donne coughed hard. It felt like his lungs were going to give out, like they would only expand so far. He could get only half a breath in. When he exhaled, he had to contract his chest to press the air out. It tasted like ash. After each breath, his chest ached. Donne called out Franklin's name again and for the first time heard it. At least his ears were starting to work again.

"Franklin!" Donne yelled again. It sounded like a whisper. And he didn't hear anything in return. If Franklin was alive, it was unlikely he could hear Donne's voice anyway.

Donne could see flashes of light poking through holes in the debris above him. He lifted his aching arms upward and some of the debris gave way, but not anywhere near as heavy as the two-by-four that was on top of him. Maybe the whole building had blown outward, but some of the rocks, wood, and mortar had still fallen inward. Or maybe that was just wishful thinking.

To his left, toward the center of the explosion, he saw fire burning and felt the heat on his face.

Donne rolled onto his stomach, more debris giving way above him and crashing to the ground next to him. He tried to push himself up against the rest of the debris, despite the ache in his arms. The sweat on his hands made them slippery and the dirt from the ground was the best remedy. Donne pushed and some more wood rolled off his back, probably from the old stairs they'd hidden beneath.

Donne finally got to his feet. He tried to stand up straight, but sharp cramps in his stomach wouldn't let him. At the same time, he got a lungful of smoke and had to crouch as he coughed. When the fit passed, he took a few steps forward, pushing through wood and concrete. He felt the jagged pieces slash away the skin on his hands.

Franklin Carter lay on the ground in the corner. A thin stream of light shone on him from above. He wasn't burned—at least as far as Donne could tell. Donne pressed his fingers to Franklin's throat for the second time in minutes and found a pulse, though it was considerably weaker. The bone of his already broken arm was sticking out of his skin, blood pouring from the wound.

Donne's hearing came back even more, the rush of water giving way to the crackle of fire. He turned to see that some of the walls had caught up and the fire was spreading. They had to get out of here, and quickly. Straining his neck, Donne could see the perfect exit. Behind him, only feet from the fire, the building had caved in on an angle. He was sure he could climb up the rubble and out into open air. The smoke at the top of the angle twisted, then dissipated through a hole that streamed the light that shone on Franklin and now Donne. It was their only option. The rest of the room was filled with thick smoke, with only a few shards of light pushing through.

"Franklin!" Donne yelled.

Franklin didn't stir. Donne slapped his face hard, and still he didn't move. Donne was going to have to carry him again. He needed a medic, and soon. His arm was bad, and who knew how much smoke he'd inhaled.

Donne tried to lift Franklin onto his back. His chest and arms were having none of it. The muscles in them stretched and tugged against the deadweight, then gave out. Franklin remained on the ground. Donne tried once more, but Franklin hardly budged. Donne sat down and tried to catch his breath, but found himself only coughing.

Not good.

If they stayed down here any longer, they'd suffocate. Firemen would dig them out by the evening and Susan would have two more funerals to plan.

Susan.

Donne remembered the pledge he'd made to himself. That she

wouldn't suffer the way he had with Jeanne. That Franklin wouldn't die. That Donne would save him.

Back in a crouch, he tried once more to lift Franklin. Donne felt his muscles scratch against his ribs, his back and legs straining against the weight. Injured and exhausted, Donne gritted his teeth against the pain. Franklin's torso was against Donne's back, but his legs still dangled against the floor. Donne shifted his shoulders and bounced on his toes to slide Franklin against him some more. Donne's arms burned, the muscles tight against his skin. His face ached, and he felt either blood or sweat stream down his forehead and cheeks. His teeth chattered as a scream tried to force its way out.

And then he stood straight up. And took one step forward. Franklin was limp against him. The pile of debris leading to safety was just a few feet away.

Each step was torture. Franklin kept slipping, and Donne had to stop after each step to make sure he wouldn't drop his brother-in-law. The fire burned against Donne's legs, searing his pants. Moving as fast as he could, Donne stepped against the first stone on their ascent toward the outside world.

Donne put his foot in the next foothold and it gave way. He nearly toppled backward, but caught his balance. The next step was like climbing a mountain. Each time he put his foot down, more debris got free.

About three steps from the top, some onlookers rushed toward them. The sun blinded Donne for a moment. Two men carefully pulled Franklin from Donne's shoulders. A woman put her hand under Donne's arm and helped him for the final steps. The moment he hit grass, he collapsed to the ground, exhausted and coughing. It felt like the fire had spread to his lungs.

"Are you okay?" the woman asked. "The ambulance is on the way."

One of the men was checking Franklin's busted arm. And then his pulse. His face was blackened and his eyes were closed. Donne hoped he wasn't too late.

His eyes adjusted to the light, and he saw a figure lumbering away along the river. It looked like he was trying to run but kept getting his feet stuck in the mud.

"I'm fine," Donne said, and got to his feet.

This wasn't over yet.

tHRee HOURS

Susan Carter opened her eyes. The smell of burning rubber and gasoline struck her like smelling salts. She was suddenly completely awake and alert. Her side burned, and when she looked down she saw she was bleeding. The edge of the console must have sliced her during the crash. The muscles in her neck had stiffened and she couldn't look too far down. She tried to turn to her right and only got a glimpse of Marshall, unconscious. Blood trickled from his lip.

The engine was still running, or at least trying to run, though it was more a rattle. The windshield was cracked, but she couldn't see much else. Most of her view was obstructed by the inflated air bag. Susan tried to move the air bag out of the way, but the pain was too great. Liquid trickled down her cheek, and she hoped it was tears, not blood.

Her left hand was free and didn't hurt too much. She took a moment to check the time. The deadline was approaching. She had to get out of here and pay Hackett.

Finding the door handle was difficult, however. As she turned toward the door, the tear in her seemed to open even more. She felt it burn and felt a warm liquid run down her leg. Meanwhile, the car was warped, the metal bent, and the frame twisted. The door was not going to open easily.

She reached out and grabbed the door handle. She pulled on it, but it didn't give. Her neck muscles screamed and the wound in her side felt as if it was opening wider with each movement. She gritted her teeth, shut her eyes, and pulled harder.

Marshall stirred.

"You . . . bitch."

The words were whispered, but the sound of them made her left hand work harder. As she pulled, she heard metal grinding on metal. It was moving ever so slightly.

"I'll kill you."

The handle gave way. She pushed at the door, but it didn't give. It was jammed. She pressed harder, ignoring the pain as she leaned into the door.

Jason Marshall reached across. He was weak, had to be, his arm moved so slowly. The fingers wrapped around the shoulder of her shirt, and Susan gave one more hard push.

The metal grinded and inched forward a little more. The door was going to open; she could feel it giving way. Marshall held her shirt tight and started to pull her back toward him. She pushed harder on the door. Marshall gave a hard tug, and Susan let go of the handle.

He must not have expected it, her body tumbling right into his. He grunted when her back hit his shoulder. Susan shot her legs out and kicked the door. It inched open a crack. She kicked it again. The door opened wider. Susan forced herself off Marshall toward the open door.

Susan tumbled out onto asphalt. She crawled back toward the sidewalk, the twisted wreck of a car next to her. Her knees scratched along the pavement, and her nails tore as she pulled herself along. When she hit the grass, she rolled onto her back. All her muscles relaxed and a sense of exhaustion fell over her. She went light-headed. She wanted to sleep.

"I'll kill you!"

Susan exhaled. There was no time for sleep. She had to get away.

But she wasn't even sure she could get up. She rolled over again and put her palms flat on the ground.

I will not die today.

Every muscle strained. Her wound burned and tugged at the surrounding skin. Sweat poured from her brow. But she got to her feet. And she let instinct take over.

Susan Carter ran for her life.

CHAPTER **46**

the ground was uneven and muddy along the river, and each step jarred Donne's legs. His feet sunk deeper into the ground, and he struggled to pull them free. The smart move would have been to run toward Hackett another thirty yards away from the river and out of the mud, but Donne rarely did the smart thing.

Sneaking up—hell, catching up—to Hackett wasn't going to be easy. Not with his body aching, not with his feet sticking. The Browning rested in his jeans waistband. He pulled it and aimed at Hackett's back.

"Bryan Hackett!" he yelled.

Hackett turned around and mumbled something that could have been a curse. Stopping in the mud, he allowed Donne to approach him. He raised his hands. Donne tightened his grip on the gun.

He'd aged in the past ten years, his hair fair but thinning. He'd filled out muscularly, as if he'd worked out hard. He had a wedding band on his finger. But he didn't look twenty-three. He looked double that. He looked like life had taken the fire out of his soul.

The stress of the past few weeks had probably done it to him.

When Donne got within five feet of him, Hackett said, "You scarred me, and that wasn't enough. Now you're going to shoot me?"

Hackett put his hand to his forehead, probably where Donne had hit him long ago. But there wasn't a noticeable scar. Nothing was there but pale skin.

What a lunatic.

"This has to end, Hackett."

"It doesn't end until your family is gone. Your mother won't last much longer. And even if you saved Franklin now, I'm sure he won't be able to survive his injuries. I'm going to kill your sister once I get my money. Right now, though, I'm going to kill you."

His voice was confident, even though Donne's gun was trained on his chest.

"Give it up. What happened between us was years ago."

"Do you really think the past dies, Jackson? What happened to my grandfather was even longer ago. But it affects everything. My father could have been rich. I could have lived a blessed life. Instead, all that's left are scars." Hackett touched his forehead again.

"Jason Marshall told me all about you."

Hackett's resolve broke just a little. The level his hands were raised lowered a bit. Next to them the river kept flowing, the odor of trash and slime the chemical factories in Clifton and Paterson dumped in it overwhelming the usual cleanliness of summer air.

"What did he say?"

Donne didn't say anything, the gun heavy in his hand. He wasn't sure how much longer he could hold it. His forearms ached from lifting Franklin. Hackett took another step forward.

"Did he tell you why I was let go? About the explosion at the office?"

"Anger issues. That was how he put it."

"I loved being a cop. I loved working for the bomb squad. I

wouldn't blow up the office. Marshall kept pushing me, and pushing me, from the first day on the job when he told me about my past. My parents never told me about that. I didn't know about it until Marshall did a background check on me."

That didn't make sense to Donne. The hatred had been in Hackett for as long as Donne had known him. But maybe that hadn't been hatred of the Donne family. Maybe it was the hatred of his parents for forcing him to live with them.

Hackett's hands were shaking now. Something about Jason Marshall had set him off.

"Oh my God," he said. "Jill."

"What are you talking about?"

"My wife, she's . . . The party . . ."

Hackett pressed his hands to his face and shook his head.

"It wasn't me who set the bomb in my office," he said. "It was Jason Marshall. He hated me too. He wanted me out."

The words cut through Donne. The conviction in Hackett's voice worried him. What if Hackett wasn't lying? And Susan was still with Marshall. He'd saved her husband, but at the same time, he'd left her in danger.

Donne's gun dropped to his side as a chill ran through him. It was exactly the opening Hackett needed.

Before Donne could raise the gun again, Hackett lurched forward and tackled him into the mud. He hit Donne twice in the ribs as they splattered to the ground, and Donne almost passed out. An explosion of pain thrust through him as his lungs exhaled the last of the air in his body.

Mud caked his face as Donne sank deeper. His clothes were heavy and he couldn't swing his arms. He was stuck. Hackett hit him twice in the stomach, rabbit punches, so fast that Donne hadn't even had time to feel the first when the second connected. Donne tried to gulp air but tasted only mud. He was going to drown there.

And he felt the fight going from him. He wanted to let go, get the whole thing over with. Die right there.

Hackett caught Donne across the chin with a right cross. He

screamed something out, but the mud muffled it. Something about family.

Donne's family.

He couldn't let go. People needed him. There was only one way out—to fight back. To reach inside and find the last ounces of strength and use it. Ignore the pain in his legs and wheel back with his knee and drive Hackett's balls right into his stomach. He swung his knee up as hard as he could and found his target. Hackett grunted and coughed. The blow hurt him enough that Donne could roll him off and sit up.

Donne opened his mouth and inhaled, gulping air down as if he'd just been underwater. As the air filled his lungs, so did pain. Could his lungs pop like an overinflated balloon? Was that possible? Donne closed his eyes and focused on the air instead.

He was caked with mud. He must have weighed an extra twenty pounds. Behind him, back toward the destroyed building, Donne heard sirens. They were close.

He found his gun in the mud, picked it up, and wiped the mud off it and onto his shirt. He pointed it at Hackett.

"Sit up," Donne said.

"Just kill me," he said. Hackett was covering his crotch and writhing on the ground. The rage had gone out of him with one blow. Or so Donne thought.

The hand that wasn't covering himself swooped out from beneath him, catching Donne in the ankle. A sharp pain shot through him, and his brain registered the knife that had been jammed in his leg. His already injured muscles contracted hard around the wound, Donne went down on one knee, and the gun went off.

Hackett didn't make a sound. He sank softly into the mud.

Donne pulled the blade from his leg, grunting as he did so. It was hard to pull it out, as if his body didn't want to give it up. It slid out, inch by painful inch. Blood spilled from the wound with each tug until it finally gave way. Pressing his right hand against the opening, Donne limped up the hill away from the river. Away from Hackett's body.

The building still burned. EMTs surrounded Franklin Carter, checking his vitals and his injuries. An ambulance careened around the corner. A few onlookers turned to face Donne, taking a step back when they saw the gun in his hand.

He should stay and see if Franklin was okay.

He should explain things to the police.

But he didn't. Before anyone approached him, he managed to get to the car, start the engine, and pull out onto the road. He was sure someone took down the license plate number.

It didn't matter.

His sister came first.

*

Bitch won't get far.

Jason Marshall undid his seat belt and pushed the passenger door open. He glanced in the rearview mirror to check his face. A large gash crossed his forehead, blood dripping from it. His left arm didn't work right, he noticed as he tried to wipe the blood away. He tried to lift it, but it barely rose past his waist. That was probably why Susan had been able to get out of his grasp so easily.

Marshall picked up his gun. Then he got out of the car and slammed the door shut. His legs felt okay. He felt like he could run. First, though, he needed one thing.

The money.

The duffel bag had bounced around during the accident, but it was undamaged. And heavier than he expected. He checked his watch. He still had time.

He slung the bag over his right shoulder and jogged off in the direction Susan had run.

CHAPTER 47

SUSAN ALWAYS HATED HORROR MOVIES. THE WOMEN always ran the wrong way, or worse, stopped running altogether and tried to hide. But that was exactly what she did. She hurt too much to run any farther. It seemed like she'd taken the brunt of the car accident, even with the air bag.

Her plan was to get home and lock all the doors. She was only a block away, after all. But she couldn't run hard; the wound at her side burned and bled more with each step. Once she got into the backyard of the gigantic brick home she ran behind, she found the closest bush. She pushed some of the branches out of the way and slid underneath and lay flat on her stomach, looking out over the yard. She pressed her right arm tight against her side, trying to slow the bleeding and relieve some of the pain.

The yard was pristine. A picnic table with an open umbrella was aligned near the back of the home, a large aboveground pool fifty feet to the left of that. The smell of freshly cut grass made her want to sneeze. She was hiding from someone trying to kill her, and the setting was a fucking Norman Rockwell painting.

Watching the corner of the house where she'd run moments earlier, she caught the shadow first. Jason Marshall came around the corner, slowly, holding a gun. He was holding on to the money too, the duffel bag awkwardly hanging from his shoulder. He surveyed the yard.

Calm, cautious. There was blood on his face, but he was walking without a limp. Both the bag and the gun were on his right side.

Her muscles tensed in fear as he turned his head toward her. She prayed that he wouldn't see her, that it wasn't her time to die. But she also knew Marshall was good. Every instinct told her to just get up and run. But she ignored them and froze, tried to sink deeper into the ground. All she wanted was to be invisible.

Marshall took a step toward the bush and stopped. Susan kept her eyes on the gun hand. That would be how she'd know. If he raised his gun, he'd found her. And she'd be dead.

✳

Donne saw the car as soon as he hit Upper Mountain Road. Smoke drifted up from the engine and the back door was open. He accelerated up to the wreck and put his own vehicle in park.

As he got out of the car, his left leg almost gave way. Not sure which hurt more, his lungs or his bleeding leg, he did his best to ignore them both. No time to even try to slow the bleeding. He instead limped over to the accident.

No one was in the car. And since the onlookers and emergency workers weren't around it yet, it must have just happened. Donne saw blood on the console, and his heart lurched. Blood on the passenger seat and the dashboard. Blood everywhere. Was it hers?

They had to be close. Donne checked the gun to make sure it was ready to be used. Sure, it had gone off once earlier, but it had also been caked in mud.

Once he was satisfied, he took a deep breath. Then opened his mouth.

✳

She was under the bush. Jason Marshall had made her easily. He just wanted to see if she'd try to run. It would be an easier shot if she was standing. After the accident, there was no way she'd be able to move too fast.

"Jason Marshall!"

The shout came from behind him. A male voice, loud and booming.

"Jason Marshall!"

It was Jackson Donne. Marshall closed his eyes and sighed. He hadn't counted on Donne's coming back. The guy was supposed to be out somewhere hiding. Marshall had counted on being miles away by the time Donne found out the money was gone and his sister was dead.

Plan changed. No time to wait for Susan to run. That was okay; he was good at improvising.

He walked over to the bush, dropped the duffel bag, and aimed the gun downward.

"Come on out," he said. Then: "We're back here!"

CHAPTER **48**

THOSE WORDS MEANT IT WASN'T TIME TO FUCK
around. Donne could tell the voice came from behind the house, a
columned mansion that probably cost millions. The owners were
probably at work. It seemed like the whole neighborhood was at work.

Or maybe they were just smart enough not to come outside
with guns around.

He limped toward the house, then alongside of it. His pant leg
and sock were caked with red and brown and moved stiffly. The gun
was heavy. Donne wasn't sure how much longer he could keep from
passing out. He'd lost a lot of blood.

When he got to the backyard, he had to lean against the corner
of the house to stay up. His grip loosened on the gun. What he saw
made him feel even weaker.

"Drop the gun," Jason Marshall said.

He had Susan pressed against him, gun pointed at her head. She was crying, screaming for Donne, and Marshall had to yell over her.

"Drop the gun or I shoot her."

"Jackson, please!"

Susan had bloodstains on her cheeks. Her left eye was swollen. Her clothes were torn on the left side, and through a hole in her jeans, Donne could see a long cut. The barrel of Marshall's gun dug into her temple.

"Let her go," Donne said.

"You are not in any position to tell me what to do. Drop. The. Gun." To accentuate his point, Marshall pressed the gun harder against Susan's skin. His finger tensed on the trigger.

"Okay," Donne said. "Okay."

The Browning clattered against the concrete patio. Donne felt like he was going to pass out and slumped against the house wall. He fought against the feeling, breathing as deeply as he could.

Stand up straight, he told himself, but he couldn't will his body to agree.

"We're going to walk right past you, and you won't do anything about it."

"Why are you doing this?" Donne asked.

"Why else?" Marshall nodded toward the duffel bag at his feet. "I need the money."

"Hackett's dead. It's over," Donne said.

"He's dead? Thanks, Donne."

Keeping the gun on Susan, he picked up the bag, slung it over his shoulder. It took him some time. He winced like his arm was hurting. Donne knew how he felt.

They stepped toward Donne, Marshall keeping Susan between them. If he could get toward Marshall's arm, maybe he'd have a chance, but Marshall was smart. He used Susan to block it. Susan and Donne made eye contact. He felt her fear, the look in her eyes tearing at his heart. He couldn't blame her. He hoped she didn't see the same thing in his eyes.

Marshall backed his way up toward the front of the house.

Donne matched him step for step. His leg still throbbed, and no way could he push off to try and tackle the both of them.

When they got to the front of the house, Donne could hear sirens in the distance. Someone had called in the accident.

Marshall got himself next to the car he'd pulled up in hours ago.

"We're going to get the hell out of here. When I get to where I feel safe, I'll let her go. I just want the money."

"Where's Draxton?" Donne asked, just to keep him there another second. To give himself time to come up with another plan.

"All you need to know is when I'm free, she's free."

"Did you kill him?"

Marshall didn't speak. Donne took a step forward, trying to run toward him, crouching like a linebacker about to tackle a running back.

Almost as if it were a muscle instinct, Marshall pushed Susan away from himself into Donne. When they collided, his legs finally gave way. Donne fell to the asphalt. Marshall got into the car.

"Take her," he said, though he sounded annoyed to let her go. "I don't have time for this shit. I'm on a schedule."

He did a three-point turn and disappeared down Upper Mountain Road.

Jason Marshall, the money, the car. Before Donne could stand again, they were halfway down the street.

Sitting back on the asphalt, Donne hugged Susan. The police showed up before anyone else. One cruiser, one uniformed cop with a notepad. When he saw them, he immediately rushed over.

He started asking questions while scribbling in a notebook, but Susan held up a hand.

"Get us an ambulance," she ordered.

"This was a hell of an accident," the officer said.

She ignored him and said to Donne, "Franklin?"

He nodded. "I found him. He was alive. When I left him."

"Oh my God," she said. "When you left him?"

"He was hurt bad. His arm was broken. Then there was an explosion. EMS showed up when I left."

She hugged Donne back. "I knew he was alive."

Donne prayed Franklin still was. For her sake.

✳

Marshall didn't hit too much traffic. Not on Route 3, not on the Turnpike. It was like the traffic gods had been looking out for him and left him a clear shot. Keeping an eye on the rearview mirror, Marshall was pretty sure he wasn't being followed.

He took exit 14 to Newark Airport and parked in long term. Even the airport seemed empty. He left the gun in the car, not caring. If they found the gun, it would be weeks from now anyway and he'd be long gone. Untraceable.

The shuttle ride to the terminal was quick, and he kept the duffel bag on his lap. Until it was time, he wasn't letting it out of his sight.

He wondered when the state police would notice he was gone. They'd probably start looking and calling when they took down Donne's statement. And if they'd checked up on Donne's investigator background and his history, they might believe him, but it wouldn't matter. Marshall hadn't left a trail, he was sure of it. No one would know where he was going.

The shuttle let him off at the terminal. Before going in, he strolled down to the corner of the building. Traffic sped past him, dropping people off, picking people up. Much busier than the long-term lot. He was sure everyone was watching him. He picked up the pace of his walk without even thinking about it. He had to fight back laughter. His uninjured arm shook just a bit. He was so close.

He had a contact at the airport. A man whose cooperation had been bought. He met Robert Steinfeld at the corner of the terminal and passed him the duffel bag, along with five hundred bucks. They'd practiced the move before, Marshall standing with his back to the security camera, obstructing the view of the exchange. Steinfeld would make sure the bag got on the plane unchecked, slipping it onto the plane personally, after saying he checked it.

Ten minutes later, he was in the terminal. This was the scary part. He got through the metal detector unchallenged. He walked up to the bar and ordered a drink. No one followed him. But he was going to be out in the open for nearly an hour, just sitting and drinking. Anyone could find him.

He sipped his beer for about ten minutes. A blond woman sidled up next to him and ordered a Malibu Baybreeze. Marshall's body flushed with warmth. He even got a bit hard. She'd made it.

"How'd everything go?" Jill Hackett asked.

Jason Marshall leaned in and kissed her on the cheek. She gave him a one-handed hug in return.

"It went." He tried to shrug, but his left arm still hurt. He sipped his beer instead. It tasted like shit. The tap needed to be changed. "We're home free. The bag's under your maiden name, in case they check when we get off the plane."

They'd met at Hackett's graduation from the academy. While Hackett was schmoozing with the bigwigs, Marshall had struck up a conversation with his wife. He liked her. She was hot, she was funny, and she was disgusted she had to be at the party. He'd asked her about Hackett's background.

After they'd been fucking for a year, she'd told Marshall she had a plan and wanted to know if he was in. He was.

And now here they were, about to start a new life together. He knew that with money and Bryan out of the way, Marshall was the one she really wanted to be with. He had a way with women, but Jill was a challenge. And he'd finally won. And now he was so excited, he felt light-headed just looking at her. They hadn't seen each other in weeks. He felt like a thirteen-year-old on his first date.

"We're going to do it," he said, then sipped some more beer. "Five hours from now, we'll be drinking on the beach."

She tilted her head to the side. "I'm getting my new life."

Putting his hand on her arm, he said, "Is the money that important?"

"You are just like my husband."

"You think?"

Jill nodded. There seemed to be a glow around her face. She really made him light-headed.

"I need to ask you a question, though," she said. "Why did you tell me to tell him you needed his help?"

He finished his beer. "I don't know. Seemed like fun. I wanted to see him. I wanted him to see me and know what he was up against. Even if he didn't know why exactly, I wanted him to know I was going to get him."

Behind them, a woman on the intercom announced their flight.

"We'll talk about this more on the plane. You ready?" he asked.

Jill Hackett got up. "I am. But I'm not sure you're going to make it."

He blinked his eyes and felt sweat at his brow.

"Why not?"

She leaned in and whispered in his ear. "I poisoned your drink."

And he realized it wasn't the way she looked that was making him feel faint.

1 9 3 9

Joe Tenant gave it six months. He let the New Year pass and
winter set in. No one ever came to ask him about Willy
Hackett, probably because the cops weren't all that sad to
see him go. Connor O'Neill retired from office and was out
of politics. After the newspaper article, he was arrested and
was currently on trial. Tenant kept in touch with Lisa
Carter, getting to know her kids, getting to know the family.
Work was horrible in the winter, the bitter-cold air off the
river freezing his ears. But it was work.

No one threatened his life anymore.

One morning after his shift, Joe didn't go to the hotel.
He went home. He stood across the street for the longest
time, ignoring the cold, just watching, hoping Caroline
would come out to him. She never did, but she must have
seen him, because she didn't leave to take Isabelle to school.

After a couple of hours, he finally got up the nerve to
ring the doorbell. It was even harder than visiting Willy
Hackett.

He rang three times before Caroline answered.

She pulled the door open a crack, standing behind it
and waiting for him to speak. She breathed heavily, staring
at him. Her eyes were darts tearing through him.

Joe Tenant had spent the night at work rehearsing speeches in his head, trying to find one that would win her back. He'd even tried three of them on Sops. All his friend did was shrug when he heard them.

And now when he finally got to see Caroline, all the memories flooded back to him: the wedding, the birth of their child, the last time they'd been together that morning in the kitchen. And finally, bringing Isabelle home and getting kicked out of the house. He was speechless.

"What do you want?" she asked. Her voice was flat and quiet. The sound of it made Tenant want to turn and walk away right then.

But he didn't. He had things to say.

"It's over," he said, his throat dry. "It's been over for a while."

"I've seen the newspaper."

"Let me in, please."

"No," she said.

"Caroline, I only wanted to do what was right. I only wanted to help. They came at me. At us. It wasn't my fault. But I've ended it."

"You?"

He didn't respond to that. She didn't need to know about jamming a knife in someone's throat. Caroline didn't need to know the images that woke him up at night. At least not now.

"Joe, our daughter almost died because of you. I can't forgive that."

"Yes. You can." He reached out to touch her face. She leaned out of range. "It won't happen again, Caroline. I love you and I love Isabelle. I never wanted anything bad to happen to either of you."

Caroline took another step backward. "How can I trust you again?"

"I didn't go out looking for trouble. It floated over to

me. I won't look for it again. I won't put our daughter at risk ever again."

"I don't know, Joe."

He took a deep breath. "Please. If not for me, for Isabelle. She needs a father."

"She misses you."

"And I miss her," he said. "Family. That's the most important thing."

Caroline sighed. And opened up the door, revealing herself. Her stomach had ballooned.

"Six months, Joe."

Joe Tenant stared wide-eyed. He didn't know what to say.

"Don't worry. It's yours," she said. "That morning, in the kitchen."

"I had Sops come and check on you. He never—"

"I know. I asked him not to."

He stepped into the house and hugged her, held her close. Smelled the soap on her skin, felt her smooth face against his stubble.

"You're going to have to prove yourself, Joe."

"I know," he said. "And I will. You have my word."

And a man was only as good as his word.

CHAPTER **49**

two weeks Later

Two airport security guards found Jason Marshall dead in the men's bathroom. He'd ingested rat poison, apparently. The state police laughed at the irony of that in their press conference. He wasn't exactly a rat—more a traitor—but no one ever said state troopers understood irony. The money never turned up. They were in the process of searching for the car and the gun.

Donne's leg was sewn up and they gave him some blood. The doctors couldn't do anything about his other injuries except tape him up, give him anti-inflammatories, and tell him not to move around more than he had to.

Franklin Carter had his arm set and spent a week in the hospital. Susan—also stitched up—was at his side nearly every minute of it, leaving only to attend Faye and George's funeral with Donne.

Donne attended Mike Iapicca's alone, as his wife wept. He wished he had some words to offer her, something nice to say, but instead he left without speaking to anyone.

The cops kept questioning him, pissed off he'd snuck out of his sister's house when they wanted to ask him about Iapicca's and Delshawn Butler's deaths. They didn't seem to have much of a case against him, because the final police report had decided it was probably self-defense. They took his Browning, and he would no longer be able to own a gun, much less carry one. And they were going to keep a close eye on him. It didn't bother him. He knew he'd done what he could. And he'd been threatened by cops before.

He was still scheduled to start at Rutgers in the fall.

His mother still lay in hospice.

✳

Susan and Donne sat in his newly repaired car in Wayne. He had the air-conditioning on, as the heat and humidity outside were stifling. The Decemberists played on the radio.

"I can't go in there," Susan said.

"Yes, you can."

"The nurses will stop me at the front desk."

"I'll make sure you get in."

"Jackson," Susan said. "They probably hate me."

"She's going to die within the week, Susan. You have to see her."

Susan's eyes filled. It was hard to keep his dry. He turned the music up.

"It must be awful," Susan said. "She's just trapped in the past. That's how her days are spent. She just talks about her dad. Franklin says Hackett visited her before I came to you. That's what set it off."

"It would have happened eventually."

She shook her head. "I can't imagine what that must be like. Her past. It's all she knows. I just can't imagine it."

For a while, they didn't speak. Donne thought about Bryan Hackett. His past drove him toward revenge. It blinded him to reality, caused him to lose his job and eventually his life.

How Bryan Hackett and Donne were more alike than he wanted to admit. And how Donne had been part of the reason he came after them. No matter how small the incident actually was, it stuck with Hackett. It pushed him. He remembered it, just like Donne remembered his fiancée every day.

"I can imagine," Donne said.

The past few weeks, he'd made a decision. He was going to start over. He hadn't had a drink in two weeks. He prepared to start college, trying to get a head start on some reading. He'd visited his sister more often. He couldn't become Hackett, driven by hatred, and dying miserably in a puddle of mud.

Donne was better than that. Too long he'd been sitting around thinking about what happened in April. And he could feel himself get caught up in these events too. He wasn't going to let that happen.

Instead he would let the past become the past.

He turned to Susan.

"Remember a few weeks ago when you told me I had to see her?"

Susan nodded.

"I went, before going after Hackett. I sat in there for half an hour and held her hand. I told her I loved her, and I said good-bye to her. I thought I was going to die before she did."

His sister put her hand on his wrist.

"Jackson, I'm so glad."

"Now it's your turn. We have to go in there, before she's gone. You have to say good-bye. She can hear you. I know she can."

Susan didn't say anything.

"You need to say you're sorry. And not just for her."

"The nurses," Susan said. "Did they say anything to you?"

"They haven't."

Donne turned the car off and opened the door. His leg still ached whenever he put pressure on his foot. The heat warmed his skin. By this afternoon, they'd have a thunderstorm.

Donne stepped around the car and opened his sister's door. Susan stared at him, not moving.

He put out his hand.

"Come on, sis," he said.

Susan got out of the car on her own, putting on her sunglasses. He wasn't sure if it was the glare or if she was covering up tears, but he didn't say anything. They stood there for a long time, the summer sun beating down on them.

She took his hand and together they went to see their mother.

ABOUT THE AUTHOR

DAVE WHITE was born in 1979 and currently works as an eighth-grade language arts teacher. He is a winner and multiple-time nominee for the Derringer Award for best short story, and was shortlisted for the 2005 *storySouth* Million Writers Award. He is a member of Mystery Writers of America and International Thriller Writers, and has contributed to many anthologies and collections, including *The Adventure of the Missing Detective* and *Damn Near Dead*. His first novel, *When One Man Dies*, was published in 2007. He lives in New Jersey.